Shieldmaiden Sisters

*Three resourceful women, not looking for,
but finding...love*

Loyalty is everything to half sisters
Valda, Brynhild and Helga. Their courageous
shieldmaiden mother has raised them to be
independent, and now that the family has fallen
on hard times, each sister must find a way to help
restore their fortunes. Being resourceful, they have
no need of men, but the right ones come along
just when they're least expected.

Read Valda's story in
The Viking She Would Have Married
Available now.

Look for Brynhild's and Helga's stories
Coming soon.

Author Note

I was inspired to write this epic tale of the silk road—or rivers, more accurately—after reading Dr. Cat Jarman's fascinating book, *River Kings*. However, it must be said that any historical inaccuracies are my fault alone. *River Kings* is a great read, and some of the artifacts Dr. Jarman discusses have ended up in my book! Like the Kufic-style inscribed ring and the carnelian beads from India. It's amazing how far these adventurers traveled!

But most of all, I was inspired by the Birka Warrior, who for many years was considered by archaeologists to have been a great and powerful warrior king. Recent DNA testing has revealed this warrior to be a woman, finally giving some credit to the belief that shieldmaidens existed in the Viking era. I really hope so, and the shield sisters of Porunn are my homage to these nameless women.

LUCY MORRIS

The Viking She Would Have Married

Recycling programs for this product may not exist in your area.

ISBN-13: 978-1-335-40789-4

The Viking She Would Have Married

Harlequin Enterprises ULC
22 Adelaide St. West, 41st Floor
Toronto, Ontario M5H 4E3, Canada
www.Harlequin.com

Printed in U.S.A.

Lucy Morris lives in Essex, UK, with her husband, two young children and two cats. She has a massive sweet tooth and loves gin, bubbly and Irn-Bru. She's a member of the UK Romantic Novelists' Association. She was delighted to accept a two-book deal with Harlequin after submitting her story to the Warriors Wanted! submission blitz for Viking, medieval and Highlander romances. Writing for Harlequin Historical is a dream come true for her and she hopes you enjoy her books!

Books by Lucy Morris

Harlequin Historical

The Viking Chief's Marriage Alliance
A Nun for the Viking Warrior

Shieldmaiden Sisters

The Viking She Would Have Married

And look out for the next
book coming soon!

For my fierce friends,
you're all shieldmaidens in my eyes.

Prologue

'**We**'ll each be married with flowers in our hair...' Helga said solemnly, seeming more like a wise old woman than a girl of only twelve winters. The slightly wilted blooms fluttered lazily in her long blonde hair. 'And the runes will tell us about the kinds of men we're going to marry.'

For some reason Helga's prophecy made Valda nervous. She wasn't sure if she wanted to know her fate.

The three girls sat beneath an old oak tree, a symbol of mystic power in its own right. The day was warm and bright. Perfect for climbing trees, or swimming in the river. The clang and bustle of their army encampment was a distant hum in the air, reassuringly close to their mother, Porunn, and her band of shieldmaidens, but also far away enough for them to spend the day in idle mischief, without interruption.

'Fine, so we say the spell three times, before we pick?' asked Valda with a resigned sigh.

'Three times and it has to be together. Then you each

pick a bone and I'll interpret your fortune.' Helga shook the bag of bones and they made a light rattling sound.

'This is ridiculous!' snapped Brynhild, who began to stand as if to leave. She'd now seen nineteen winters and seemed to think herself in charge of them—even though Valda disagreed.

Valda grabbed her arm and tugged her back to the forest floor with a thump. 'Sit down. I'm not doing this without you! Besides…she'll never be happy unless we do it together.'

'Correct!' sang Helga with enthusiastic delight, as she held the bag out in the centre of their circle and gave it three sharp shakes. The dappled light of the trees shone on her pale hand, causing unusual patterns on her milky skin, and Valda wondered if there really was magic in her sister's veins. She certainly looked like a creature of the forest with her blonde hair and blue eyes bright with determination, beauty and a strange wisdom.

Soon their long days spent together would come to an end. Brynhild was training with their mother for longer periods of time and—if she proved herself worthy— would soon enter the ranks of the other shieldmaidens. Valda was certain she would.

Valda would follow soon after. There was less than two winters between them, and her training had also increased significantly since spring. There was talk of more battles with the Franks, more land to control and raid. Valda and Brynhild hoped to join the next fight, rather than stay behind with Helga and the other children. But that was up to their mother and Porunn was always cautious when it came to her daughters—even if she wasn't in any other aspects of her life.

'Where did you learn this spell anyway?' grumbled Brynhild.

'Aunt Freydis.'

Brynhild groaned. 'The Volva? That explains it. So, you want to be a witch roaming the world telling fortunes and casting spells then?'

Helga's chin jutted up slightly. 'So, what if I do? I'd be better at it than swinging a sword.'

Brynhild laughed. 'That's for certain!'

A flash of hurt ran across Helga's features and Valda elbowed her sister in the ribs.

Brynhild grunted, but looked contrite. 'Sorry. You'll improve…with time.'

Helga was not built like them—she was small and delicate, and though she showed promise with a bow, she struggled to wield even the lightest of wooden swords, much to their mother's dismay.

Helga's slim shoulders shrugged, then she smiled slowly. 'Ready?'

'But I don't want a husband!' Brynhild sighed stubbornly, crossing her long legs. Valda wondered if Brynhild felt awkward; she was far taller and stronger than any of the boys, and as bad tempered as a wounded boar most days.

'I cannot change what I have seen,' Helga patiently explained. 'There is one in your future…but by using the runes you will be forewarned about him.'

'But why bother if it makes no difference?'

Helga frowned. 'Because…it will help you recognise him.'

'Oh, let's get on with it! We did promise her,' Valda said. This was all taking far too long in her mind and the arguing didn't help.

'Fine!' huffed Brynhild.

When Helga nodded, they all spoke together as one, chanting the ancient words slowly, so as not to make a mess of it. With a flourish Helga moved the bag in an arc as if she were stirring a pot. Then she gave it another three swirling shakes and the sound of magic shivered through the trees, as a sudden gust of wind blew across them. Valda swallowed down her fear and rubbed her arms to take away the sudden chill.

A cool breeze from the north, nothing more.

'Take one,' Helga urged Brynhild, who scowled at the sack as if it were filled with poisonous serpents.

'I'll do it,' Valda said, taking pity on her. She reached in and pulled out the first thing that touched her fingers.

It was a sheep's rib. Meticulously cleaned, but it looked as if someone had gnawed on it a little too thoroughly, as there was a light crack running down its centre. It was blank, so she turned it over looking for more. Helga had painted one side with a Laguz rune. The design was simple and striking against the white. A thick straight line broken at the top like a snapped arrow head.

'Water, love, growth and travel. Maybe your husband lives across the sea?' pondered Helga cheerfully, pleased by her own insight.

Valda gave a weak smile in response and tried to hide her disappointment.

The Laguz meant all of those things, that much was true, but Helga wasn't the only one who'd listened to Aunt Freydis. Valda recognised it and as a water rune she knew its meaning was unpredictable. Especially as Valda had drawn it upside down. Reversed, it could also mean fear, insecurity and loss.

Those were uncertainties she already felt in abundance living in Rollo's army as they did. When she'd dreamed of her future, she'd hoped for stability, a hall or farmstead of her own…a home. Maybe even a husband and children to share it with? But…conflict and travel? They were two things she had never hoped for.

As her sisters drew their own runes and laughed at their possible meanings Valda told herself over and over again. *It's only a child's game. It doesn't mean anything.*

Chapter One

AD 913—Jorvik River Dock

'What do you mean there are *no* ships?' snapped Valda, glaring at the sweaty man in front of her with growing displeasure. She gestured pointedly around her; the dock was filled to bursting with all manner of longships, knarrs and rowing boats.

The vessels were so tightly packed you could hop from one boat to another down the entire length of it, without stepping foot on dry land. To say there were no boats was like saying there were no trees in the forest.

If the markets were the city's beating heart, then Jorvik's docks were its lungs, continually in motion—where all manner of goods and people flowed in and out to trade.

It was also the only place where she might find enough work to help her family, ideally as part of the crew on a raider or merchant's ship. Her family needed silver and lots of it—more than she could currently earn as a mercenary.

The man spoke slowly, as if he were talking to a child,

punctuating each word with an exaggerated display of his weathered jowls. 'I. Mean. There. Are. No. Ships.' He leaned back on the barrel he was using as a stool, as if to look at her better. 'Not for passengers.'

Clenching her jaw tightly, she hissed, 'I'm. Not. A. *Passenger.*'

Her hand dropped to the hilt of her sword for emphasis and the man had the audacity to look bored.

She should spill his guts on the jetty and see if he believed her then!

Valda had probably seen more warfare under Jorund's banner than this man had or would ever have the misfortune to know. She flexed her hand to ease the tension as she reminded herself that this was a new land and that her reputation could not swim across the sea—as much as she wished it would.

Why had Porunn insisted on bringing them here to this smelly and endlessly wet city? At least in Rouen her name held meaning. She was known as 'Valda the Blade'—quick and lethal in battle. Here she was no one. A young woman in tattered clothes, her sword the only possession of real value. Not for the first time she wished they'd stayed in Northmannia.

But reputation was a double-edged sword and Porunn had been too humiliated to stay. Bjorn had taken everything from her, including her pride.

And who was she to criticise? Hadn't she also run from Jorund rather than face a life under the leadership of a man who could never love her back?

Both mother and daughter were pitifully poor sighted when it came to men.

Her hand wrapped around the hilt of her weapon; the lobed pommel and gold inlay felt cool and solid beneath her fingers. It had been a long time since she'd had to prove herself in the world of men. Before, she would have enjoyed the spectacle, but today she just felt tired and in low spirits, sick of having to constantly prove herself worthy when no one cared either way.

In Jorund's army no one had questioned her place. And like a love-sick puppy she'd followed him for years, eagerly awaiting the scraps of his affection. Hoping that one day his admiration for her as a warrior would grow into love for her as a woman. But he'd never felt the same way and had viewed her only as a friend—or a sister at best.

The bitterness burned and her fingers flexed.

She didn't need another sibling, she had two already!

She wanted a partner, a lover, an equal. Someone who put her needs above his own.

The impossible.

All she had left now from her time with Jorund was a sword. A gift he'd given her when she'd become his second-in-command.

Cold, hard steel, nothing more.

Through gritted teeth she spoke to the man, her voice low and menacing. 'I can fight. Shall I demonstrate?'

Frustration caused her anger to snap and she whipped out her sword. She slashed the air in bold strokes with an easy roll of her wrist, the steel hissing like a serpent as it cut through the air. The sword was a work of art, beautifully balanced and a pleasure to wield, the ornate garnets winking from the base of its hilt promising a glorious death to any challenger.

The man flinched and wobbled on his barrel. She was almost tempted to cut him...just a little. Except it would have been unfair as the man was both stupid and unarmed. That didn't stop her from frightening him, though.

Maybe it would teach him never to doubt a shield-maiden again.

When she returned her steel to its scabbard the man gulped and nodded. He recognised her worth now. 'But...' he said apologetically, 'most spring crews are already decided. You could try one of the larger ships? They may need extra crew... Harald!' His thundering bellow carried across the dry dock, causing many men to look up from their tasks.

Harald answered with a bad-tempered, 'What?'

'Do you need any more crew?'

'No!' Harald shouted back, already turning away.

Another man stumbled past, and said, 'I'm going raiding...' He had an oily smile, sharpened teeth, and was obviously drunk by the way he swayed from side to side as he peered at her with glassy eyes. 'I don't need another sword...but you can pay for your place in...other ways.'

Valda wouldn't have rowed across the river with him, let alone gone raiding. Disgusted, she turned away with a dismissive snort. She heard his wheezing cackle of laughter as he staggered onwards.

What else did she expect? A man of honour and integrity? Raiders were slavers and petty thieves these days—there was no bravery in what they did. She'd told Helga last night that she was willing to do anything for her family, but faced with this man, and the grim reality of it, she felt her resolve crumble.

Could she really go raiding? She'd fought in wars to win land and respect, but could she go back to the old ways? *But what choice did she have? After ruining things in Francia?*

She'd had an honourable life before, as Jorund's second-in-command. He'd been the best of men and had been rewarded for it. Now, he was Lord of Évreux—gifted with land, power and a noble wife.

A wife who loved him and whom he—more importantly—loved back.

If only she'd never confessed her true feelings for him. Then she could have stayed and remained Jorund's second and never stepped foot in hateful Jorvik! She'd still have a home and could easily have offered her mother and sisters a place by her side when things had turned sour for them.

But instead, she'd confessed her unrequited love like a babbling idiot! Burning away her future in a single breath. Those years fighting for a land to call home *wasted!*

Valda's spine straightened with pride. What good was there in wallowing in self-pity? *Her sisters and mother were relying on her!* Brynhild had been their main provider for all those years Valda had spent with Jorund. It was time for her to help her sister and accept her own share of responsibility. She would do whatever she had to do to earn enough silver to secure their farmstead… although, there was no harm in looking for a more honourable position first.

'Are there any merchant ships?' she asked some men hopefully.

The first shrugged and opened his mouth to speak.

But it was another voice that answered. A rich, deep voice from several feet away, although it carried clearly across the distance between them. As if every man and woman in Jorvik had put down their tools and stopped speaking at that very moment.

'I have a ship, Valda. Where would you like to go?'

Then, all at once, the silence ended, the blood and sounds of the dock rushing forward and into her ears, making her dizzy.

Surely not... Halfdan?

Memories crashed through her. Sweet promises whispered between hot, stolen kisses. For a moment she thought she was back on his boat, the smell of oak in her nostrils and the tender kiss of her first love's touch on her neck.

Her stomach twisted painfully and reflexively she gripped the hilt of her sword again for comfort and balance.

Halfdan had been the first to break her heart, long before her most recent disaster with Jorund. In fact, Halfdan had been the reason she'd looked for a man like Jorund in the first place. A dependable, loyal and honourable man. Not driven by the desire for adventure, but by the need for a home and a family. Only, she'd learned too late that Jorund would never want it with her.

Were the gods mocking her?

To weave her past and present together in such a painful and laughable way?

Strangely, she was reminded of the Laguz rune she'd picked out as a youth and the terrible fate it had predicted for her.

Uncertainty, insecurity, a fickle love that would always leave her lost and broken—like flotsam on the sea.

They'd all come true with him, her first romance. And she'd searched every day since to find the opposite...only for that to crumble, too.

It was inevitable, really, that she would have to face him again. She turned slowly, determined to meet the past with an unconcerned smile. After all, she was a grown woman now. He could not break her again.

Halfdan's heart still hammered in his chest. He'd seen Valda's fiery hair from halfway down the dry dock and had almost winded himself pushing through the crowds to reach her. He'd been worried that if he lost sight of her, even if only for a moment, he might lose her for ever again.

Why had he done that? Why should he even care after all these years?

Now, he felt foolish and he pulled back his dignity with hard resolve. No matter what, she would never know what she'd meant to him.

It was odd that their paths should cross once more.

He'd thought never to see her again and especially never here. Her family were based in Francia and had no reason to come to Jorvik. He himself only ever came here to trade, as he preferred to avoid his father's hall whenever possible.

But there was no eluding him now.

He had a deal to strike.

One that would secure his brother's future and end their father's tyranny...he just had to tread carefully with the older man.

Now, with Valda in front of him, all of his careful plans were forgotten in the blink of an eye and he was offering to take her anywhere she chose.

What was wrong with him? Why could he not forget her and move on with his life? Why, when it came to his heart, must he always have one foot in the past?

And more importantly...would she even accept his offer this time?

Would she sail away with him? As he'd asked her to do once before, long ago.

Valda turned towards him and his heart burned with desire. He'd thought she would seem different somehow after all these years. Less intoxicating…

That his wide experience as a man would diminish her in some way. That his age and wisdom would dull her vitality and shining beauty, leaving behind something far more ordinary and dull. He'd imagined, and hoped, that the shieldmaiden he'd idolised in his youth would be nothing special after all. A pale beauty in comparison to the varied and exotic women he'd met on his travels.

But that was not the case.

She was still…*perfect*.

Annoyingly so.

If anything, age had only polished her beauty to a brighter lustre. Her hair shone like copper in the sunlight, her features, once soft and rounded with youth, were now sharp with confidence and strength. A scatter of adorable freckles ran across the bridge of her nose like a dusting of spice on milk. Intelligent hazel eyes scrutinised him, sweeping up his body with meticulous care, missing nothing and judging everything. Her full, pink lips twisted into a dry smile of amusement, as if she had always known, like him, that this moment would one day come.

He was a fully grown man now. No longer burdened by the heightened emotions and passions of his youth. But seeing her again *hurt* and he couldn't understand why. It wasn't as if he was going to make the same mistakes again.

There would be no declarations of love this time. Never again would he beg for her to sail away with him.

She could either take his offer or refuse him. It did not matter to him either way.

Except it did.

His spine ached to straighten from his casual lean against the barrels of the dock, to show her that he, too, had changed. That he was no longer an awkward youth, but an assured and confident man. Of course, his pride refused to let him preen before her. Couldn't bear for her to know the effect she still had on him. That the very sight of her caused his old passions to burn with renewed yearning.

Indifference. That's what he'd hoped he'd feel if he ever saw her again, and even if that wasn't the case, he would do his best to pretend it was.

'Halfdan, is that you?' She laughed with bemusement, the easy smile widening as she stepped towards him. Her lack of concern at seeing him only reinforced his opinion that she'd never truly cared for him at all, not deeply. What she'd felt was passion and, like any blazing fire, it could burn down to nothing but ash if left to die.

A fiercely independent woman, she'd loved her freedom more than him. That must still be the case, as any man would have considered himself lucky to win a woman like her. But he knew from his idle enquiries— whenever he'd travelled past Rouen—that she'd never married and the lack of a ring on her hand now confirmed it.

His eyes swept greedily over her body. She still wore the manly attire she'd worn in her youth. Boots and wide woollen trousers, her calves wrapped in leg-bindings for warmth, the fabric billowing out at the knees to allow ease of movement around her hips and thighs. A green tunic was cinched in at the waist by her sword belt, and a matching heavy mantle draped over one shoulder, a pack and shield strapped to her back.

Still the perfect Valkyrie he'd dreamed of for more nights than he liked to admit. If, right now, she grew wings and swept him away in death he would die a very happy man. Whether he dined in Odin's Hall or Rán's sea kingdom beneath the waves, neither fate mattered to him. He cared only in whose arms he would lay.

Of course, in those dreams her hair had always been loose, like it had been that summer. Liquid fire rippling around her, burning his skin with its agonising softness. In his mind, she would reach for him, stroke his face and promise never to leave. Then he would drown in her kiss.

He forced the dream from his mind and did as any wise merchant should—he focused on the details that would give him an advantage. That's when he noticed her clothes were well worn and the cloak was knotted rather than pinned with a brooch.

Had she had to sell it? Was she poor?

But how could that be? She was Jorund Jötunnson's second-in-command—and that man had had great success in Francia.

She wore an ornate sword at her side…so maybe his first assumption was wrong? Possibly, she needed to return to Rouen and currently lacked the silver to do so. But why had she left Jorund in the first place?

So many questions and they'd barely even spoken… yet.

A knot pinched in the muscle of his shoulder and he rolled it to ease the ache.

'Valda!' He beamed, using a warm and carefree tone as he eased leisurely away from the barrel.

He gave her a lighthearted tap on the arm, hoping it

would convey that he was both friendly and unconcerned by their past. Nimbly, she danced away from him, landing an equally playful blow to his lower ribs. It took all of his skills in subterfuge and negotiation to hide his wince. She still had a mean jab.

She laughed, but as she pulled away her smile stiffened slightly, as if realising something unpleasant. 'I need work, not passage. But maybe you know of someone who can help me? I want to join a merchant ship for the summer…or anything, really. I need to earn silver for my family.'

He paused, weighing up the price of such a trip. Not in silver, all of his voyages were ultimately profitable, but in the cost to his heart.

Dared he risk it?

Loki would have been proud of Halfdan's trickery, as he feigned a surprised gasp after a moment of hesitation. 'Oh! How strange a coincidence this is! I could do with another sword on my ship. I have a long voyage planned this summer.'

A trip he'd only just this moment decided upon. One that might cause problems with his father… But he was confident he could figure it out later. What mattered now was getting Valda's agreement to join him.

She bit her lip. 'Are you sure it won't be…odd?'

Halfdan laughed and hoped it didn't sound as hollow as it felt. 'Why would it be odd?'

She smiled as if she were reassured. 'Well, I can row and fight much better than in my youth. If you need proof of my skill, I can always demonstrate it…' Worry crossed her face. 'I have nothing to trade, though, except a few pelts. Will you still have me?' she asked, her jaw tilted up in proud defiance, as if daring him to reject her.

He waved away her words with his most charming of smiles. Truthfully, he would have accepted her aboard his ship even if it had meant throwing his own cargo in the river.

'No need! I know you are a fierce shieldmaiden, old friend.' The word *friend* tasted bitter on his tongue. He added a carefree shrug of nonchalance as he continued. 'All of my crew receive an equal share in the profits—after my cut, of course. Even with little to trade, you should still earn a good amount of silver.'

'Thank you, Halfdan. You were always generous.' Her eyes softened a little and he breathed a sigh of relief that she didn't hate him for not offering her more, either then or now. The awkwardness he'd feared at seeing her again was slowly vanishing like the morning mist on a summer's breeze. There was only one problem…

'Word of my arrival will reach my father soon. I should meet with him,' he said.

'Oh, of course. Best not to keep him waiting… I would hate to cause him offence by delaying you.' Her worried tone spoke loudly of his father's influence in Jorvik. Ulf was a bully and a tyrant so Halfdan wasn't surprised that Valda would be nervous of offending him—especially as she had her mother and sisters' welfare to consider.

'You haven't delayed me…but come to my ship tomorrow, and we'll discuss the details. It's docked by the ale house further down from here. Walk with me a little? At least until the Jarls' square…or wherever your home is?' He waited, hoping that she would explain where she lived, and therefore disclose who her current overlord was, but she only nodded in response.

Falling into an easy rhythm, side by side they walked together along the jetty and into the muddy veins of the

city. She moved—as always—with certainty and purpose, her arms swinging freely by her sides, a slight
swagger to her step. Bold and as hot headed as her fiery
hair, she was resourceful and brave.

Valda the Blade.

She looked a little thinner, though, and he hoped she
and her family had enough to eat.

To distract himself, he looked out towards Jorvik to
the workshops, churches and markets that made up the
chaos of the city and swallowed the horizon from view.
Smoke and the settlement's many smells filled the air
with both the best—but mostly the worst—that life had
to offer.

He'd been here less than a day and already the salt of
the sea called to him.

Unable to contain his curiosity a moment longer, he
asked, 'Are you still with that giant…what's his name
again?' He feigned forgetfulness, even though he knew
perfectly well the man's name—he'd cursed it often
enough.

'Jorund Jötunnson?' she asked quietly and he noticed
the way her lips pinched at the mention of him.

His pulse quickened in anticipated outrage. He
clenched and unclenched his fists to ease the tension
building within. 'Ahh, yes, *Jorund*. That's it! Fights
under Rollo's banner?' He'd heard fine things about the
man, but refused to praise him…not if he made Valda
bristle like that.

It had been a while since he'd asked his Francia contacts for news of her. Mainly because he'd thought her
happy and settled, which always lowered his spirits.

I can never be yours, she'd said to him once, long
ago…and he was still trying to accept it.

He often wondered what would have happened if things had been different. If their own fierce independence hadn't won the battle.

Maybe they would have married as she'd wished and settled on land? In Gotland, the place of his birth and his mother's untimely death.

Would he have been happy there? He wasn't sure.

But dwelling on such things was pointless.

After their final, terrible argument, she'd returned to Francia as she'd said she would and become a shield-maiden in Rollo's army. When he'd learned that she'd left her sisters to live as Jorund's second, he'd drunk himself near half to death. Knowing that separating from her mother and sisters could only mean one thing...another man had her love.

A man who by all accounts was unburdened by familial duty and honoured for his actions alone. It was one of the reasons Halfdan had built up such a vast amount of wealth for himself. To prove, if only to himself, that he was worth more than the name his father had given him.

'I'm no longer with him,' she said quietly.

Did that mean they were no longer together? He'd suspected as much when he'd seen her, but the confirmation caused his stubborn heart to kick like a mule. He moved aside to allow a cart of fish to pass while he gathered his thoughts. When he returned to her side, he managed to restrain his curiosity enough to mutter an unbothered, 'Oh?'

Pain flashed briefly across her face. 'He's Lord of Evreux now, and...married. There's no longer a place for me there... In fact, there probably never was.' She laughed as if it were a sudden and bitter surprise that she'd only this moment acknowledged. 'I can't believe

I just told you that! But I guess you know better than anyone my disastrous choices when it comes to men.'

He frowned, confused at his warring thoughts and emotions.

Sympathy, anger, pain, delight—each emotion washed through him with equal force. 'Forget about him. You deserve better.' He stared at her profile for a moment longer than he should have, entranced by the strong, yet beautiful features of her face, and the glowing embers of her hair. *I should have married her.* 'You always did.'

Her eyes darted to his and he looked away, cursing the slip of his tongue. It was far too late for regrets. Valda had loved Jorund enough to follow him, a feat he'd never managed. He might still have some uncomfortable feelings towards her. Might even be compelled to help her despite their past. But nothing else could happen between them. She wanted stability and security—two things he could never offer.

With a forced laugh he added, 'Besides, you will be far happier than he'll ever be. Marriage is a shackle on a man's freedom—one that should be avoided at all costs!'

'You never married? I thought your father had you promised to Olga.'

'Who?'

'Jarl Olaf's daughter?'

Halfdan frowned, wondering why Valda would bring up such a weak connection. One he only remembered vaguely himself…and only then because of the lies Olga had spouted about him after Valda left.

'No, I couldn't stomach the girl. She married one of her father's men in the end. A babe followed soon after… too soon.' He laughed at his own pitiful jest and immediately regretted it.

Valda's lips tightened in a pinch of disapproval, but she remained silent. 'Sounds like a lucky escape,' she said drily.

Seeing Valda's clear condemnation of him and realising how hard it must have been for her as a fatherless child, he felt suddenly guilty and found himself sympathising with Olga's situation, something he'd never imagined possible.

He chose his next words carefully. 'I hear she's happier now—less spoiled.'

'So, a lucky escape for her, too.' There was no malice or anger to her words, yet he'd never felt more worthless.

'I hope the babe wasn't tarnished by the mother's mistake.' Her words were oddly bitter and he frowned.

'Olga and her family are happy…at least as far as I'm aware.'

'Good,' she snapped. 'I never liked her, but I wouldn't wish…unhappiness on her.' Valda looked away.

For some reason her support towards Olga made him spiteful and he found himself telling her in an overly bright tone, 'Well, despite my best efforts, it appears marriage will ensnare me eventually.'

Curious hazel eyes looked up at him. 'You're getting married?'

He'd hoped to see something else there, too, but she seemed unbothered by the news and that hurt far more than he'd liked to admit.

'Not yet. But…it's likely.' That wasn't entirely true. His father was keen for him to accept an alliance, but he'd not agreed to anything yet. He'd heard about a proposed match, though; it was the reason why Ulf had requested a visit from his eldest son. Regardless, Halfdan found himself labouring the point—if only to make her realise how difficult he found the idea of marriage to be, both then and now. It wasn't that he hadn't loved Valda enough to marry her, it was that he'd loved her too much. Marriage to anyone not of his father's choosing meant hardship or even death to those Halfdan loved.

Although, as was his way, he explained it in jest rather than reveal the true pain behind it. He sighed with mock misery. 'I am like Fenrir—bound in unbreakable chains. I believe my father wishes me to marry a Briton, the sister of a lord from the Western Mountains—the Saxons call them the Welsh and, according to them, they are impossible to deal with. However, my father wishes to make a deal with them and I will no doubt be his sacrifice.'

'Poor Halfdan.' Valda laughed. 'What a terrible life you lead as a powerful jarl's son.'

Halfdan laughed. Of course, she was right to tease him. He was luckier than most and more fortunate than his half-brother, Erik, who had lived most of his life as a slave and an outcast.

But he couldn't help it, he'd still rather his life were different. That he'd been born a simple warrior without a title. At least then he'd have been free to court the woman he'd always loved. Instead, he'd had to make do with his second love…the sea.

'I'll see you tomorrow, Halfdan.' She bit her lip in hesitation before adding with a sigh, 'I truly am grateful for your offer.'

For a moment he worried that she would disappear into the crowd and he would never see her again. He reached out and squeezed her arm lightly. 'Promise me you will come tomorrow… I swear, I can help.'

She hesitated, the sweet tongue he remembered peeping out to lick her lips as she stared into his eyes and considered his words.

'I will,' she eventually whispered in a hoarse voice, as if the agreement hurt her pride.

Maybe it did?

Then she turned away, slipping from his grasp and disappearing out of sight as easily as she'd done all those years before.

Chapter Two

Valda moved swiftly through the alleys and markets towards home, weaving through the buildings and people like a salmon heading upstream. When she was confident that she'd put enough space between herself and Halfdan, she leaned against the wall of one of the less rickety buildings and waited.

Although she had taken great care to check several times that he wasn't following her, she had to be certain. Several carts and people passed her by, but no tall, handsome man wearing extravagant silks and a charming smile. No Halfdan.

She let her head drop back against the wall and closed her eyes against the dreary path and darkening sky.

If accepting his help after all these years was hard, then leading him to the hovel she shared with her family would be unbearable. They were even poorer now... which was an impressive feat in itself.

She pushed away from the wall, her breathing suddenly laboured and tight.

Memories whispered through her veins.

'Sail away with me.'

Lazy summer days spent making love in his half-built boat…

Lost in the past, she could almost smell the wood shavings. The aromatic curls of oak that clung to her hair as he laid her down on the deck. The smooth warmth of his skin beneath her fingertips and the soft pelts beneath her naked back.

The heady desire, the longing, the *torment*.

She'd thought those days were behind her, a misstep of her youth.

But the *feelings.*

They were still there and as strong as they ever were. Not even with Jorund had she felt such all-consuming passion. As if her body would scatter like leaves on the wind if she could not have him.

Her first taste of love and loss.

But to have those feelings still, after all this time? Maybe it was just the shock of seeing him again that had poured salt on to the open wounds left by Jorund. She'd hoped to feel the same mutual desire with Jorund, but that had been a fruitless hope. Fire needed both fuel and air to burn and there'd been nothing solid between them.

At least she could mask it better now. Age had given her some wisdom at least.

They'd gone to Gotland for a distant relative's wedding. She couldn't even remember their names now. Halfdan had been the son and heir of the terrifying Jarl Ulf—but he was nothing like his father and people said he had his mother's way about him.

The islanders had shivered and flinched as Ulf passed. Halfdan, in contrast, was loved and worshipped by everyone. He owned that small trading post as surely as if he'd held it in the palm of his hand. Valda had not been able to understand how two men could be treated so differently by those under their rule.

It all became clear one day when Ulf had beaten a man to death for merely knocking into him by accident. Halfdan had tried to save the man, had fought with his father to let him go. But Ulf was a monster that could not be stopped.

She'd found a broken Halfdan huddled in his boat the next day, reminding her that he was still so young despite his bravery, and her heart had bled for him. She'd held him tight until the pain had been washed away by lust.

She'd thought love could heal all ills and failed to heed Brynhild's warning.

'He is destined to be a jarl and jarls do not marry the nameless daughters of shieldmaidens.'

He'd begged her to leave with him. To sail to distant lands and visit the greatest cities in the world. But she'd refused to leave her family and they'd argued about it.

Halfdan had said he could not join with her family— his father would never have accepted it. Neither would he have accepted their marriage. *'Not yet,'* he'd said and Valda had grown uneasy, afraid that his promises of love were weak, that he would eventually tire of her and walk away—as so many of her mother's lovers had.

She'd struggled with the choice for days. Changing her mind over and over until she was driven half mad by it.

Then Brynhild had heard a terrible rumour and she'd convinced Valda to seek out the truth of it.

Together they'd waited and watched in the sand dunes until they'd seen Olga, Olaf's daughter, leaving Halfdan's boat with a smug smile on her lips.

Valda still hadn't believed it. Not until she'd gone to the boat and seen for herself Halfdan sleeping naked on the deck, an empty bottle of mead and two cups in the furs beside him.

Their special place...or at least it had been to her.

Valda hadn't been his only love that summer and her heart had shattered in that moment.

She'd sobbed so hard that Brynhild had had to drag her away. She was grateful to her for it; if she'd woken Halfdan with her tears she would have been even more humiliated. No shieldmaiden cried; they were warriors. She'd realised then that the only loyalty she could rely on was that of her mother and sisters.

They'd left the next day and she'd prayed to the gods to never again see his treacherous face.

To think she could have been like Olga. Carrying a child that he would never acknowledge. She was disgusted with him. But also not surprised. It was not uncommon for powerful men to walk away from their responsibilities like that...

She'd thought better of Halfdan, but hadn't his betrayal proved otherwise? He was not a man to be trusted...and yet his offer today had seemed genuine.

She only had to look at him to realise how successful he'd become; he wore silks fit for a king. A voyage with him would be a great opportunity...and she didn't have many of those to speak of...

Could she really sail away with him now? After all that had happened between them? Forget the past...

'Heill!' came a grunt from behind her and Valda almost jumped out of her skin when she heard the blunt, husky voice of her elder sister. Shame heated her cheeks and she tried to shake the unnecessary guilt from her thoughts.

'Brynhild!' Valda smiled brightly as she turned

around to face her—a little too brightly, judging by her sister's alarmed look. But Valda wasn't quite ready to explain the strange events of her afternoon. 'How was the Jarls' assembly?' she asked instead.

Brynhild rolled her sapphire eyes with a grimace. 'The King of Wessex continues to encroach on Norse territory, and the Jarls are still undecided as to how to proceed.'

'And Gunnar?' asked Valda, curious as to what their new overlord felt regarding such an obvious insult. So far, most of the Jarls seemed more focused on internal struggles and backbiting than the creeping tide of Saxons reclaiming the land.

It was worrying.

'He said very little,' Brynhild replied with a pointed look and Valda sighed.

Gunnar was weak. It would not be long until he fell beneath the axe of another jarl. His inaction was dangerous, not only for himself, but for Valda and Brynhild too. As part of his paid retinue, they were duty bound to protect him. It was one of the many reasons Porunn and her daughters needed to leave Jorvik and secure land of their own. Ideally further north and away from the Saxon border.

If only another jarl would accept them.

A fly buzzed past Valda's ear and she swatted at it with a curse. It wasn't even fully spring yet and already Jorvik swarmed with them. 'Odin's teeth! How I *loathe* this place!'

'Rouen wasn't much better.'

'At least the weather was warmer. It's rained endlessly here since we arrived in the autumn!' Valda dragged her boot up and out of the churned earth, scowled at the filth that covered it and then dropped her foot back with a wet slap. 'Today is the first dry day in weeks! But the city still looks like a swamp!'

Brynhild raised an eyebrow at Valda's rant. As if she knew full well that the only thing Valda missed from Rouen was her old life. 'You just hate Jorvik.'

Valda shrugged—she couldn't deny that. Jorvik's foul stench felt like a suffocating shroud against her skin and she was miserable here and longed for change.

'Any luck at the docks?'

'Possibly…but let's get home first, so I can tell you all together.'

Brynhild gave her another curious look, but remained silent as they walked back.

It wasn't long before they reached their tiny wattle-woven hut in the Tanners' stretch of the city.

Even if she covered her eyes, Valda would always know when she was close to home…because of the stench. The acrid smell of hides being cured filled the already stale air with the foulest of odours. But it was all they could afford with Gunnar's silver.

As they entered their plot, their younger sister waved at them from the tiny vegetable patch. Helga grew some herbs and a few root vegetables—only she could manage such a feat despite the appalling soil.

Helga was the only one of them who wore an apron dress—she'd always been more feminine than her older sisters—but the wool was looking a little old and tattered. The toggle fastenings were also visible as she'd had to sell her turtle brooches weeks ago.

Seeing her younger sister so diminished by their circumstances was the hardest thing to bear. Probably because she didn't moan and whine about it as much as

Valda did—which somehow made it worse. She wished she could buy her new brooches, maybe even some glass beads to string across them, but that was impossible. They barely had enough food to fill their bellies. Valda's hand guiltily touched the hilt of her grand sword before moving away.

They all had to work hard to put food in the pot, just in different ways.

Valda and Brynhild earned scraps of silver from Gunnar. Porunn, who was too old to sell her sword, hunted in the woods surrounding the city. They ate the meat and sold the pelts. Helga was the best at selling them, quickly charming the local tanners with her pretty smile, offering them an occasional fortune telling, or herbal remedy alongside their furs, and she also ran the home.

Valda glanced in at the empty room and then frowned at the setting sun. 'Where's Mother?'

'Here!' called Porunn, walking in from the opposite direction, her limp heavier than usual and a single hare hanging from her belt. *Poor pickings on her snares tonight, then.* Either that, or someone else had taken her prey. The city children did that sometimes. Who could blame them? They were hungry, too.

They all took it in turns to squeeze into the hut and sat around the fire, keeping the door open to help remove the smoke. The room was small and bare except for two wide benches either side of the fire pit.

The benches doubled up as their beds at night. Brynhild slept with Helga as they were the smallest and largest of the group, and seemed to balance each other out, while Valda slept beside their mother. It was cramped and uncomfortable, but at least with them crushed together it was reasonably warm, even in winter.

Valda had nothing to offer the pot today, so she lit the fire and filled the cauldron with some rain water from the barrel. She'd lost a day's work by going to the docks. They'd agreed last night though that it was worth the risk. They couldn't go on like this.

'Well?' Porunn asked Valda with a raised brow as she skinned the hare and dropped the meat into the pot.

'There's a merchant ship that might take me on. I'll find out tomorrow.'

The chorus of relieved sighs that filled the tiny hut made Valda's stomach twist painfully and it wasn't only from hunger. There was no way she could reject Half-dan's offer now, no matter how uncomfortable the prospect made her.

'A merchant ship, too? That *is* good! You would never have been happy raiding,' Helga said, adding some chopped parsnips and herbs to the stew.

'Will you need goods to trade?' Porunn looked at their bedding with a frown. A few old furs and blankets were all they had.

'There's my sword…' said Valda.

Her mother and sisters stared at her with wide eyes.

Valda shrugged. 'It's just a sword.'

'But…it's…' Brynhild couldn't seem to find the words, but Valda knew what she meant. It was her last gift from Jorund. A thank you for her service and a token of his respect for her.

Valda nodded. 'At first it made sense to keep it. It's Frankish steel, after all, and I needed a weapon to join Gunnar's guard. But… I have felt bad holding on to it. Helga has sold all her jewellery. You and Mother have traded everything you could and left yourselves with only basic weapons while I have had this the whole time. It was wrong of me to keep it. I should have traded it long before—I'm sorry.'

Porunn shook her head firmly. 'No. We have taken enough from you. You paid for our passage here and we have lived off the remains of your hoard throughout the winter. I insist you keep it. After so many years of loyalty and service, you deserve it.'

Helga nodded, her eyes brimming with sympathetic tears. 'I would not wish for you to sell it, either. My jewellery meant nothing to me, they were just trinkets. Your sword does…'

Valda sighed. 'I'll have no need for such an elaborate weapon if we secure a farm.'

Porunn patted her arm. 'At least wait until after your voyage. You may need it.' She turned to Brynhild then. 'What of the Jarls?'

Brynhild took out a loaf of bread from her pack and began to slice it, offering them each a piece in turn. 'I asked around… Ivar is the only Jarl that might consider us. His territory is the strongest and reaches up into the land of the Picts. But…' She paused with a miserable sigh.

Helga finished the words for her, as was her way. 'One of us needs to be married…so that he has a sworn allegiance from a man.'

Porunn swiped aside an errant strand of silver hair that had tumbled out of her braids. 'Something I might even consider…if anyone would have me.'

'You would?' Valda asked, horrified that her mother would even consider it. How many years had she spat on the idea of marriage…and now she would give up her treasured independence…for a farm?

Helga leaned forward, touching her mother's shoulder in a comforting caress. 'There is more love in your future. I am certain of it.'

Porunn smiled sadly and stirred the pot. 'I would be glad of even a loveless marriage if it meant a better life for you three. But I fear it will be you supporting me instead. I am too old to sell my sword, or bear children, and I have no silver. I doubt it will even be an option.'

'You have a lot to offer,' Valda reassured her, although a small part of her agreed. It was true, Porunn was not a great prospect for a husband—even though she was still beautiful in her own wild way.

'Then one of us should marry...' suggested Helga, without much enthusiasm.

Porunn shook her head vehemently. 'No! You have no bride price and I refuse to give *any* of you away to an unworthy man. Odin will not forsake us. We have fought too well and too hard on the battlefield for him to forget our loyalty. If only I had followed the advice I gave you girls when you were growing up. *Never rely on a man for your happiness. He will only ever disappoint.*' Porunn tossed another log on to the fire and the flames rose hungrily to claim it. 'I *curse* Bjorn for this!'

As was their custom, all four women spat into the fire at the mention of his name.

The curses aimed at Bjorn would follow him until Ragnarök, the end of days. Their mother's relationship with him had been the cause of their downfall. For years Porunn had valued her independence and refused to accept any man. But as she'd got older she'd started to desire a companion in spite of herself. She'd thought she'd found one with Bjorn, but her lover had disappeared in the middle of the night with every scrap of silver the family had accumulated over the years. Then Valda had arrived from her own misadventure with Jorund and they'd ended up here, scrabbling in the muck trying to survive.

'What if we bribe him? Offer him enough silver that he can't refuse?' asked Helga.

'It's possible…' Brynhild said. 'But I think being in Ivar's service first might help our cause. He seems an honourable man and is at least considering my request to join his retinue. I feel Gunnar's power waning and I do not wish to be pulled into a hopeless fight.'

'Do you think he will accept you?' asked Porunn.

Brynhild smiled coldly. 'Gunnar has been crowing about the Valkyries in his guard for weeks. I also demonstrated my skills at the assembly when one man got too heated with Gunnar. Hopefully that will impress Ivar.'

Valda couldn't help but laugh. 'I'm sure it will.'

Gunnar had accepted Brynhild into his ranks on looks alone. With her big, menacing body she looked as close to a Valkyrie as any living woman could. It had been a pleasant surprise for Gunnar when she'd proved herself worthy in both likeness and skill.

Valda, on the other hand, had had to fight two men before he'd accepted her. She'd won both matches, of course, but it still irritated her.

'So, tell us of this merchant ship. What are the crew like—are they trustworthy?' asked Porunn as she gathered the wooden bowls and began to ladle out the stew.

The moment to confess had finally come and with all their plans so heavily reliant on Valda's income she felt more confident to speak. 'I know the merchant…as do all of you. It's Halfdan Ulfsson.'

The sound of the fire cracking filled the room as her mother and sisters stared at her with shocked expressions.

Brynhild was the first to awaken from the trance.

'That betraying *swine*! Are you mad? He can't be trusted!'

'That is in the past… And he *can* be trusted…just not when it comes to…matters of the heart.' She laughed lightly, although it sounded bitter in the silence and she wasn't even sure she believed her own words. At least there was one thing she could be certain of. 'There is no risk of me making the same mistake again,' she said firmly.

Brynhild snorted. 'I hope so! We can't afford another mouth to feed. You had the luck of Loki not to fall heavy with a bastard last time—'

'Enough!' barked Porunn, tapping Brynhild lightly on the head with a wooden spoon to silence her. Then quietly she asked Valda, 'Are you sure you want to do this?'

'I don't think we have much choice, do you?'

'No.' She sighed. 'I suppose not.'

Chapter Three

'Strange he agreed to your terms for Erik's freedom without complaint,' mused Tostig with a frown.

Tostig was his mother's only living kin and a distant one at that. Still, he was more of a father to Halfdan and Erik than Ulf and Halfdan trusted his counsel in all matters, *especially* when it came to dealing with his *real* father. They sat at a table further away from the Jarl's raised dais. Ulf preferred to sit alone, up and away from everyone around him.

'Yes…that was surprising,' Halfdan said thoughtfully as he considered the day's events. He'd finally succeeded in persuading his father to accept payment for Erik's freedom. It had been easier than he'd expected, a little *too* easy. 'Maybe he's realised he was wrong?' Halfdan suggested, although the idea that Ulf would do such a thing was preposterous.

'You think so?' Tostig asked, looking pointedly past Halfdan and at his father.

Ulf was in an unusually jovial mood tonight, laughing and feasting as if he'd won a great victory. A stranger might presume it was because of the return of his favoured son—but Halfdan knew better. He'd probably been triumphant in one of his many schemes with the other Jarls. Either that or he knew he could get more from Halfdan… Why else had he insisted Halfdan come to Jorvik to discuss a potential betrothal?

With hard lips and a badly scarred face that spoke of his many battles, Ulf's blue eyes were hawklike in their predatory perusal. With his tall physique, dark blond hair and equally bright blue eyes, Halfdan had been told more than once that he matched his father in likeness if not in spirit.

It was both a blessing and a curse. His father liked him, viewed Halfdan as a more cheerful version of himself and so had always behaved better towards him. But Halfdan could not respect or love him in return. He'd seen how his father could so easily turn on those around him.

As had most of Ulf's retinue of warriors. The celebration in the Hall lacked depth and sincerity. The tables gleamed and the delicious food was heavily spiced with exotic seasoning, yet people ate quietly at their tables with their heads down.

A precious glass pitcher with matching chalices sat on the Jarl's table, Halfdan's latest gift to his father. It was filled with the strongest, finest Frankish wine Halfdan could offer—all to sweeten the deal. In fact, everything of value in the Hall had been provided by Halfdan over the years. The silverware, the beautifully carved chests and benches, even the rich tapestries—decorated in silk and gold thread—had been bought from Halfdan's purse.

Ulf had always been a minor jarl and had only won this land in Danelaw through violence and Halfdan's silver. His power and wealth had grown because of his sons' hard work. But he gave no praise or thanks for it. Their tributes to him were an expected display of loyalty and subservience.

It always left a bitter taste in Halfdan's mouth whenever he met with his father.

He knew Erik wanted to kill him and would probably have done so without hesitation if Halfdan had allowed it. He could even understand his brother's wish to murder his father. Maybe he would have felt the same if he'd had Erik's life. But his mother's words always came to mind whenever he contemplated such a monstrous crime: *'Be better than your father. Be the man he should have been.'*

Oblivious to his son's thoughts, Ulf dragged a thrall into his lap and kissed her hard. The girl looked terrified and Halfdan looked down at his platter, repulsed. It was better not to intervene directly, especially for the slave girl.

'Erik will be free, that's all that matters,' Halfdan muttered as he pushed a succulent piece of meat around with the tip of his dagger.

'Yes…and all it has cost is one hundred pounds of your silver!' Tostig replied in a scathing tone.

'It will be worth it.'

Halfdan had chipped away at his brother's enslavement for years, slowing carving out his freedom piece by piece, firstly by taking Erik with him on his travels and now by buying his freedom from their father.

'Your half-brother should *never* have been a thrall!' snapped Tostig. 'Your mother would never have allowed it.'

Halfdan nodded, but remained silent.

He'd only known his mother six winters, but those days had shaped him into the man he was today. Sigrid had been a beautiful, kind and compassionate woman. Ulf hadn't deserved her and everyone knew it. When Ulf had returned home from raiding with a thrall carrying his child, Sigrid had welcomed the frightened girl into her home and cared for her.

Erik's mother had not spoken a word of Norse at first, but the two women had quickly formed a friendship that Ulf found peculiar and infuriating. Perhaps he'd expected jealousy instead? But Sigrid didn't care enough about Ulf for that and she was content to bring up the two boys alongside each other, as brothers.

When Sigrid had become ill carrying Halfdan's sister it was Erik's mother, Anahita, who tried to save them. But mother and child had died in spite of her efforts. In Ulf's raging grief, he'd murdered poor Anahita for her failure and enslaved their son—punishing her in both this life and the next.

Their father was a cruel and bitter man and did not belong with decent people. But as a powerful jarl no one questioned his actions or his choices, such was the privilege of his position.

Halfdan suspected that Ulf had gladly used his younger son's bond with Erik to ensure his obedience. That his ever-increasing wealth and influence as a merchant would be kept in check by the vast sum he'd had to pay for his brother's release.

Which brought him to the problem of arranging his 'one last trip'. The trip he'd planned solely for the benefit of a certain red-headed shieldmaiden from his past.

Valda Þorunndóttir: *The Blade.*

Lethal with a sword even in her youth, she'd developed a reputation in Francia for being sharp, direct and pragmatic in battle.

She was all those things...*and more*, he thought with a rueful smile.

Meeting her again had felt too much of a coincidence. The gods were giving them a second chance and you did not ignore the will of the gods.

He remembered fondly those desperately passionate days. How she'd clung to his arms as he'd sank into her wet heat. The way she'd whisper his name against his neck to urge him on. Throughout that summer they'd learned each other's bodies and pleasure so thoroughly he'd felt lost with anyone else. As if no one could ever know him quite like Valda.

His feelings had not changed. Today was proof of it.

But had hers? She'd loved another man since... Could she have forgotten her feelings for him? Their last argument had felt so final.

He'd had dreams of them sailing away together, living a life of adventure and travel. Who better to have at his side than a brave warrior like Valda?

But she'd wanted the impossible first.

'I don't want your love or your kisses or...stupid promises!' she'd said.

'Then what do you want?' he'd asked.

But in truth he'd been thinking about himself. How desperate he had been to escape Gotland and his father's Hall, to seek out his own wealth and glory, to help his brother leave, too. He couldn't do any of those things if he took a wife. The defiance against his father would have had disastrous consequences. Ulf would never have allowed Erik to leave his Hall, might even have killed him, or Valda, as a way of punishing Halfdan for his disobedience.

And a voice of doubt had whispered, *'If she wants*

marriage, does she really want you? Or does she only wish to be the wife of a future jarl?'

He was ashamed to admit it now, but he'd had a little too much to drink that night. Hiding his own insecurity with humour, he'd laughed in her face.

'Surely the dull life of a wife is not what you really want? I thought better of you...'

'I want loyalty and respect. I want—'

'Marriage.' He'd spat out the word as if it were rotten fruit.

She needed proof of his love. In that moment it had felt as if a hand had closed around his neck and choked the air from his lungs.

He'd spent years persuading his father to let him sail away. To let him explore the life of a merchant—at least until he was ready to settle down, marry and follow his father as Jarl.

The unfairness of it all had made him so angry.

'And if I wasn't a jarl's son, would you demand marriage then?'

'Of course...'

He'd snorted with disbelief. *'Your mother never did.'*

It had been the worst thing he could have said and he still regretted it bitterly.

Immediately she'd stiffened. 'Goodnight, Halfdan!'

'I only meant—I admire her!' he'd tried to explain, but it had been too late.

He'd not meant to insult her. It was well known that Porunn was fiercely independent and had spurned all offers of marriage. Even having a jarl's babe—Valda's sister, Helga—had not tied her down.

He'd followed Valda, but his drunken steps had been

as clumsy as his words. 'I never took you for a coward, Valda! If you truly loved me, you'd be willing to wait!'

Valda had struck back like a serpent. 'You are so ignorant! You have no idea what it's like to be a woman. No idea what you're asking of me!'

Even though her words had rung true, he'd been too young and arrogant to heed them. *'I will not marry... not yet!'*

She'd stared at him for a long moment, her expression changing from raw pain to stubborn ice. The sudden change in her heart still plagued him today. It was as if he'd watched her love for him die.

'If all you want is a concubine than I will never be yours!'

He'd made the only choice he could, although he should have been more honest with her. Explained better why he feared his father's retribution.

Maybe he could make amends by helping her now?

Tostig's voice brought him abruptly back to the present. 'There is something very odd about this alliance your father is proposing.'

Halfdan thought for a moment before answering, 'You're right. It feels more like a hostage negotiation than a marriage proposal.' He nodded to the slim, dark-haired man in the corner who watched the feast with narrowed eyes. 'They send a representative to offer terms—but he does not look happy about it, does he? And no one has met this lord of the Western Mountains—or his sister, my proposed bride—but he has a reputation that is fierce. My father has land on his borders—a small settlement, I believe, nothing substantial. Why would such an ambitious and powerful man propose a marriage alliance with Ulf? Unless Ulf holds something against him or covets his lands… It does not make sense and I do not like things that do not make sense.'

Tostig smiled, his teeth gleaming in the firelight. 'And there I was worrying why you'd agreed to this meeting so readily.'

'If my father wants me to marry her, then I will have a better deal first. I will only accept if it guarantees Erik a better future. Now, let us see how far his *generosity* will stretch.'

Halfdan took a large jug of ale and made his way over to the bride's representative and not his father—a deliberate action ensuring he would draw Ulf's attention.

'Tell me about your lady, sir. What's she like?' Halfdan asked loudly. 'Young…pretty…clever?' He drank from his horned cup, portraying the drunken, entitled son of a jarl to the stranger before him.

The man looked up at him with tired, pained eyes. 'She is all of those things…and more.' *Interesting*, thought Halfdan, a little surprised by the repetition of his own thoughts from earlier. He looked at the man a little more closely. Handsome, in a youthful and earnest sort of way. The type that might turn a young maiden's head.

'*More?* Then tell me…' He poured the ale into the man's cup until it was practically overflowing, then set the jug down next to him. 'Is she blonde like me?'

'Dark.' The man's fingers tightened to match the ivory cup in his hands.

'Blue eyes, or brown? My mother had brown eyes… earthy and warm… I rather like them.'

'Green, like the sea,' the man muttered, taking the cup and draining half of it in one long gulp.

Very interesting.

Ulf's voice boomed across the Hall. 'Why do you care

what she looks like, Halfdan? I want you to marry her; that should be enough incentive for you! I am determined this time, Halfdan, I want you to marry, or maybe I will forget my earlier kindness regarding your brother.' The last was said as an empty threat. In truth, Halfdan had already warned his father that all 'gifts' from his trades would cease if he didn't at least agree on a price for Erik.

Halfdan smiled tightly, but kept his attention on the man in front of him. 'It pleases me to know that my *potential* bride will be beautiful. Bedding her should be a pleasure, rather than a chore. And I do so hate chores.'

Halfdan watched with approval as the man's face flushed with anger.

There was promise there.

He turned away, leaving the man to muse on his own misery while Halfdan joined his father at the high table. The slave girl was roughly pushed from his father's lap and she scampered away as quickly as she dared. A small burst of satisfaction warmed Halfdan's heart. The mention of his mother had been enough to cool Ulf's lust for the night. It was a sly trick that didn't always work, but when it did, it saved the female thralls from an unwanted night in his father's bed.

'Well?' snapped Ulf.

Halfdan eased on to the stool beside him, being sure to refill his father's chalice of wine first. 'You seem keen for me to accept this alliance…far more so than the others you've offered me in the past.'

Ulf's voice was low and filled with barely concealed fury. 'It could be good for both of us. Now, will you accept it or not?'

Halfdan leaned closer so that only he could hear him.

'You want this *a lot*, don't you? Enough to accept another deal?'

'What *deal*?' he snarled.

'You've agreed the price for Erik's freedom. How much to buy his future, too?'

Ulf frowned at him and took a long drink of his wine before answering, 'Go on.'

'I want Erik to have land and a title.'

A slow smile of disgust stretched across Ulf's face. 'Fine. If you agree to marry her, Erik will have a settlement of his own.' He leaned forward, his hot, stale breath hitting Halfdan's cheek with a hiss. 'Now, speak… Will you do it?'

Halfdan paused, Valda's beautiful face filling his mind. *Was he making a mistake by agreeing to this? Was there still hope for them? No, he could not risk his brother's happiness on a wishful dream. But he would try his best to help her, it was the least he could do.*

'Yes,' replied Halfdan, meeting his father's eyes with a heavy heart. Then, with a light smile he added, 'As soon as I return—'

'Return?' Ulf's eyes narrowed into vicious slits.

He knew his father would argue it, but if Valda was to have her voyage, it was crucial for Ulf to agree to the delay. Halfdan feigned surprise. 'Father, one hundred pounds of silver for Erik's freedom is a substantial amount, even for me. I could give you half the amount now, but I will need to get the rest from my Dnieper settlement.'

Ulf scowled darkly. 'You could marry *now* and pay for Erik's freedom later.'

'But where is she—this Welsh bride?' He'd heard from

one of Ulf's men that she would not leave the safety of her brother's land until the alliance was agreed.

Ulf frowned. 'She can be here in a matter of weeks.'

Halfdan smiled. 'Weeks? Then you should definitely have your full payment before—besides, it will give you time to decide on Erik's land. I want good, fertile land for him, nothing less than you would give to me. And all details should be clear from the start... You taught me that, Father. I am a shrewd merchant, after all, and we never pay unless we have the goods first. The wedding can take place the winter after next, at the latest.'

'It will not! You must marry within the year!' Ulf bellowed, causing everyone in the room to lower their voices with a flinch.

All except Halfdan, who had already anticipated the outburst. It was the reaction he wanted because it would soften the blow of the agreement he had really been seeking all along. 'But Erik is in the east, along the Volga route,' Halfdan said innocently. 'Then he will no doubt spend the winter in our settlement, which means he's not due to sail here until the following summer.'

'Then collect him on your way back!' shouted Ulf, his frustration clear.

Halfdan gave him an admiring smile that almost turned his stomach. 'Of course! Why did I not think of that? I will send word for him to meet me at the Dnieper settlement. There, I can collect him and your silver and be back by autumn...long before your deadline.'

Ulf leaned back in his throne-like chair and stared at his son with deep, menacing eyes. 'By this autumn...or your brother will never see the following year. Is that understood?'

Halfdan nodded. He'd got what he wanted, but his

heart felt as heavy and cold as a block of ice. He refused to let fear enter his voice and replied as positively as ever.

'If you provide the bride, I'll be there!' Then, to be certain his father would not change his mind as he had so often done in the past, he said loudly so that all could hear, 'In the autumn, I will return with one hundred pounds of silver. That silver will buy Erik's freedom. You will then gift Erik with the title of Chieftain over a fine settlement and I will marry this Welsh bride on the day she arrives in Jorvik. Those are the terms. *Swear it!*' He held up his hand and gripped his bronze arm ring as he made his oath.

Ulf did the same. 'I swear it!' he snarled, with a bitter glare.

They spat and shook hands, sealing the deal in a gloomy feasting Hall as silent as the dead. Everyone watched the exchange with wide eyes, amazed that Ulf had finally agreed to free his eldest son. Word would spread quickly through the Halls of Jorvik.

It was a vague hope, but maybe Halfdan could buy Erik his title as well as his freedom. If, for example, the bride never arrived for the ceremony? Ulf could not punish either of them for it. Then Halfdan could offer twice the sum and gain both for his brother without having to marry after all.

Later, Halfdan decided, he would have another word with his bride's representative.

He could subtly suggest that maybe she shouldn't be here when he returned in the autumn, that if this man loved her—as it appeared he did—then he should take her by the hand and run.

As Halfdan should have done.

Chapter Four

'Welcome aboard!' shouted Halfdan as he strode purposefully from his ship's ramp to greet her.

Valda looked up at the impressive dragon boat and smiled.

It certainly suited him.

Unusual in design, and much larger than any of those surrounding it, the ship appeared built for long trade voyages, but was also equipped for battle.

Round red and black shields ran along its sides, with sea chests placed at thirty pairs of oars, suggesting a crew of double that. A magnificent mast soared up into the sky, rigged with a glorious red sail that made Valda's back ache to look up at it. The snarling head of a dragon was carved at its prow, with black tar-covered teeth, bright green eyes and a face of flaming red, the colour trailing down and along the ship's sides to a swirling carved tail decorated with runes. There was also a red tented canopy area near the animal's head, the kind of luxurious accommodations a king might have had.

Halfdan certainly looked as if he were a king. His clothing looked even more extravagant and opulent than the day before, but he wore them with such an easy manner that it seemed natural on him.

She found herself dazzled when she looked at him, there was so much to take in.

His tunic was heavily trimmed with silk and embroidery, the vibrant red bringing out the gold in his hair. His cloak was also red—although a darker shade—and made from a fine wool that would be the envy of any man. A large, gold, penannular brooch held it in place on his left shoulder. Even his dark breeches were luxurious, trimmed with extravagant bands of embroidered silk along the waistband and down the seams. A thick belt in a buttery leather, covered with intricate decoration, kept his weighty purse as well as a sword at his side. A weapon was not an uncommon sight on a Norse merchant, except that his was a curved Saracen blade. She'd never seen one before and it fascinated her. It also had an elaborately decorated pommel and sheath with jewels winking from it. He wore similar boots and leg wraps to her, but his were of a far superior quality and she stared at his footwear for a little longer than would have been considered normal. They put her own worn-out and leaky boots to shame.

A finely twisted, gold neck ring held a Thor's hammer in place around his strong throat. It was nothing like the crude bone hammer she wore and, as the frayed piece of twine that held hers in place suddenly began to itch, she resisted the urge to touch it.

'It's beautiful!' she said with honest admiration. 'Your father must be very proud.' She'd heard Halfdan's father was a very wealthy man now, but this ship surpassed even her expectations.

Was he trying to impress her? But why? It was obvious she had nothing—a man with only a pair of weather-proof boots was more impressive than her. She felt like a beggar.

Halfdan shrugged and scratched his neck, an array of silver rings shinning on his fingers in the sunlight, and she wondered if she'd soured his mood by mentioning his father. Then she noticed it. The simplest piece of decoration on his entire body.

A bronze arm ring, the one he'd worn in his youth. He'd told her once that it had been a gift from his mother's side of the family and that it was all he had left of her.

Seeing it calmed Valda's nerves.

There was something oddly reassuring about it, that despite the obvious luxuries he now enjoyed there was still enough of the old Halfdan left for her to recognise him. That beneath all the glittering silks and jewels there was still the same boy who loved and missed his mother.

'And it's magnificent compared to your first ship,' she added and he laughed.

'Anything would be better than that bundle of sticks.'

For a moment she wondered what had become of Halfdan's first ship, the boat where they'd stolen precious moments together among the wood shavings. What had happened to their names on the prow? The shaky carvings made by Halfdan's knife as they'd laid together under the summer sun. Had he shaved them off after their argument? Written Olga's initials instead?

She banished the unwelcome thoughts from her mind. It was probably an old fishing boat by now or had been used for firewood. She doubted Halfdan would have been sentimental over it. Surely he would have wanted to look to the future and the tantalising possibilities just beyond the horizon.

He'd probably forgotten all about it, as she should have done.

Meeting him again had rekindled her past memories to torturous effect.

He was her first love, forged in the fires of youth, and it was bound to still hurt.

Those passionate days burned more brightly than even her happy times with Jorund. Except, of course, nothing had ever happened with Jorund. She'd pined for him. Admired and loved him from afar, but he'd never returned her feelings, or even kissed her.

Halfdan, on the other hand...

'Come aboard, let us toast to our new venture together!' he said with a hard clap of his hands. The noise woke her from her daydream and she realised with a hot flush that she'd been staring at his lush mouth for far too long.

The word *together* finally sank into her mind and caused her to pause for a moment.

Was she really going to do this?

But no other ships were begging for her to join them. The man on the dock yesterday had been right; many crews had already been decided and she would not find many opportunities available to her, especially not one on a grand merchant ship such as this.

But could she bear it?

She shook her head to clear her mind and followed him.

Of course she could! She was no longer in love with him. No longer a naive girl unable to resist a handsome man's charms.

Besides, she would guard her heart against him. Now that she was older and wiser it would be far easier to do so. All she had to do was remember how he'd betrayed her with Olga—she didn't need any more reason than that to avoid an entanglement!

Halfdan turned back to her and offered her the choice of boarding first with a flourish of his arm.

'Still the charmer,' she said drily.

'For you? *Always*.' His face broke into a devastating smile that would have had her blushing in her youth. But she was no longer a stupid girl led by her heart and so she arched her brow instead and ignored his arm.

In a way, she was glad he'd already broken her heart. His flirting had no effect on her any more. He could no longer seep into her heart and bleed away her resolve. She knew the truth.

Always meant nothing to him.

Her gaze swept over him, trying to see the serpent beneath.

But that was unfair, it was part of his nature. He'd survived a childhood under his father's roof by being likeable and charming—he probably didn't even realise he was toying with her. She could not blame him for it, especially now that she was wiser.

As she'd ignored his arm, he swept back his errant locks with a swipe of his hand instead. Some of his golden hair had fallen from the hastily gathered knot at the back of his head. He had a well-trimmed beard that accentuated the strength of his jaw and there was a masculine beauty to his face and body that could not be denied: impossibly broad shoulders and narrow hips, long muscular legs and the confident stride of a seasoned helmsman.

It was then she realised the similarity between Jorund and Halfdan. Halfdan was also tall—not as tall as Jorund, but Jorund was known as *Giant's Son* for a reason—and their similar colouring was unmistakable.

She'd loved Halfdan first. Was her subsequent taste in men determined by that first flush of love? Was it fate, or would she have always preferred big, blond and blue-eyed men? Yet Jorund and Halfdan were so different in character.

Halfdan was like the god Loki. A handsome trickster, full of humour and adventure. Taking nothing and no one seriously. A spoilt son enjoying his freedom for as long as possible before responsibility caught up with him.

Jorund, in contrast, had been a tormented man, silent and brooding, with a steely resolve for honour and justice. He'd never have played with her affections as lightly as Halfdan had. He'd simply never loved her at all. She'd only realised how hopeless her affection for him was when she'd seen him with his wife. He'd looked at his lady with such adoration that Valda had despaired of ever possessing even half as much devotion from another soul. Thankfully, she'd left before she embarrassed herself any further.

Maybe it was these bitter thoughts of the past that made her needle Halfdan further as they walked along the ramp to board his ship. 'I bet you're going to miss sailing her once you're married. I can't imagine there's much opportunity to sail in the Western Mountains.'

It was a spiteful comment and she wasn't quite sure why she'd said it.

Jealousy, perhaps?

She already despised the woman who would, without any effort, secure a man as handsome as Halfdan for her husband. All because of the advantage of her birth, an advantage Valda could never possess.

Whatever the reason, she immediately felt guilty when he looked back at her with a wince. Then he seemed to shrug off the sobering thought with a grin that stole the breath from her lungs.

'Perhaps I will manage to keep on trading after all... who knows what fate the Norns will weave for me? But... you're probably right. I suspect my father will want me to begin ruling his lands. They are spread out too far as it is.'

He sounded depressed and for some reason that saddened her. 'You are a jarl's son. You can do whatever you want,' she reminded him.

He jumped down into the belly of the ship, and she followed. The crew's sea chests were placed at regular intervals, the oars pulled in. It was tidy and well organised— which suggested a reliable crew.

Some men, presumably part of his crew, played dice at the far end of the deck. Halfdan gave them a wave, which they quickly returned, before he spoke to her again. 'I have given my word I will marry her.' He absently touched his bronze arm ring, the sacred object most men swore their oaths on. She stared at the coiled sea serpent and felt oddly disappointed and sorry for him. No one should be forced to marry someone not of their choosing.

Except why should she care that he was forced to marry another? As a jarl's son, it was inevitable.

She looked up to find Halfdan staring at her, his lips slightly parted, his eyes intense, as if he were waiting for her to react in some way.

'Such is fate,' she said with a carefree shrug, guarding her emotions from him.

He smiled sadly, as if she'd disappointed him, then

cleared his throat and the curious moment vanished like fog under a brilliant sun. 'Come!' he called, as they headed towards the tent at the prow of the ship.

Valda followed, trying her best not to feel sorry for the boy who'd dreamt of sailing to distant lands. He'd managed it for a few years at least—before his father's tyranny caught him in its snare. She couldn't imagine Halfdan as a jarl, dealing with the harvest and the storing of grain, or worse, ordering the deaths of men. The dull, heavy weight of it would probably crush his spirit in the end.

Growing up, she'd sometimes wished to have her father in her life. But never someone like Ulf. She'd rather no father than have a man like that.

But as a grown man Halfdan could make his own choices. If he wished, he could ignore his father's plans for him, leave the luxury of this ship behind and forge a new life. He must have earned enough independent wealth to do that at least.

No, she refused to pity him.

Inside the tent, Halfdan's chamber was surprisingly spacious and as well organised as the deck. There were sea chests lining the walls, a large bed covered in lavish grey and white furs from the far north, as well as an iron brazier beneath an air vent. At the head of the ship was a table and a stool that appeared to be nailed to the floor, no doubt to stop them flying around in turbulent seas. The table was scattered with what looked like several parchment charts and cargo lists, as well as a sun stone and a large dish of water she knew was used for navigation.

Halfdan struck a flint to light the brazier and the tent filled with a soft flickering light. Next, he closed and tied the tent flaps. At Valda's raised eyebrow he explained innocently, 'To stop a draught.'

She laughed, unable to help herself. 'You forget I know you, Halfdan. I remember your constant fear of draughts...and crowds.'

He sighed wistfully. 'Happy times between the furs. I always remember them fondly.'

She snorted. 'Furs? I don't remember it being so grand as that.'

'As if I could lure you away to a proper bed with your guard dogs surrounding you! How is Brynhild by the way? Still reducing men to ash with a single look?'

'Of course,' she responded with a smile.

'I'm surprised you all left Northmannia. Does Rollo have no use for warriors now that the treaty has been signed?'

All joviality disappeared from Valda's voice, leaving only bitterness behind. 'He has given land to his most loyal *men*. Even a great shieldmaiden, like my mother, was denied a small farm. Unless she marries one of his warriors, of course.'

'I see.'

'Do you not think it unfair?' she cried, irritated by his easy acceptance. 'That we will receive nothing but silver despite our years of loyalty?' She should not have asked—she could tell by his surprised expression that he did not wish to answer her.

'I do...' He paused, looking as if he were about to say more, but then thought better of it.

'But...?' she prodded.

He sighed. 'But...your mother was always a flighty creature, unwilling to settle in one place for too long. Maybe Rollo knew this?'

Did he think the same of her? Was that why he'd so easily cast her aside?

'So she does not deserve a reward for her service? All because she has never accepted a man as her husband? Has never *shackled* herself, as you so rightly put it? No, we must bribe a jarl to give us a farm, when she deserves so much more?'

'But she received silver…that's a reward,' he said, a golden brow lifting slightly with barely concealed amusement.

She silently cursed him; he must know they'd had some terrible misfortune. *Why would he make her say it?* 'She did…but it was stolen.'

'Ah… Well, I'm sure things will improve, especially if you join with me on this trip. Do not worry over your mother. She has a strong, adventurous spirit and the freedom to choose her own path…she will be fine. In truth, I have always envied her.'

I will not pity him! Valda silently vowed. *He has chosen his fate.*

'What's she like? Your bride?' she asked, desperate to remind herself of the facts.

'Small and dark, like the rest of the Britons in the mountains.'

'Beautiful?'

'Apparently so… I have never met her,' he said with a non-committal shrug and Valda laughed.

'I'm sure she is. Your father wouldn't accept anything less for you.' Not because Ulf loved his son, but because he would view anything less as a personal insult. 'I refuse to pity you, Halfdan Ulfsson. I know you. You usually get your way in the end.'

A mock look of offence crossed his features and he

bristled dramatically. 'As I refuse to pity you, Valda Þorunndóttir! You who have always succeeded in everything you do!' His face broke into a smile. 'You'll have your farm within a year. I'd wager perhaps even less time than that if you wished it. I just never thought any of you would want such a life…except Brynhild. Possibly she'd be happy to…settle.'

Valda rolled her eyes. 'You and Erik were always so horrible to her. How is your brother—still boring and bitter?'

It was Halfdan's turn to laugh. 'I was never unkind to her, you know that…and, honestly, I think my brother is ashamed of his behaviour back then—especially to Brynhild. But he had his reasons. My father treated him poorly…still does. I wouldn't be surprised if Erik sought her out to apologise when he comes to Jorvik for my wedding.'

'Good.' Valda huffed; she'd always hated Erik for hurting her sister—even if Brynhild never spoke of it. Then again, Erik had been an outcast in his own home and that couldn't have been easy.

He gestured her towards the only stool in the tent. 'Please, take a seat. I'm afraid what I lack in furniture and home comforts, I make up for in *excitement and pleasure.*'

She sat down with a huff which changed to a laugh— he really was a terrible flirt. 'I do not need or *want* excitement or pleasure. I only need enough silver for my mother's farm.'

'How much?'

She said an amount, one that she and her family had decided on the previous night. Valda hoped to earn enough for the bribe, while her mother and sisters would try to earn enough in her absence for the seeds, tools and animals.

Halfdan barely blinked at the huge sum. 'You will earn that easily from this voyage. All going well, of course.'

Valda sighed with relief; her plans no longer seemed impossible. She couldn't wait to reassure her family later. 'When will we sail?'

With a disapproving click of his tongue, he filled two silver chalices from a cask and passed one to her. 'Is silver all you care about? You sadden my heart, Valda. We all need some pleasure in our lives. Otherwise, what is the point of living? Here, drink this and have your first taste.'

She took the chalice from his hands, their calloused fingers brushing against each other and igniting the air between them. Her breath caught in her throat and to cover the sudden flush of her cheeks she raised the chalice to her lips and took a long drink. Smooth wine coated and seduced her tongue, delivering a rich and sharp taste, with the added fragrance of oak and blackberries. She sighed with pleasure.

'Delicious,' she murmured.

When she raised her eyes Halfdan was looking at her with a knowing smile, as if he remembered her sounds of pleasure from long ago. She remembered, too. Those memories had kept her warm on many a lonely night. Heat pool between her thighs and she tried her best to ignore the intoxication of the wine and the man.

'Exquisite, isn't it? The best wine from the south. And if you eat it with fruit and cheese, it brings out the flavour even more.' He opened a nearby chest and began assembling a plate. His hands were quick and nimble despite their weathered roughness. She stared at them as they worked, remembering how those same hands had touched her so intimately in the past.

In no time, he was presenting her with a large platter of exotic dried fruits, bread and cheeses. His body curved over hers in the small space of his tented chamber. Awkwardly, she put the platter on the table behind her, becoming more suspicious with every passing moment. Things were going too well and she always grew nervous when that happened, as if she were waiting for Thor's hammer to fall. 'So, when do we sail?' she asked again.

Halfdan sat back down on his bed, his knees pressing against her thigh. She shifted slightly so they were no longer touching. A small glimmer of amusement flashed on Halfdan's face before he spoke. 'Tomorrow, when the rest of my crew return from the markets.'

She felt the tension in her shoulders slide away. 'Good.' She cut some cheese and laid it on a chunk of bread with the blade of her dagger. Then she stifled a groan as she popped the creamy delight in her mouth. She hadn't eaten so finely in months—and never anything as luxurious or rare as these delights.

Had Halfdan hoarded every delectable food and beverage from across the known world?

And if so, why was he offering them to her now?

Was it to remind her of what she'd missed by rejecting him? But then, his faithlessness had proved that they could never have been happy.

No, it was just posturing and crowing.

Then another thought occurred to her.

Had he noticed how thin her body had become?

He'd never liked to see people go hungry. Ulf sometimes starved people as a form of punishment. She knew that because once, during that summer, they'd crept out in the middle of the night to give grain to a nearby blacksmith's family that had displeased Ulf in some way. She'd never forgotten the look of gratitude on the children's faces, or the tears in the burly smith's eyes as he'd embraced Halfdan before he'd left.

Not that her family were starving. It hadn't got that bad—not yet at least.

As if to confirm her suspicions, he casually nudged a large, linen-covered basket with his foot. 'A few samples for your mother and sisters to try.'

'Thank you,' she said quietly, hating the mixture of shame and admiration she felt at his generous offer. She focused on the plans ahead and tried to ignore the memories that disturbed her sense of conviction. 'And which markets are we going to? Hedeby, Birka, Kaupang?'

'Ahh…not quite,' he answered, with a slight hesitation that he quickly covered with a smile.

An uneasy feeling washed over Valda. With regret she stopped chewing and swallowed the tasty morsel so that she could speak. 'What do you mean?'

Halfdan waved his hand as if he were swatting away a fly rather than her obvious concerns. 'This will be a long voyage—my last adventure before I marry. Full of great riches and reward! Firstly, we will travel to our old trading post in Gotland, then to…' He paused, catching her eye and holding it, the blue of his eyes like precious sapphires winking at her across the gloom. 'Miklagard.'

'Miklagard!' Valda choked on her wine and sprayed half of it on her tunic. 'What?' She gasped. 'But… that's…that's…at the very edge of the world!'

He laughed, a low rumble—it sounded like distant thunder, a promise of wicked pleasures to come. 'Surprisingly, the world is much larger than you think. When you reach the end…you discover it's not the end after all. There's always some other place further still…just beyond the horizon.'

She'd never have believed it and yet here they were— together again and about to embark on the epic voyage he'd always promised her.

Her head suddenly filled with the vibrant images Halfdan had tempted her with nine winters ago. At that time, Halfdan had never been to the places he'd spoken of, but he'd heard tales from passing travellers as well as from Erik's mother and he'd elaborated on them for her benefit.

'The Great City, The Golden City, the Byzantine capital! The Christians call it Constantinople and it is meant to have a stone church so large it could only have been built by giants or gods. There is nowhere like it in the west, not in Francia, England, or the motherlands. It is unique.'

The rich flavours on her tongue were only a seductive promise of yet more new experiences to come. Miklagard, at the furthest edge of the world, was said to be filled with every exotic and luxurious wonder from across the world.

She would see it! The thought rushed through her veins, riding on the intoxicating wave of Frankish wine. *Valda, fatherless daughter of Porunn, a shieldmaiden with no land or silver to her name, would see the greatest city ever built!*

The air felt suddenly hot and stifling as she realised the implications of such a journey. She gulped in a lungful of air, hoping to steady herself. 'But… I just wanted to earn enough for the farm. How long will we be gone? A year? I can't leave my family for that long.'

'Not a year. With me, it takes half the time to get there and back!' he said smugly. 'It's not so long a journey, not really. We'll be back before winter.' He paused, leaning forward and placing a hand on her thigh that seemed to burn through the fabric to her soul. 'Wouldn't you like to see it? The Great City? See the church I told you about? It's as grand as I thought it would be. Gilded with gold and covered in marble! The weather there is dry and hot, the air, filled with the scents of flowers, fruit and spice!'

The air closed in around her as she stared into his eyes.

'Yes,' she whispered, and it shocked her to the core that she'd answered him.

He smiled slowly with triumph. 'I promised I would take you there one day, didn't I?'

A flush of heat crept up her neck. 'Some things are best left in the past.'

'Don't say that.' He moved closer, crowding her with the bulk of his body. He reached out and cupped the side of her face. His expression was soft, as if he was fondly remembering their time together—when she'd allowed him such privileges without a thought to their consequence. His thumb swept against her lower lip, causing her to gasp. She retreated with a jerk of her head.

'To be clear,' she said firmly, 'I will be a member of your crew. Nothing more!' She sobered, placing the chalice firmly on the table beside her before turning back to him. Thankfully, he'd leaned back to allow her the space she desperately needed. 'You are going to be married. I refused to be your concubine then and I refuse it now. Nothing will happen between us on this voyage, Halfdan. Nothing! Or... I won't go!'

Halfdan sighed and a look of regret or guilt—she

wasn't sure which—momentarily crossed his face. 'Nothing will happen.' With a teasing smile, he added, '*If* that's what you want.'

Somehow, that worried her more, because now he knew she wasn't quite as impervious to his touch as she'd led him to believe.

His teeth flashed like pearls in the dim light of his tent. 'I am glad you are here, Valda. I can't imagine a better woman to spend the last days of my freedom with.'

Chapter Five

'What are *they* doing here?' Ulf's voice was quiet and low, but with enough bite of menace to send a shiver of awareness down Halfdan's spine. He looked over at the group of women boarding his ship and winced.

They were early.

Ulf was always deadliest when he appeared quiet and brooding. It would not take much to strike the spark of anger within.

It was what made him such a deadly and formidable jarl. Halfdan wondered sometimes how his father stomached having a son so averse to war as himself. But then, Halfdan had made him very rich, so he supposed he was forgiven for that failing at least.

His father was unpredictable, dangerous and cared for no one. But he also had a good memory and was quite perceptive when sober. It was clear he knew exactly who they were, as well as Valda's significance to his son. Of course, at that time, his father had not cared about their relationship or their separation, as long as they didn't marry. He'd made Halfdan swear on his brother's life that he had no plans to offer her that. If there was even a rumour that he was willing to marry her, Erik would have been murdered in his sleep.

And he'd known his father had meant it.

How many times had he beaten, starved and humiliated Erik, sometimes punishing Erik for the deeds Halfdan had committed? When Halfdan had denied helping a starving family his brother's hand had been plunged into boiling water. The lack of infection days later had apparently proved Halfdan 'innocent' of the crime. It was a horrible lesson he would never forget. His actions had consequences, not just for himself, but for others.

And his half-brother Erik would always suffer the worst. He'd been shunned by everyone except Halfdan because of his birth—the islanders had not wanted to feel Ulf's wrath out of hopeless sympathy for a dead thrall's child. Halfdan had tried to intervene, but he was two winters younger than Erik and could only offer a diversion most of the time. Things had changed as they both grew bigger and stronger. Ulf became more hesitant in his cruelty. But Erik was still a thrall, who could be beaten and killed by his master at will. It had been a relief for both of them when Halfdan had left, taking Erik with him.

'Valda is joining my crew for this trip. Her mother and sisters probably came to say goodbye,' he answered smoothly, while continuing to pack his father's trade goods as quickly as possible.

He wished his father hadn't insisted on seeing him off. He didn't usually, but Ulf was probably keen to remind him of his promise.

In the hopes of distracting his father, Halfdan patted the parcel of goods. 'We should get a good price for these furs, especially the bear pelts.'

Ulf's eyes narrowed as he turned to face his son. 'Why would you add *her* to your crew? I've heard they've been begging for scraps at every jarl's table. You are too soft.'

Halfdan straightened his spine and faced his father for an inevitable battle of wills. He hated it, always had, and though he was no longer a youth afraid of his father's wrath, he was still afraid of who his father might turn against in his absence. 'She is an excellent shieldmaiden and there is a rumour that more nomads are raiding the ships returning from Miklagard. I could do with another experienced blade.'

Ulf snorted with disgust. 'Do not pretend you want her for her blade!'

Halfdan rolled the tension out of his shoulders, trying to ease the irritation his father's dismissal of Valda's ability had sparked. Valda was an experienced fighter, far better than any of the men under Ulf's command, but there was no point arguing it, so Halfdan tried another tactic to ease his father's temper.

'I admit, maybe, a little amusement for me, too.' Halfdan gave one of his most mischievous smiles and a light shrug. His father could forgive lust—it was one of the few aspects of human nature he understood. It would be better for Valda and her family if Ulf dismissed her significance to him. Threats to his plans were always dealt with a sweeping scythe's blow, cutting down any and all opposition.

Ulf's snort of laughter eased the tension in Halfdan's neck. 'So be it.' But then he fixed him with a hard, cold look. 'As long as it is only an *amusement*. You have given me your word this time, Halfdan. There can be no squirming out of this match. I have brokered a deal with the Dragon in the West and he will not forgive betrayal…' His voice lowered, to a whispered threat. 'And neither will I. *Not this time.*'

Halfdan rarely felt anger, but he felt it now, like a noose tightening around his neck. 'I know,' he snapped, matching his father's hard eyes with his own.

Ulf looked away first, his voice oddly mild when he spoke, as if his next words had been carefully considered. 'There is your brother's future to think of, too.'

Halfdan crossed his arms over his chest and stared at his father with barely concealed disgust. 'I have given my word, as you have given yours.'

'Yes.' Ulf's tone softened for a moment and Halfdan saw a flicker of the man he could have been. 'A man must keep his word, or all his actions are meaningless. *You* are my son and heir—even if you are not my eldest. It is *you* that I want to become Jarl after I die.' He looked away, his eyes hardening. 'It is time for you to end your dalliances and stand by my side as a leader of men.'

Halfdan stared at his father, his heart heavy with disappointment.

Did Ulf fear that Erik would steal his inheritance, a title he didn't even want? Was that why he despised Erik so savagely?

How awful that he'd rejected one son in the hopes of protecting the other…when his sons loved each other and hated him for it. His cruelty had only strengthened their bond, even as Ulf tried to use them against each other like game pieces on a Tafl board. His motives could not be trusted.

His father could never understand their friendship or their brotherly bond because he didn't understand love.

Ulf's final words before he left the ship were said without emotion. 'Never forget.'

After watching his father leave, he focused his attention on the group of women still on board. They had a pitiful number of dirty pelts with them, furs he wouldn't have allowed anywhere near his ship under normal circumstances. But it was obviously all they had to trade and he didn't want to insult them by rejecting them.

At least they'd be fed in Valda's absence, as he'd agreed with a local merchant to send two fresh loaves and a haunch of meat to them each week until he returned. It hadn't taken long to find out where the family of shieldmaidens lived.

'Let me,' he said, taking the bulky parcel from Porunn as if it were a bolt of the finest silk. He put it carefully in a chest he'd bought especially for Valda by the mountain of his own cargo, before turning back to the four women.

Age had weathered Porunn's beauty and a long scar ran down her cheek and neck, but it only highlighted the defiance of her jaw. Her white hair still shone with health and vitality, and her body was lean and strong despite the slight limp to her walk.

He smiled at Brynhild, who looked at him with her usual disapproving glare. She was almost as tall as him, her shoulders broad and her arms heavily muscled. There was no mistaking her womanhood, however, as she had developed full breasts and flared hips since he'd seen her last. Wickedly, he hoped that Erik would see her at some point when they returned to Jorvik. He suspected the sight of her would drive him mad.

Then he smiled at Helga, who gave him the only genuine smile he'd received from all four of the women since they'd boarded his ship. Helga looked how he imagined an elf from Álfheimr might look—fairer than the sun and as fragile as morning light. Beautiful and yet other-worldly. Her pale blue eyes missed nothing and she smiled at him with affection and amusement as if she knew his fate already. He looked away and back at the one woman he could never ignore for long.

Valda, with her fiery hair and courageous spirit. Currently she was frowning at her sisters and mother as if they were a plague on her life. 'Thank you for coming to see me off,' she said, looking meaningfully towards the dock.

Her mother laughed and pulled her into a tight embrace, ignoring Valda's squeak of protest. 'Come here! Let me hold you—it will be so long until I can do so again. May the gods keep you safe!' Porunn's eyes were wet with tears as she pulled away and Valda responded by pulling her close once more. Helga and finally Brynhild wrapped their arms around the two of them and all four stood in a silent embrace for a long time.

The demonstration of love and kinship pulled at a loose thread in Halfdan's heart and he swallowed hard to ignore it.

When they finally pulled apart, he was busying himself with tidying the already tidy piles of cargo.

Porunn turned to him before she left. 'I will make a sacrifice to Rán for a swift and safe return.'

He straightened and nodded, grateful for the sentiment. A ship's return relied on the whims of the sea goddess. 'Thank you.'

Then Porunn, Helga and Brynhild left and Halfdan began shouting orders as the crew prepared to leave the river dock for the long voyage ahead. Valda sat at one of the oars and began to pull in a steady rhythm with the others. Using the steering oar, Halfdan navigated them through the congested dock and out of Jorvik. Soon, they caught the flow of the river and no longer had to row.

The fresh air flooded his sail as well as his nose and he breathed it in deeply, grateful to leave the rotten, oppressive weight of Jorvik and his father behind. Valda came to join him and, as the wind whipped back the stray hairs from her face, he'd never felt happier. She was finally with him.

'I've never been further east than Gotland,' she said softly, staring into the distance ahead.

A strange pride filled his chest at her admission. He was glad he could offer her more. It was all he had ever wanted—to see the excitement and joy of new places in her eyes. 'We will stop at Gotland first, although we will camp along the coastline most of the way. It saves on time and supplies. Then we go to the rivers and lands of the Rus, down through the flatlands of the East and then finally to the sea north of Miklagard. But do not worry, I am an experienced traveller these days.' He wished he could promise that no harm would come to her, but life on the seas was turbulent and dangerous.

'I'm not worried. I am glad to be here. Thank you for accepting me.' Her eyes briefly met his before going back to stare at the horizon. 'As you said, it will be nice to have one last adventure before we settle down.'

'Indeed,' he replied cheerfully, but the idea of them both going their separate ways afterwards made him weary.

A sour voice in his head whispered *She can never be yours*. But he refused to listen. He'd seen the desire in her eyes when they'd touched yesterday. The door to her heart was not closed and there was a chance they could still be together… Maybe…

There had to be a reason why they'd reunited at such a pivotal moment in both their lives!

It was fate. It had to be.

Chapter Six

They were out in the North Sea in a matter of hours. The winds were fair and flowed eastwards with enough bite to make their journey swift. Valda acquainted herself with the crew and the ship, discovering that many of Halfdan's men were from Gotland and had stayed with him since the very beginning.

Would she have stayed with him if she'd accepted his offer?

Probably not. He wouldn't have been faithful and she wouldn't have been able to accept a life without his complete devotion. It would have broken her eventually, as it had in Rouen.

It was a pity, though, that her heart had kept her from experiencing this life. The ship was impressive and Halfdan worked alongside them to ensure its smooth sailing. Whenever a task needed doing, he was always close by, either jumping in to help or preparing to meet the next challenge. He didn't act like a spoiled heir, like many men might have done on their father's ship.

He'd taken off his tunic and worked bare-chested in the spring sunshine, a sight that dried her mouth and had her staring—more than once—as his bronzed muscles rippled and flexed. Excitement flooded her veins as it always did when she was with him. There was never a dull moment with Halfdan and she both loved and feared it.

The whole crew moved with efficient purpose and skill. More than once, she worried she was in their way, or not helping as much as she could. Most of the men barely spoke as they worked, so comfortable with each other and the ship that there was no need for words, especially in such fine sailing conditions.

One of the men, Tostig, was more conversational than most. He liked to talk and she liked to listen—or at least she did with Tostig. He was friendly and fatherly and had a relaxed manner she found endearing. He was older than most of the men, with a snowy-white beard that he wore in a tapering braid all the way down to his waist. In contrast, he didn't have a single hair on the top of his weathered head.

Early on he'd noticed her squinting into the light and he'd offered her some of the black kohl paint he used around his own eyes to soften the glare. She'd accepted and he'd painted around her eyes while chatting amiably to her.

'This will be my fifth trip along the trade routes with Halfdan. I am not sure if I will do another. I have so many hoards buried—too many, really. I will need at least two horses sacrificed on my funeral pyre, just to help me carry it all into the afterlife. My daughters will think it such a waste… They're Christian now, but still respect my ways.'

Valda laughed at Tostig's jovial description of his own demise. He had the sort of dark humour she always found amusing. 'Maybe you should spend your share instead?'

'Perhaps,' he said thoughtfully. 'But on what? My girls are married to good men and need nothing more from me. My wife is gone and I could never replace her. I'll probably gamble it away on a bad wager. That seems fitting and it will give me an excuse to keep on sailing.'

'You like trading with Halfdan, then?'

'I would sail with no other man. Halfdan is fair and generous, but also willing to take risks! I like that—it leads to an interesting life and hopefully an interesting death. Although he is very lucky and I have yet to die in his service...which is a pity. What about you, shield-maiden, daughter of Porunn? I thought you found glory in Francia? Why do *you* wish to sail with him?' He asked his last question with an odd expression—piercing and as all-knowing as Odin himself. It reminded her of Helga's gift.

'For my mother and sisters. We wish to run a farm, but we will need the approval of a jarl to do it and silver... plenty of silver.' She tried and failed to keep the bitterness from her voice.

'Ah.' Tostig nodded with understanding. 'Well, you will have more than enough by the end of this trip. And you can have my share, too...if I survive.'

She blinked in disbelief at his generosity. *Surely he did not mean it?*

Tostig misunderstood her shocked expression and went on to explain the perils of their journey instead. 'You see, there are war bands and raiders that could attack us at any time, both at sea and along the rivers. Or the locals may turn on us...and there's always the possibility we may drown in a storm.' He pondered the potential manner of their death with a fond smile as if he were imagining a lover's caress.

'Well, I hope to live to see my mother and sisters again. They are relying on me,' said Valda, tugging a cap on her head to keep the sun off. She walked over to some ropes that looked as if they needed tightening and began to work. Tostig had helpfully explained the tasks as they did them and she was beginning to get the hang of what needed doing. She hoped in a few more days she could work as silently and as confidently as the others. If she were busy, she wouldn't be as distracted by the presence of Halfdan's bare chest.

Tostig shrugged. 'I'm sure you will. The gods love Halfdan.'

Unable to help herself, she followed his gaze to where Halfdan stood at the helm. He squinted at the horizon with concentration, his blue eyes also surrounded by black kohl. He was so handsome he made her heart quicken just by looking at him and their eyes clashed for a moment before her eyes darted away in embarrassment.

This whole trip was a bad idea, but it was too late now.

'I'm sure they do,' she replied, clearing her suddenly dry throat loudly, and focusing her attention back on the ropes. 'Will you show me the ship and rigging? I want to be of use if the weather changes.' If they were attacked, she could fight. But if there was a storm, she needed to know how to help and, frankly, she needed the distraction.

Tostig shrugged. 'There's no need for you to do anything. Relax, enjoy the journey.'

Valda bristled at the implication and looked around at the men toiling so diligently side by side. Not only was she the only female, she was also the only newcomer, too, by the looks of it. Everyone else seemed comfortable and familiar with each other.

She caught a few glances her way and felt her stomach churn.

What did they think of her?

Her skin crawled with uncomfortable awareness. But she raised her chin and spoke a little more loudly than normal. 'It is true I am a warrior and know very little about sailing. But I enjoy learning new skills and I am determined to be useful, and earn my place among you.'

Tostig raised his eyebrows with an amused smile. 'Fair enough, shieldmaiden. Let's put that strong sword arm to good use.' He threw her a thick rope and she began to pull on it with all her might.

Halfdan tried not to stare as Tostig showed her his ship. The men were curious about her presence and there was no man alive more curious than Tostig, so he wasn't surprised he'd taken her under his charge.

Tostig was wise and noble and appeared to have a soft spot for red-headed shieldmaidens. Although Halfdan wasn't surprised at that. The man adored his daughters.

Ulf had repeatedly questioned him as to why he kept Tostig as part of his crew. Trading was a young man's sport in Ulf's mind. But Halfdan had been glad of Tostig's experience over the years and his crew respected the older man's wisdom—it had saved them more than once. He could read the temperament of the sea as if there were runes carved upon its surface and he'd taught Halfdan about the stars and navigation. But more than that, he'd taught him how to be an honourable man.

Tostig feared nothing but a long life and that made him brave, but not reckless. When Tostig was, eventually, reunited with his wife, Halfdan would lose the only kin, apart from his mother, he'd ever looked up to.

Halfdan admired and loved him far more than his own father if he were honest. Seeing Valda laughing and talking with him made his heart ache with longing. He wondered if Tostig had already guessed her significance to him. That she was the woman from his past who had spoiled his heart for all others.

As night began to fall, Tostig joined him at the steering oar.

'I will take it for a while. You should go eat. Spend time with your woman, maybe even sleep a little.' Tostig's words were light, but Halfdan knew better.

'She's not *my* woman.'

Tostig took hold of the steering oar and checked the position of the emerging stars in the twilight, unconcerned by Halfdan's declaration. 'Aarne will be pleased to hear that—he's already considering a marriage proposal.'

Halfdan's mood considerably darkened as he looked towards the youngest member of his crew. He was playing dice with Valda on one of the sea chests. She'd ingratiated herself with his men with surprising ease. But then she'd always been a likeable woman, willing to mix with all manner of people as long as they treated each other fairly. The only people she could not stand were those who thought too highly of themselves. He remembered how she'd initially mocked his advances, believing them to be the arrogant desires of a spoiled heir. Maybe she'd been right. He *had* been a little proud and self-righteous—he could see that now, with age and hindsight.

She deserved a man who would commit to her without reservation.

Sadly, he was not that man and he should leave her be.
Except he couldn't.

Aarne spotted Halfdan's dark stare and flinched. The youth quickly excused himself from the game and left and Halfdan heard Tostig's knowing chuckle following him as he walked towards Valda.

'Sleep in my tent tonight,' he said, before realising how odd that must have sounded to her and the others around them. Part of him didn't care what they thought and only wanted to claim her as his own. To throw caution aside and never let her go. But he'd sworn his oaths and she'd never accept him as he was.

Valda looked up at him, the flecks of green and gold in her hazel eyes appearing brighter surrounded by the black of her kohl and the flash of anger in her glare.

'I can't do that,' she replied firmly with an upward tilt of her jaw.

Damn Tostig! He'd made her even more beautiful than Halfdan had ever thought possible. It caused jealousy to swell within him, overpowering in its intensity and speed, like the rush of a storm.

He had to control it.

He sat down on the sea chest opposite her, trying his best to appear as mild tempered as a lamb. 'You are not used to the sea—'

She interrupted before he could finish. 'I'm a member of your crew. I sleep where they sleep.' She leaned forward, her voice a quiet hiss between her teeth. 'I am not here as your…lover. Understood?'

He waved away her concern. 'That's not what I meant. I thought we could share it…we will be in different watches and so shall sleep at different times.' He paused, hoping the mention of different watches would pacify her. Leaning forward, he closed the short distance between them, drawing her in like a fish in his net. 'I thought it might save you some *awkwardness* with the crew.'

'How would sleeping in your bed do that?' she asked mildly, her mouth twisting into a half-smile she was fighting not to show.

'Aarne has taken a liking to you.'

'I can handle *Aarne*,' she said with a roll of her eyes that pleased him. She didn't consider the youth a potential match at least.

'But it might help for you to have a little privacy… when seeing to your *needs*.'

A flash of shock entered her eyes and for a moment they both remembered the *need* they'd felt for each other before. Of course, that's not what he'd meant, but it was satisfying to see the spark of desire in her eyes. Then she frowned as she realised his true meaning.

I have her there! he thought triumphantly.

He'd seen her awkwardly carrying a slop pail behind the cargo a couple of times since they'd left Jorvik. He went on, 'Why would you reject an offer anyone else would gladly accept?'

She rolled her eyes, but nodded in agreement. 'Fine. I shall use it for that, but I will not sleep there.'

'You have a bedding roll, then? An oiled one to keep out the rain?'

'I have my shield. I have slept beneath it before.'

'So, you would leave a perfectly good bed empty and sleep beneath a shield? I promise you my tent and bedding are clean.' He hoped that logic would change her mind. Valda could be stubborn, but she also valued reason and common sense. He liked that about her, the calm thought she gave any problem. So different from his chaotic father and even Erik's unpredictable nature, to a certain extent.

She sighed. 'Very well. I shall sleep in your tent... alone.'

'Of course!' He smiled, trying to ignore the strange thrill of excitement that ran through his veins at the thought of her sleeping in his bed.

'What feast are we having tonight?' he said, changing the conversation now that he'd managed to get her agreement.

'Bread, cheese and salted herring. All washed down with buttermilk,' she replied drily as she handed him a clean platter from a nearby pile. 'No wine or fruit today, I'm afraid. Your men said they sold all of that in Jorvik.'

He sighed. 'The food on the journey to Miklagard is always less interesting than the food on the way back.'

'I'm sure it is.' She laughed and they began to pick at their meal as the stars came out to shine above their heads. It reminded him of their long talks on his little boat and he shifted in his seat, trying to ignore the physical reaction those memories ignited within him.

He longed to kiss her again. To taste that full mouth that had once gasped against his. He wanted to kiss away the cynical twist that had been added to her lips in the many winters since they'd parted.

Nine to be exact. Nine was a sacred number, filled with magic and meaning. It felt right that it would play a part in their relationship. Almost hopeful...

'Tell me about your life, Valda, since you left Gotland,' he asked, longing to learn all that he could. He knew the facts, of course, and the rumours from his contacts in Francia—but it wasn't enough, he needed to know more.

She put aside her trencher and picked up her bone cup, sipping from it slowly and carefully. 'There's not much to tell. I fought under Rollo's banner—'

'How did you end up with Jorund?' He wanted to cut out his tongue for bringing up the name of her lost love, but he couldn't help himself. He was compelled to know the truth. Maybe it was because they were under the darkness of night? He could ask her the questions he didn't dare ask in the light of day.

'Oh!' she gasped. 'Erm, I knew him as a child. His mother fought with our mother, but after she died he went to fight with his father for a while. Then, when he returned under Rollo, we became friends again. He's a strong leader and he'd grown up around shieldmaidens, so he valued my experience and skills.'

'Not many do?' he asked, already knowing the answer, and cursing the fragile egos of weaker men.

She chuckled. 'Not many do, and even when you prove yourself they still don't like it… You have no women in your crew,' she pointed out.

He shrugged. 'You're our first. When I left Gotland, no women wished to join with me…' She was avoiding the subject of Jorund, he could tell, and he wanted to avoid talking about the end of their own relationship. 'What did you mean when you said there "wasn't a place for you there" with Jorund?'

It took her a while to answer. The boat creaked and the sail rustled in the wind, but other than the occasional movement of his crew, the ship remained peacefully quiet. He wished he felt at peace, but behind his calm mask was a wounded heart waiting with half hope and half despair for her reply.

Did he want to know the truth?

'I grew to have feelings for him. Then, when he married, I realised I would never be anything more than a friend.'

Halfdan had never hated a man more in his life. 'He put you aside?'

A bitter laugh escaped Valda's mouth, as if she were horrified at the implication. 'There was nothing to put aside! My feelings were not returned. He saw me as a friend and nothing more.'

Realisation slowly dawned upon him. 'Then you two were never…'

'No,' she said firmly, taking a deep drink of her cup.

'I'm sorry, that must have been hard for you.'

'It was harder when I realised how much I was giving up.' She sighed. 'If I'd not allowed my heart to rule over my head, I might have been happy in Francia. I'd still have had a place as Jorund's second and my mother and sisters could have come to live with me when their silver was stolen. As it is, we are now scrambling around, trying to build a future from the ashes. All because of my pride.'

'I quite like your pride…and your heart,' Halfdan found himself confessing. 'I hope you are not too sad over his loss.'

'No' she said softly. 'In all honesty, I think I loved him for the wrong reasons.'

'How can you love for the wrong reasons?'

'Because he represented everything that I wanted.' Her words were like a slow blade across his chest, stealing the air from his body. 'He was dependable, independent and honourable. He wanted land and a home more than anything. I thought I had finally met my equal.'

'There is no man equal to you. At least no one I would consider worthy enough.'

A bitter laugh filled the space between them. 'Not even you?'

He smiled sadly. 'Especially not me. You deserve so much more than I can give you.'

Valda stood, breaking the unbearable tension between them. 'I think I shall go to bed. Goodnight, Halfdan.'

That night, Valda lay in Halfdan's bed and wondered about everything he'd said to her. She tossed and turned, but could not shake his words from her mind.

Was he teasing her? Mocking her? Or did he truly believe himself unworthy of her?

His bedding smelled of him. Rich and musky with a hint of sea and spice. In frustration she sat up and shook the furs to straighten them out. That's when she noticed the bedframe was marked just below the head—presumably it was normally covered from view by the bedding. She peered at it, but could not make out the meaning of the cuts in the darkness, the moon and stars offering little light through the thick canvas. She ran her fingers across the surface of the wood. The oak felt polished and smooth beneath her fingertips, as if Halfdan had run his own fingers over the marks many times. A habit to help him sleep, perhaps? She found the start and end of the strange markings and followed the lines, drawing an image in her mind.

It couldn't be!

She gasped as the realisation struck her hard. They were runes. Initials to be exact, woven together in a swirl-

ing, entangled design. Their initials, the ones Halfdan
had lazily carved into his first boat all those years ago.

He'd obviously used some of the ship's timber to make
his furniture. But it couldn't be a coincidence that he
would choose this particular plank for his bedframe.

It meant something to him. Their love had meant
something to him and possibly...still did?

The thought frightened her, because it made her feel
weak and vulnerable, opening her heart to memories
she'd thought to leave firmly behind her and in the past.
Her hands flew along every side of the bed, but there
were no other carvings.

Why would he keep it? Was it just a fond memory of
his first infatuation?

That had to be it. He couldn't possibly still pine for
her. He'd bedded another woman the same summer he'd
professed his love for her. But maybe he'd thought himself in love with her? Was that why he spoke so roman-
tically about their past, believing himself more affected
by their parting than he actually was? People could easily delude themselves when it came to love. Hadn't she
already done so herself...*twice*?

However, she couldn't decide if she was lucky or un-
lucky in matters of the heart.

She'd fallen twice for men who did not love her back.

But then again, she'd not met Olga's fate at least.

She shuddered when she thought of poor Olga. She'd
not liked her, had thought her spoilt and arrogant, but
no one deserved to be cast aside. Especially when they
carried their lover's child. How could he have been so
callous? It did not fit with the memory of the boy she'd
loved, but then, neither had his unfaithfulness.

It might have been her. Pregnant and unmarried. Her

family would have protected her, though, and she would not have had to marry a stranger to appease her family's pride, but life would have been very different. She wouldn't have been able to fight, would have had to rely on her sisters and mother for support. All of their futures would have been affected by her mistake.

Thankfully, she'd avoided such misery—though not through wisdom!

She'd been lucky.

She could not risk her luck a second time. Hadn't Brynhild warned her about bringing home Halfdan's bastard? Her eldest sister had more wisdom than her, always had, and probably always would.

It felt as if her life were like the moon's cycle. Love and hope fading in and out of her endlessly miserable night. She feared she might lose her mind if she had to go through it all again.

No, she would avoid any more conversations with Halfdan and their different watches would certainly help with that. Ignore the pain of the past and move forward. They would sleep and work at different times of the day and she could almost pretend he wasn't even there.

Couldn't she?

Yes, she had to remember her family's future and focus on that!

The past was a land she no longer wished to explore.

Chapter Seven

They would arrive in Gotland within a week of leaving Jorvik, due mainly to Halfdan's remarkable ship and his competent crew.

Valda had got to know the men well. It was unavoidable when you were constantly in each other's company. They were amusing and boisterous at times, many of them were related and reminded her of her own sisters when they squabbled among themselves.

There were a couple of father and sons, like Frode and Aarne, and some brothers like Bori, Odger and Svend. But other than physical similarities, it was difficult to tell who was related and who was not, so comfortable to jest and quarrel with one another as they were.

All of them, she was relieved to discover, were good men, bound by the common desire for adventure and a better life for their families.

They'd only stopped once along the coast to replenish food and water and they'd barely had to land the ship as it was a coastal village with its own jetty. The people appeared to know them well and were happy to trade with the crew for supplies. In no time they'd been back on the open sea again, Halfdan's dragon ship cutting through the spring waves with surprising agility.

'We'll reach Gotland today?' Valda asked Bori as she spotted the shadow of land on the horizon.

Bori nodded with a grin. 'Our quickest arrival yet!'

His brother Odger moved to stand beside him. Odger was his reflection in every way, except his red beard was a little longer than Bori's—much to Bori's annoyance. 'Rán is pleased with us, the winds are unusually favourable—even for this time of year. Did you say your mother made a sacrifice?'

Valda nodded, but Bori interrupted his brother with a friendly slap to her back. 'Valda has brought us luck! We should have more women on board. I might ask your warrior sister to marry me when we return. That way we'll have even better fortune on our travels.'

Valda laughed. 'I wouldn't wish my sister on you, Bori. Brynhild would eat you alive!'

Bori's smile widened with glee at the prospect and Odger thumped his arm. 'You were promising Astrid marriage only a few weeks ago! Set your sights on one woman at a time and give the rest a break!' Then Odger glanced towards Halfdan at the steering oar. 'This is the fastest we've ever dared sail. He is determined to return by autumn for his marriage, so it is fortunate the journey has been swift. Let's hope it continues that way.'

It was a timely reminder for Valda who'd been shaken by the discovery of the engraving on Halfdan's bedframe. No matter how sentimental he might be over their past relationship, he was still bound for marriage to another woman. She'd heard from the crew that the wedding was to take place on the very day they returned to Jorvik.

She had to remember that! Not allow herself to become distracted by the past.

However, as they sailed alongside the coast of Halfdan's ancestral home, she couldn't help reminiscing about their first summer together. Bittersweet memories leapt into her mind as she saw the island again for the first time in nine years.

The land was reasonably flat, filled with mostly pine trees or farms, and dotted with fresh, shallow lakes. Rocky beaches dominated the coastline, interspersed with the occasional sandy dunes like the ones around Halfdan's settlement. Her mind flew with each curve of the island to all the many places she and Halfdan had explored together.

Further north, for example, there were enormous pillars of rock, as if a giant had scattered his broken teeth among the shingle. They'd first kissed beneath the shadow of one of those stones after Halfdan had rowed them there in a tiny fishing boat so that she could see them. They'd then feasted on sour berries and drunk sweet mead before heading home.

A small part of her hoped they would pass them tomorrow, on their way out of Gotland, as they headed onwards to the land of the Rus.

Her spine tingled with awareness as Halfdan came to stand beside her. He didn't say anything and she watched the horizon with intense interest. After a deep bend in the land, they sailed into the shelter of the trading post's harbour.

Was this why he stood beside her? Was he waiting for the first sight of his home?

But when he didn't move away the silence became

too much for her and she found herself making light conversation.

'Your father's settlement has flourished since I was last here,' she said.

'Yes, it must look strange to you now...nothing like what you remember.'

That was certainly true. It no longer looked like the small farming and fishing community it had once been. She couldn't even see the Jarl's Hall any more. The purpose of the settlement had been transformed. No doubt its position, straddled between the Western and Eastern routes, made it an ideal trading post.

The boat sailed serenely into the harbour like a swan and the crew leapt to action. Aarne jumped from the ship with a thick rope and began to lash the vessel to the wooden jetty while others tied up the rigging and brought down the sail. Halfdan, Tostig, Valda and Aarne were the only people who would leave the ship to trade so they waited with Halfdan's parcels of goods until they were safely docked.

Valda took a moment to assess the changes to Gotland since she'd last been here.

It was similar to Jorvik with its multitude of small buildings, all closely built together in a grid formation. The hum and metal clang of craftsmen filled the air as heavily as the smoke billowing from several workshops. The general filth was the same, too, trodden so thickly into the wooden walkways she could barely see the timber beneath. At least being on the coast gave it one advantage that Jorvik didn't possess—a sea breeze to ease the stench.

The settlement sat on a hill and was surrounded on three sides by huge earthen defences, with the harbour and wooden jetties the only access to the market within. The buildings and people ran up and over the hill like ants, busily occupied with their livelihoods.

Outside the walls, the only rise in the flat landscape was made by the low funeral mounds, the graves ebbing and flowing in earthen waves and stretching out to the forest beyond. It was as if the settlement were a rock thrown into a pool, sending ripples of death in its wake.

Valda thought them both beautiful and sad in equal measure. There hadn't been this many the last time she'd visited, but then, neither had there been this many people. She supposed with the port's expansion, it was inevitable that the dead's population would grow in number, too.

'Your father must be pleased with it.'

'He is.'

She'd expected more of a response, but there was nothing in Halfdan's expression. No pride or censure, only acceptance.

'Do you miss it? How it used to be?' She wondered if his mother was buried among the rolling hills; she suspected she was. Valda knew very little about his mother, only that Ulf's wives never lasted long after they were married—either through cruelty or misfortune—and their graves rippled in Ulf's wake.

In fact, Halfdan's mother had lasted the longest out of all of his wives, the ones before and after her only lasting a year or two at most. When Valda had visited his settlement all those years ago, there'd been rumours even then that the other Jarls had started to refuse marriage alliances with him. They were no longer willing to send their daughters into a match that would end in certain death.

Valda only had one parent and Porunn had made many

mistakes in her life, but at least her mother had always been loving and supportive of her family. The same could not be said for Ulf.

Halfdan surprised her by smiling broadly. 'No. Change is always a good thing. New experiences enrich you. They give you a greater understanding of the past.'

Heat crept up her neck as she wondered what 'new experiences' had shaped his thoughts on *their* past. *Did she pale now in significance?*

'And what have you learned in your time away?'

He laughed. 'Very little…' Then his face became sombre and he looked out at the graves. 'Except that life and freedom are the only treasures really worth possessing.'

She hadn't expected something so thoughtful and wise to come from Halfdan's lips. He was always the jovial prince, spoiled by wealth and privilege. It conflicted with her hard-won beliefs and made her doubt herself, like when she'd found their carved initials on his bed.

Now that the boat was docked, the group headed out with their sacks and chests of treasures. They carried with them some pottery and jewellery made by the Jorvik craftsmen, as well as several Frankish weapons. It appeared Jorvik was a melting pot where raw goods from all over the world arrived and left as polished, crafted items of greater value. Greater than what could be created here, for example, although she wondered how long that would be the case.

Halfdan walked beside her, seemingly unwilling to end their conversation, yet saying nothing more either. They'd not spent much time together on the ship, which sounded strange considering the confined space. However, he'd kept his word about sharing his tent and they'd lived almost separate lives. It had led to an uneventful journey—which she was grateful for—but it did mean she found herself staring at him on the few occasions their paths crossed during the changing of the watch. Particularly as he spent most of his time on the sea half-naked, his golden chest on display, or wearing little more than a linen undershirt and woollen leggings.

Being around him was still a shock to her senses. She looked around at the rest of the harbour to distract herself from the warmth of his big body beside hers. At least he was back in his fine merchant clothing today.

They weren't the only arrival that morning. Two other ships were also docked, and they passed them as they were in the midst of unloading their cargo. There was one clear difference between Halfdan and the other merchants who had sailed into the harbour.

Halfdan had no slaves.

Valda had spent many years in Francia under Jarl Rollo whose only goal had been the creation of Northmannia and to rule over his own land. His campaigns had been more focused on military strategy, than capturing slaves for the markets. It was a difference Valda had never fully appreciated, until now.

Maybe she had a different view because she'd lived among the Franks for so long? But as she watched the wretched huddle of frightened people being led by the ropes of their masters, she couldn't help but pity them. And yet it was the main form of commerce in their land. Throughout most lands if she were honest. But something Halfdan had said earlier gave her hope. He believed in freedom after all… Did that extend to all? Including the weak?

She decided to ask him now, rather than face an unpleasant surprise later on. 'You have no slaves for trade. Will you…be taking captives at some point?' she asked.

He glanced at her and then at the auction block the slaves were being led to, his expression giving nothing away. *Who was she to question him if he did capture slaves?* It was the Viking way, yet her stomach recoiled at the thought.

'No, I have no need of them. I make enough silver trading luxury goods.'

'Your father always had thralls and they are meant to fetch a lot of silver in the East…doesn't he have a say in your cargo?' she prodded, suspecting there was something more behind his decision.

Halfdan frowned at her in confusion. 'Why should he?' She had the odd sensation she'd disappointed him in some way, but then he sighed and added, 'I am not my father. And when this place is fully mine, *that*—' he stabbed an angry finger at the raised wooden dais '—will be the first thing to go.'

Relief and respect bloomed inside Valda with equal measure. 'I'm glad. Not many feel the same, especially traders. Maybe I have lived among the Christians for too long, for I cannot see how trading in people can ever be seen as honourable.'

He shrugged. 'You forget about my brother.'

'Of course, it must have been hard for Erik—growing up as a thrall's child…' She hesitated, unsure if she should bring up questions from the past. No one had dared ask Ulf why one of his sons was treated so much worse than the other. 'I know your father…and the islanders tended to…ignore him.'

A pulse jumped in Halfdan's jaw, then he sighed. 'He

was more than an outcast. He was…still is…a *thrall*.' He spat the word with disgust.

'He's a…thrall, a slave?' she gasped, bewildered and outraged.

'Yes, a child of a thrall is still owned by its master.'

'Yes, but…most men free their own children! Surely…' She paused, as she considered everything she knew about Ulf. The man had no compassion or love in him. A twisted reflection of an older, crueller Halfdan, it was a wonder his son was so…*good*. Admitting that fact disturbed her almost as much as the news about Erik's upbringing.

Halfdan grunted in acknowledgement. 'My father is convinced that Erik's mother was responsible for my mother's death and that Erik—because he is older—is a threat to my position as heir. *All nonsense*.'

'We never realised,' she said, wondering how Brynhild would feel knowing the truth. Suddenly, Erik's behaviour that summer made far more sense and her heart ached for him. She'd never expected to ever feel pity for Erik.

Halfdan laid a hand over her shoulder and gave it a light squeeze. The caress felt far more heated and sensual than it should have and Valda's spine stiffened with alarm.

She did not want to respond to his touch.

'It is never openly discussed,' he said softly. 'But he has no arm ring and does not carry my father's name. My father either acts as if he does not exist or punishes him brutally when he realises he does. If my brother ever ran from his service, he would be killed on sight and my father would richly reward the man who did it. I would not wish that life on anyone. But…there is finally hope.

My father has agreed on a price for Erik's freedom…
which is partially the reason for this last trip.'

Before she could delve any deeper into that strange
reply, they were interrupted by the very loud cry of excitement from a woman rushing towards them.

'Heill, Halfdan! Welcome! I heard your ship had
docked! What a wonderful surprise!'

The woman had come from a large Hall close to the
market. Valda assumed her to be a merchant or noble-
man's wife by her elaborately embroidered apron dress
and the heavy weight of jewellery she wore.

'Dagrun!' shouted Halfdan in greeting, his voice and
manner filled with warm admiration. It made Valda's
teeth grind, as he continued, 'It has been too long since
I saw you last. And I swear you are even more beautiful now than the day I left!' Now Valda could see why
Halfdan didn't need to trade in slaves—he was a master
of charm. She sighed as she realised he always had been.

She'd thought she was special? Ha!

Dagrun's array of silver shivered with a light melody
as she rushed to join them. She wore a headdress made
with pierced dirham coins that cascaded around her face
in a waterfall of exotic wealth and four thick silver neck
rings stacked one on top of the other shone at her throat.
Her dress was embroidered with the finest silk embel-
lishments and her turtle brooches were intricately decorated with precious gem stones and laced together with
a string of colourful glass beads.

She was pretty, Valda supposed—if you liked your
women shallow and weak, which Halfdan obviously did
by the way he was beaming at her.

Were they lovers?

It felt odd to see him with another woman. It hurt and angered her far more than it should.

Dagrun clasped his hands within her own and gasped, 'You must stay with us while you are here.'

'I was hoping you would say that. Your Hall is always the most welcoming!'

Dagrun preened with pleasure at Halfdan's bright smile.

Valda wanted to scratch the woman's eyes out. She'd not even acknowledged Valda or any of the others. She only had eyes for Halfdan.

Dagrun leaned forward, her voice a seductive whisper. 'I hope you have something special for me?'

'Oh, I do!' he whispered and Valda honestly wasn't sure how she could bear it. Were they going to make love right in front of her, too? Although…why should she care? Halfdan was not hers…nor was he Dagrun's; he belonged to some nameless woman far away across the sea.

Dagrun squealed with excitement at a terrifying pitch and ushered them towards her Hall. 'Come, come! We will feast; my husband joins me from our lands tonight.'

Valda wondered if the news of her returning husband would disturb Halfdan. But his smile didn't falter; if anything, it brightened as he caught Valda's disapproving eye. 'Dagrun is the wife and daughter of a jarl from the far north. She and her husband stay here during the summer to trade and…they're one of my best buyers. Everything she wears she bought from me,' he whispered in her ear and she swore she felt his breath all the way down to her toes.

'She certainly has a taste for silver,' grumbled Valda, unable to keep the disdain from her voice.

Halfdan brushed his hand down her arm in a sooth-ing gesture. 'Do not be jealous, *sweetling.*'

Valda scowled at him darkly. 'I'm not!' she retorted, but he was already walking away and Tostig was staring at her with sly amusement.

She stalked after Halfdan, her hand on the hilt of her sword and her chin held high.

The evening in Dagrun's hall with her husband, Harald, was not as unpleasant as Valda had first imag-ined it would be. The goat stew, bread and ale were plen-tiful and delicious, which was a welcome break from the salted meat aboard the ship.

Harald was older than Dagrun by many years, but seemed happy to indulge his young wife with whatever she wanted, and her desire seemed genuinely focused on Halfdan's treasures rather than himself. It appeared Dagrun was obsessed with jewellery and had a keen hun-ger to possess the exotic. She was delighted by the car-nelian beads from Persia, admiring the pink and orange glow they gave as Halfdan held them up to the firelight.

Valda learned quickly why Dagrun preferred to buy her precious treasures from Halfdan in particular and it wasn't what she'd presumed.

He sold more than just trinkets. He sold stories, like a travelling Skald. Both Dagrun and her husband listened to him with gaping mouths of wonder as he spoke of the silk road and his epic journeys.

She even found herself falling into the dreamworld he created, so vivid and exciting were his words. The cyni-cal side of her had tried to remind herself that's all they were…stories. But he wove such a colourful and vivid picture she began to wonder how much was real and how much was embellished. The people and places he spoke of sounded so real, and soon, she thought with a thrill of excitement, she would experience them for herself.

'Each bead...' he said, stroking them with such a loving caress that Valda felt her own body tighten with longing. She couldn't deny it, she still desired him, physically at least. She rolled her shoulders back and tried to concentrate on his words '...carved by a master. Look at the cuts...so sharp, so focused and precise. Mined from a distant land in the furthest reaches of Asia. They have travelled through humid forests and lands so strange you would not believe me if I told you...' He paused and the fire cracked in the silence.

'Tell us!' urged Dagrun, practically bouncing in her seat with excitement.

He smiled slowly and leaned forward, his voice hushed as if even speaking of it were a dangerous feat. 'There is a sea that no boat can sail...a sea of sand.' He raised his hand and sand poured slowly from his clenched fist; the crowd gasped in awe.

'How long has he been holding that?' muttered Valda drily to Tostig and someone in the crowd hushed her.

Had he taken it from the bag at his belt? Did he always carry around sand?

Valda stared in shock and wondered if Halfdan was the son of the god Loki, as he was so full of tricks and deceit. She'd thought she was seeing another side of him, a more honourable, noble heart... But these tales—although inspiring—were beginning to shake her trust in him once more.

Could she ever believe in anything he said?

'There is no water there. Nothing but sand, an endless beach so dry that nothing can grow there, not even a blade of grass. The heat is unbearable, so intense you could bake your bread without lighting a fire. A man would easily die of thirst before he was able to walk across it, so vast and endless are the dunes. Many have tried and become quickly disorientated and maddened by the heat and thirst. Sometimes you see their pale bones, crumbling beneath the sun.'

Dagrun gasped with horror, but Halfdan was not finished.

'To cross it, I had to make friends with the local tribes. They own strange, ugly, hunchbacked horses that need very little water to survive and these strange creatures know the path by heart as they have crossed the sand many times. But you have to be courageous and trust them to guide you.' He looked thoughtful for a moment, then held up the beads to the firelight until they were lit within with the pink and orange fire. 'This colour... it reminds me of the sunrises I saw there, on those endless fiery dunes.' He shook his head, as if waking from a dream, and then offered them to Dagrun. 'Such a long and perilous journey. All to reach the beautiful Dagrun... so that she could hold the sunrise of the East in her precious hands...'

Dagrun's hands slowly tightened around the beads as she took them. A loving gaze to her husband was all she needed to secure the deal. The men agreed a price and Halfdan moved on to the next of his treasures.

While Valda was still reeling from the huge price the Jarl had agreed to pay, Halfdan was busy offering up the next item with equal charm.

It was a large precious gem ring inscribed in a strange language that Valda had never seen before. The language of the Saracens, Halfdan said, and the inscription praised their God.

'How did you come by it?' asked Harald curiously and, like a fisherman with a heavy net, Halfdan reeled them in once more. It appeared half of the joy of these precious items was in the outlandish tales behind them. She imagined Harald and Dagrun would tell their friends and neighbours these stories with great pride when they returned to their lands. It was part of the prestige in owning them, she supposed. She did not covet them in the same way, but she could appreciate their unique beauty.

'This,' he said holding the purple stone up to the flickering flames, so that it glowed with an inner light, the inscription a strangely beautiful scar across the surface of the gem, 'I did not buy...'

If anything, his admission only caused a low murmur of interest to run through the crowd. Even Valda was curious—as she'd thought him a merchant, not a raider.

'Let me explain...' Halfdan handed the ring to Harald so that he could take a closer look. 'We were sailing down the Dnieper, only a day or so away from the sea that leads to the great city of Miklagard. When we saw a caravan up ahead racing towards the river from the east, they were being closely followed by a pack of nomadic raiders. Usually, we would sail by and let these strangers face their fate. But we'd had an easy journey and frankly Tostig and I were a little bored of our good fortune.'

Tostig huffed in agreement at this and Valda laughed—she could just imagine how sour an uneventful journey would make him—but part of her suspected that it was Halfdan's sense of honour that had caused him to go to a stranger's aid—although she couldn't be certain. She wasn't sure what was true any more. The principled, loving brother, or the cunning, faithless liar? He truly was the son of Loki, a shape-shifting trickster.

'We decided to lend our swords,' continued Halfdan with an easy shrug. 'We fought hard and won the day.' For once he didn't expand on the details. Maybe because a jarl would never be impressed by tales of fighting, or maybe it was because Halfdan himself wasn't impressed by the glorification of death? She hoped it was the latter. As a warrior herself she'd always noticed the men that crowed the loudest about their victories were usually the furthest removed from them. Only the cruel or stupid could walk away from battle and brag about it.

Halfdan paused for dramatic effect before adding, 'But one of the raiders…he was intent on reaching one of the caravans. A richly decorated one, covered with the finest silk and leather dripping with liquid gold. I killed him before he could attack the person within and then discovered a Persian princess inside. She was grateful for our aid and admired our skills in battle. She gave me this ring in gratitude for our help. We travelled on together to Miklagard. Of course, the princess wanted me to join her, to become her guard and lover.' Valda choked on her ale and had to cover it with a cough. Halfdan gave her a secretive smile before giving a mournful sigh. 'I could have lived in a beautiful palace surrounded by wealth and luxury…but I could not accept her offer.'

'Why?' whispered Dagrun, as if she was afraid her question would break the spell he'd cast upon her.

Halfdan took a slow sip of his ale, as if undecided about revealing the truth. Valda wondered for a moment if he wouldn't say any more. But then he spoke and the whole room appeared to lean closer in anticipation. 'Because… I could never give her my heart. You see… I no longer possess it. It was broken in two long ago. Half of it belongs to the sea…' He stopped speaking and Valda felt her chest tighten painfully.

'And the other half, what happened to it?' Dagrun gasped, her eyes misty with the romance of it all.

Halfdan sighed, his smile bittersweet. 'Long ago, when I was a naive and foolish youth, I fell in love with a beautiful shieldmaiden, but she would not sail away with me. She still holds the other half.'

Valda gasped and gripped her cup until her knuckles turned bone-white. The world seemed to tilt and shift as if she were on that sandy beach once again watching all of her dreams die.

'Oh, Halfdan! How sad!' Dagrun sighed and Valda closed her eyes. The smoke, the heat of the Hall, his lies. It was all too much, but she couldn't move. It was as if her body were shackled to the bench.

He didn't love her. How could he?

Halfdan's voice was soft and gentle, oblivious to the torment he caused within her. 'Don't pity me, sweet Dagrun, I do not deserve it. I was arrogant and selfish and, like most stupid young men, I let her slip through my fingers and have regretted it ever since. Now, I must fill the emptiness of my heart with travel and bringing joy to beautiful women in the form of precious treasures.'

Dagrun smiled brightly in response and Valda felt her stomach twist as if she were going to be sick. All at once she felt the blood rush back into her veins and she was able to break free from the invisible chains that held her.

She quickly slipped from the room as the final exchanges were agreed. Dagrun and Harald were not the only ones to buy that night. Others rushed forward and asked for simpler, more affordable treasures of their own.

It was no wonder they bought everything he offered. He'd sold them an exotic dream, a fantasy. The kind he'd tried to sell to her all those years ago.

Chapter Eight

Outside the Hall, Valda sat on a barrel overlooking the harbour, a cup of ale she'd absently brought with her forgotten at her feet. Perspiration beaded her brow from the suffocating feast still taking place within.

She sharpened her sword with a whetstone, using hard, fast sweeps, and wishing it were Halfdan's face she pressed against the blade. She hoped the grating sound of stone on steel would block out the merrymaking only a few feet away. Without Halfdan's permission she couldn't leave—her duty was to guard him and his property—but she refused to sit there and listen to any more of his lies. At least outside she could pretend to be keeping watch and have some peace before she had to face him again.

If she were going to leave, here, in Gotland, would be her last opportunity, as it was still within easy reach of the trade routes to Jorvik. She had no silver to buy passage, but she could sell her sword…

Her hand paused as indecision waged a war within.

But then her family would have nothing.

She'd have failed them and why—because her tender heart couldn't stomach a little discomfort?

Wounded on the battlefield she'd been braver than this! Had faced unreasonable male pride and constant criticism for many years—some even by those *under* her command. Yet she'd never faltered or doubted herself. Not until now.

She would do anything for her family.

A statement and a promise. She had to continue forwards because without the income from this trip they would never get out of the pit they were in. She *would* get them their farm, even if it meant a miserable three or four months for her. It would be worth it…eventually.

So what if Halfdan had a romanticised view of their past relationship? *It wasn't real.* Even if he believed it was. He could reminisce all he liked about their lost love, but she knew the truth!

She might have cleaved his heart in two by leaving. But that was nothing in comparison to the agony she'd felt after seeing Olga leave his bed. And was it just Olga? How many other times had he betrayed her that summer? The pain of it was so utterly humiliating and shattering she could not speak of it without shameful tears for years afterwards.

With a screech she dragged the stone once more down the blade. The familiar disappointment was a bitter weight on her shoulders. After Halfdan's betrayal she'd never thought she could love again. Then she'd met Jorund…

Why were men so disappointing?

First her nameless father, then Halfdan and finally Jorund.

The sword screamed again beneath the stone.

Jorund had been different. He'd been trustworthy, loyal, disciplined, but he'd not wanted her.

Was she the one at fault?

She knew some men would struggle to love a shield-maiden. They were too independent and fierce for ordinary men. She'd seen it over and over again with her mother.

Jorund had not loved her, that was the will of the gods, and he'd been blameless in her suffering.

But Halfdan…

How could he say such things? Claim an undying love he could not possibly feel!

The shieldmaiden of his past? He'd been talking about her—she was certain of that. There weren't that many warriors like her family in the world, even fewer who were stupid enough to fall for hollow promises.

Anger burned like a fever deep within her chest until she swore her eyes might burst into flames.

Since when had he become the victim of their relationship?

She had been honest and loyal. She'd given her body and heart when she really shouldn't have, while he had taken her love and thrown it away, as if it were nothing. How *dared* he claim to be the wounded party!

He had betrayed her! The injustice of it all still enraged her.

How she wished she were a Valkyrie—one of the truly awful ones with a name like 'Bone Crusher'. She would crunch that arrogant worm under the heel of her leaky boot until there was nothing but a pile of dust remaining.

The wind rose as if sensing her need for vengeance. The fresh breeze cleared the night air with the tang of the salty sea and the possibility of rain. She wished they hadn't stopped at Gotland—it had stirred up too many memories and made Halfdan sentimental.

If it wasn't for his presence, she'd be happy to live on the sea and travel the world for ever as she rather liked living aboard ship. The work was vigorous and interesting, with enough danger to suit her nature, and the crew—with one exception—were easy to live with. The days were pleasantly tiring, while at night she was rocked to sleep by the sea, like a babe in its mother's arms.

She blinked in surprise.

Was she falling in love with the sea?

A familiar fate for her at least, to love something that could never love her back, she thought with dry amusement. She straightened her spine. This journey would be an adventure, nothing more. She wanted land, security, and a future. A solid one, not this volatile and dangerous life on the sea. She was done with instability; her family needed her home.

She had to remember that!

A deep masculine voice interrupted her thoughts. 'Are you well?' asked Halfdan, full of concern and she fought the urge to throw the whetstone at his eyes.

'I should ask the same of you. I'm surprised you can walk and talk with such a broken heart!' She'd tried to sound sarcastic, but it came out as resentful.

'Valda,' he said, a gentle coax as well as an apology— all rolled together in a single word.

Valda glanced over at Halfdan by the Hall doors. She couldn't see his face clearly in the shadows, but she gave him a bitter smile anyway. She refused to let him see her pain. 'It was getting too hot in there.' She sheathed her sword and put away her whetstone. The blade was now so sharp it could probably cut out the stars.

He moved and sat on the barrel beside her. Far too close as always and she hated that her body responded to him. Already she could feel shivers of anticipation across her skin, her heart beating a little faster as the salty spice of his musk filled her nose.

The darkness shrouded her in memory. They'd spent many nights looking up at these same stars, their arms draped around one another, her head resting against his chest. As if sensing the loss, she rubbed her arms to fight off the sudden chill.

'Are any of those stories even true? It's so difficult to tell.'

'I meant what I said about you,' he answered and she turned her head to peer at him through the gloom.

How could he mean that? After what he'd done? Was this his idea of an apology?

The moonlight shone on his face, there was no pretence any more, no deliberate charm…just Halfdan. The boy she'd loved and the man she couldn't help but desire. Sincerity and regret were plainly etched across his face, like the runes carved into his bedframe.

For whatever it was worth, he meant it.

Sighing, she said, 'You may have given me half of your heart…but you had *all* of mine.' The air was sucked from her body, as she realised how vulnerable such an admission made her. Quickly, she added, *'Then',* before looking away.

'I did?' Halfdan whispered, as if awed by the possibility, and frustratingly ignoring her last word.

'Then,' she repeated more firmly, staring down at the harbour below, wishing he would leave her alone to gather her emotions and shield them once more.

When would he finally stop raiding the past? She didn't need to be reminded of her own lack of wisdom—every day she woke in his bed she felt it.

It felt as if he were toying with her, like a cat with a half-dead mouse. Never sinking his claws in enough to give the death blow, but enough to make her wince.

He didn't love her—not really. *How could he?*

Even in his declaration of love he'd admitted to only half loving her. Not to mention his current betrothal.

Halfdan sighed. 'But no longer?'

'No.'

'Because you love Jorund now?' he asked quietly, his voice rough in the darkness, and she wondered if the idea hurt him. Probably his pride, nothing more.

She almost lied, but found she couldn't. 'No.'

He sucked in a deep breath and they sat silently for a moment, listening to the waves and the calls of owls.

Then he reached for her, taking her chin between his fingers to force her to face him. To face their past.

'I should have married you,' he said and she tried to fight the pathetic fluttering of her fragile heart.

'It's probably for the best you didn't.'

He wouldn't have been faithful. A fact she couldn't have accepted. As a warrior, loyalty meant everything to her.

He leaned in and pressed his lips lightly against hers, a questioning caress that she should have pushed away. But she didn't. She couldn't. She'd longed for it, for him, for his touch.

Memories flooded her senses and it felt as if she were falling into both the past and the future, all at the same time. The taste of his mouth, the scent of his body, were so familiar despite their separation. She leaned closer, her body aching with the need to be held by him once again. To feel the searing pleasure only he could provide.

'I should have married you,' he whispered again,

and she found her hands reaching up to grip both of his biceps. To pull him closer or push him away, she still wasn't sure, and so instead, she just held them. She'd wanted to hear those kinds of words so badly in her youth, for him to offer her undivided and enduring love.

Her body and soul yearned for him and she wished she could believe him.

His fingers stroked up her cheeks and ran over the braids of her hair. Then he dragged her close and all she could manage was a resigned sigh of relief as she opened her mouth to his.

All at once the fire ignited between them, their breath mingling, hot and heavy in the cool night air. Their tongues stroked against each other, instinct taking over as their bodies eagerly welcomed their reunion. She pulled him closer, her body racing ahead, impatient for the climax she knew he could so easily wring from her body.

It had been so long.

She twisted on top of her barrel to face him and his muscled thigh pushed between hers, claiming the space between them. Greedy hands slipped beneath tunics and feasted on hot skin. She moaned as she ran her palms up his rough chest. His muscles felt bigger and more developed since she'd last touched them. Excitement flooded her veins in anticipation. She would delight in the man that he'd become.

His own hands were around her waist, measuring her with possessive indulgence while his mouth ravaged hers with increasing intensity.

She dropped one hand to his groin and stroked the rigid bulge with wanton satisfaction. His masculine growl was enough to send a new wave of pleasure down her spine.

Soon, they would need to stand, find some place to satisfy their lust. She squirmed in her seat, rubbing herself against his thigh. The idea of him taking her right there, in front of the busy Hall, was almost too tempting to bear. She knew that if he laid her down on the ground, she'd open for him gladly, so needy was she to end the years of abstinence.

Was she mad?

Thought and reason had flown long ago like Odin's ravens.

What would they report to the All Father tonight? That Valda, daughter of the fierce Porunn, had fallen once again for Halfdan Ulfsson's charms, as easily as an apple falls from a tree?

There was a cheer from inside the Hall, followed closely by the beating of a drum and the first notes of a drunken song. As if woken from a dream, she pulled away, groggy and shaken, struggling to clear her thoughts with laboured breaths.

It had gone too far.

Impatient, Halfdan's hands began to tug at the bindings around her breasts.

'No!' With a mighty push she threw him away from her. His barrel toppled immediately and with a satisfying thud he landed hard in the dirt.

'I can't do this! Not *again*! And... And... You're to be married, you've given your word,' she cried, jumping up from her barrel and striding a short distance away. For air, or to stop herself from going back to him, she wasn't sure which. Just needing space between them, so as not to drown.

Halfdan remained where he was sprawled on the earth, raising his head and shoulders enough to see her from his prone position. He didn't seem bothered by the way she'd so harshly rejected him.

Which was surprising. Most men's vanity would have been hurt beyond repair. Not to mention how angry they'd be at the spoiling of their fine clothes. Any other man would have cursed and raged at her, but not Halfdan. He brushed a blond lock from his eyes with a resigned sigh and sat up slowly, resting his strong forearms on his knees as he looked up at her.

'And I will keep it.' His voice was pained but resolute, as if the acknowledgement tore at his insides. Someone must have opened the door to the Hall because a golden light fell on his handsome face, illuminating it. 'And I'm truly sorry for that. If I could change it, I would…but we could still be happy…' he said softly. 'Together, at last.'

She scowled at that. 'So, you would dishonour *her* instead?'

He frowned and looked a little guilty at that. 'I doubt she is keen on the idea of marrying me either and things could change… Maybe she might change her mind?'

More false promises. Valda snorted with disgust.

'Or…' He rose to his feet, smacking the dirt from his clothes before taking a step towards her. 'Let us enjoy what little time we have together before family and duty separate us once more… One last taste of freedom.'

He reached for her arm, but she shrugged him off angrily. *How dared he speak of family and duty after what he'd done?*

'You have not changed, Halfdan. You are still as arrogant, selfish and disloyal as you ever were.' She looked towards the Hall—a man and woman were stood flirting in the doorway. They looked young and flushed with love. Exactly how she'd been once, before Halfdan had broken her heart. 'I'll sleep on the ship,' she said, turning away from both the couple and the man she couldn't seem to forget.

'*Disloyal?*' muttered Halfdan, confused, and then with more anger, 'Disloyal?' He seemed annoyed for the first time since she'd pushed him. 'I did not walk away, Valda. I offered you a life with me, all that I could offer at that time, and you said no. I could not marry you then; my father would never have allowed it. I asked only that you give me the time to find a solution. But you left me, hoping for something better. That's what you wanted from Jorund wasn't it? Land and a title? Do not be angry at me because you made the wrong choice!'

'*Choice?*' The rage inside her boiled over. 'You never gave me a choice, Halfdan! You offered me nothing! I wanted a life of stability. You knew that and all you could offer me were weak promises.' Dragging in a shaky breath, she looked up at the star-strewn sky and tried to focus on what was important. 'What happened just now…will *never* happen again. It was a mistake. One I deeply regret. I am not interested in being your…anything! Those days are behind us. If you cannot accept that, then maybe I should leave.'

Breathless, she waited for his response. Would he agree? Throw her aside as easily as he'd done nine years ago? As easily as he'd walked away from his own child…

Halfdan stalked towards her, his jaw tight and his sapphire eyes glimmering in the starlight. She raised her chin, her hand going to the hilt of her sword—not because she felt threatened, but because it reminded her of who she was. All her past failures and her hopes for a better future…with her family and, more importantly, no more *men*!

'You are part of my crew, Valda.' His words hung in the air between them, a claim of ownership as if he'd branded her with an iron.

'Then *treat* me like a member of your crew! Do you make indecent offers to Tostig? Do you kiss him, too?'

His nostrils flared, but then he smiled a slow lazy smile. 'Tostig would not have me and neither, it seems, will you. So be it. Tonight, you can sleep on one of the benches in the Hall with the rest of my guard.'

With a firm nod she strode towards the glowing light of the Hall, pushing between the lovesick couple to re-enter and ignoring their hisses of outrage as she barged past them.

They were fools.

Chapter Nine

Halfdan was a little surprised, but mostly relieved, that Valda had continued with them after she'd rejected him so thoroughly in Gotland.

He cursed himself for allowing his lust to get the better of him. He shouldn't have pushed her so hard. Realising all was not over between them should have been enough for her to digest in one go. Valda was a prickly creature at the best of times, so strong that she saw even the smallest display of emotion as a weakness. He knew that about her and he loved her unbreakable resilience, but it also made her outer shell hard to crack.

He should have allowed her a small retreat, time to accept the significance of their relationship. But, no, he'd indulged in his desires and had ended up flat on his back for it—as he deserved.

He knew he'd taken it too far, but hadn't been able to stop himself. Her admission that she no longer loved Jorund had lit a fire within him similar to the burning need he'd felt as a youth wanting to travel the world. He wanted her back. He couldn't deny it—no more than he could deny the sea was wet—so he'd needled and prodded until he'd had the answer he yearned for. She *had* cared for him and still desired him. Elation had given his heart wings and it had soared with hope when she'd kissed him back.

There was a chance for them. A tantalising possibility that he couldn't shake from his mind. But…she'd been right. There was no hope of marriage, not really. He was betrothed, bound by honour to fulfil his oath. He could offer her no more than he could before, although this time for different reasons.

Conflicted by what he wanted and what he'd promised, yet he wanted it all—it was the merchant in him that made him greedy. Maybe there was a chance that his bride would never arrive, or that he could make some other deal with his father? But they were pitifully distant hopes.

First, he needed to be sure that Valda still wanted him, all of him—the good and the bad. He wanted her to love him not for what he could offer her, but for all that he was and that included his loyalty to his brother.

He would give her time, a chance for the desire to rekindle into something more meaningful.

She was avoiding him again, but he didn't mind. They both needed time to consider their actions and words.

What better way to do so, than while sailing? Your hands were always busy, your mind as wide and as free as the endless horizon.

He wanted her back in his life. But he refused to risk his brother's future happiness if she didn't love him.

She did care for him a little.

Why else would she react so passionately in his arms? Lust had once led to love, maybe it could again? Given time… Something he unfortunately did not have a lot of.

'*I am not interested in being your...anything!*' she'd said, but her beautiful eyes had betrayed her. Whenever he stripped off his tunic to work—as was his custom at sea and in fine weather—he'd caught her staring. Those hazel eyes had skittered away as soon as they'd met his, but it had been enough to reassure him that he was heading in the right direction. She couldn't force herself to ignore their physical connection any more than he ever could.

Although she seemed determined to try, thwarting him at every opportunity to talk with her in any depth. Even rudely ignoring him at times, focused only on eating, sleeping and working—preferably all while he was nowhere near her. It was infuriating.

They'd sailed across the Eastern Sea for several days now. Usually, he would hop along the coastline, but he'd promised both Valda and his father they'd be back by autumn and it was always wise to follow the fortune of swift winds for as long as possible.

However, as dawn broke across the grey sea, Halfdan noticed the wind changing direction and a sharper bite to the air. In the distance, dark rolling clouds predicted what was to come. They would hit a storm before the end of the day, he was sure of it. He joined the next watch as they sat on the deck to break their fast. He would not rest yet—the ship would need him later.

As usual his eyes strayed to the closed tent by the prow and he frowned. Valda was normally awake by now.

'She'll be out soon enough,' Tostig said between bites of salted fish on dried biscuits.

'What?' Halfdan asked, too distracted by staring at his tent to fully appreciate what Tostig was saying until it was too late.

'Every time the watch changes you sit here and wait for her,' Tostig said, pointing to the tent with his finger.

'It's only because I'm ready for my own bed,' Half-dan replied.

Tostig snorted with amusement. 'You've not seen the change in weather then? It's about to turn. They'll be no sleep for any of us soon.'

Embarrassment turned his insides into squirming eels. Was his obsession with her hopeless? He could not break his oath to his father and Valda seemed determined to ignore him anyway. Why should he even bother to win her back?

'Pathetic!' snarled his father's voice inside his head and he flinched.

He glanced at the other men and they avoided his eyes with knowing smirks.

It was obvious, then.

He shouldn't be surprised. How many times had he been distracted by the sight of Valda on his ship? Watching her for so long that he'd forgotten what he was doing, or even who was talking to him at the time.

Closing his eyes, he took in a deep, cleansing breath of salty air and remembered his mother. *'Never be ashamed of who you are. Your father is. Let that be a warning to you.'*

When he opened his eyes again, he felt better. Looking over at his friends, he smiled and then gave a wry shrug of acceptance.

He could not change what his heart wanted.

One last taste... It would be worth it, for both of them. And who knew how quickly their fates could change? So much had changed already.

The tent flap opened and out strode Valda. There were

small dark smudges beneath her eyes, but otherwise she appeared as fresh and as fearless as normal. Their eyes met across the deck and he thought he heard a few chuckles from his men. Valda's eyes followed the laughter with a narrowed glare and it died quickly.

She made her way to the oars and began to check them—a fruitless task as he could see they were all in perfectly good order. No doubt she was waiting for him to enter his tent before she joined the others. He grabbed some food and made his way over to join her. The food looked stale and unappetising, but as it had been a while since they'd replenished their supplies it was to be expected.

Valda looked up immediately, sensing his presence, and gave a long-suffering sigh as he approached, as if she already knew why he was there and was frustrated with him for it.

'You look tired, maybe you should sleep a little longer?' he asked. 'I slept at the oar—last night was uneventful—I won't need much sleep today.' He didn't mention the storm in case she insisted on helping to prepare for it.

'I'm fine,' she replied sharply. 'I have fought battles on less sleep than this. I'm used to it.'

'Then you should eat.' He thrust the dish of food into her hands and she took it, realising too late what she'd done when he sat on the oar bench in front of her.

'I wish you wouldn't do this.' She grimaced, tearing a chunk of biscuit off with her teeth. He had the unhappy feeling she wished to rip the flesh from his own bones in exactly the same way.

'Do what?' he asked innocently.

'*This!*' she hissed, gesturing wildly. 'Seeking me out at every opportunity. The men will think…' Her hands, still full of food, dropped to her lap, her words trailing away as if she were afraid to voice them.

'Why should we care what they think?'

Her eyes jerked to his with a flash of anger lighting up the green and gold in her eyes like jewels. 'I care!'

'Why?'

'*Why?* Because I don't want them to think less of me!'

'Why would they think less of you?' He smiled at the irony. *Hadn't he had these same fears?* It was strange how similar their minds worked.

She gave an exasperated sigh as she looked out at the seemingly calm sea beside them. The heavy ripple of waves was the only indication of what was to come. 'They'll think you only brought me along to warm your bed.'

'You *do* warm my bed,' he teased.

'You know what I *really* mean! They'll think I'm not good enough.'

He laughed and she stared at him as if he were mad.

'Why does that amuse you?'

'You are a famous shieldmaiden—your skill and courage in Francia is legendary. If anyone is not good enough it is me, not you! Besides…the men already *know* what I want. They know me too well. I cannot hide my feelings from them.' He sighed. 'Valda, I would love nothing more than to have you *really* warm my bed. But they will not judge you harshly for *my* weakness. I cannot help my desire for you, but I will not act upon it. Not unless you change your mind, of course, and then I will happily join you in *our* bed. I would like to see if there is a chance for us…a future…if the gods are kind.'

She must have the seen the engraving by now. She must know its significance.

He waited, hoping she would throw aside her doubts and take him as he was. But it was too soon for that, and like all clever deals he had to convince her she was making the right decision. Then, if he was lucky enough to win her heart, he could deal with the problems that awaited them back home…later.

Valda stared at Halfdan in disbelief.

How could he speak so casually? She had rejected him. Twice! And still he insisted on wanting her. It would be pathetic if he wasn't so *reasonable* about it.

'Are you mocking me?' she asked, her voice barely a whisper to her own ears.

He smiled in response. 'No. Why would you think that?'

She sucked in a deep breath, but there still wasn't enough air to clear her head. 'To admit your *supposed* feelings so freely…when nothing can come of it.'

'I have not lied to you, I want you. As much as I did nine years ago. We will be together on this ship and in close contact for months. In my experience it's always best to be honest with your crew.'

'When you desire them?'

The shout of Halfdan's laughter reverberated around the ship, causing several to glance over at them. 'Oh, yes, *especially* then.'

'I joined your ship to earn silver for my family, nothing more.'

'And yet you will have much more than that, I hope. Adventure and excitement. The life I'd always wanted to show you. Why not some pleasure, too?'

To remind them both, she said, 'We had pleasure before and it didn't end well.'

'No, it didn't,' he said with a pained smile as if the memory wounded him as much as it did her, which was impossible. 'We wanted different things then.'

'Nothing's changed.'

'Has it not? Not even after your disappointment with Jorund?' His words slipped through her ribs like a knife, piercing her wounded heart.

'Especially after Jorund.' She bristled. 'You're still to be married, are you not?'

He nodded. 'I am. But I prefer to take whatever joys life offers me before it's too late. Wouldn't you? Bad things can happen as well as good. Life is too fleeting to not enjoy everything it has to offer. I understand your refusal to be my concubine, but why not take some pleasant memories with you to your farm?' The light amusement of his expression dissolved into a serious expression. 'For all my faults, I know I can make you happy.'

'Yes, for a short time.' Her words were meant as a rebuke, but too late she realised she'd revealed her only weakness. Him.

'It's all that I can offer at this time. But I swear it will be worth it.' Something about the look in his eyes struck something deep inside Valda, leaving an invisible imprint on her soul. When she thought of the time ahead—farming with her sisters and mother—it filled her heart with dread and not the peace she hoped it would. Part of her didn't want to think that far ahead. Thinking too much about the endlessly lonely nights ahead depressed her.

He was right, she did want one last taste of pleasure... more than anything else in the world. Their incredible kiss days ago had proved that. How many nights had she tossed and turned, longing to feel his body pressed against hers? Like old times—when she'd not felt quite so alone.

She wanted him, and his offer was…tempting.

Pride flared red hot down her spine, like a newly forged sword plunged into water.

He betrayed you!

And there it was. The heartache that held her back. The grief she could not stomach again. It didn't matter how pleasurable their time together could be. It was the ending she could not bear. She was done with being a man's *second*! She'd decided after Jorund that she would be the first and only in a man's heart. She would accept nothing less.

Halfdan had said she'd made the wrong choice in the past. But if Olga's life was to have been her fate, she was glad she'd walked away.

Today, she was making a similar decision, one that hurt, but was also the wisest.

She smiled coldly and the hope in his eyes dulled a little. 'Miklagard is enough adventure for me. I look forward to the peace and security of returning to my sisters and mother.' She leaned forward, her voice hard when she spoke. 'That's where we've always differed, Halfdan. In *loyalty*. You always wanted to escape your family. I never did.'

Punched in the gut by her words, Halfdan dropped his head as she walked away.

They hurt because they were true.

He *had* been desperate to escape his family…even the responsibility and guilt of Erik, if he was honest. He'd never even considered how difficult leaving her family would have been for her.

But that was then. She'd lived apart from them since— her time with Jorund proved that. So why the insistence that she wished to stay with her family? Unless she no longer wished to follow a man, especially one that currently could offer her nothing more than pleasure... He could understand that.

It wasn't ideal for either of them. He wished he could offer her more, but he couldn't, only his heart and soul.

But why wasn't that enough?

Another thing he couldn't understand was her wish to settle for the life of a farmer. She was a shieldmaiden, she'd fought and killed men in battle. She wouldn't be happy tending livestock, weaving cloth and growing crops. So why did she claim to want to return to her family to work the rest of her days with them, when he could offer so much more than that? The sea was filled with endless excitement in comparison and he'd seen the glimmer of anticipation in her eyes when he'd first mentioned Miklagard. He knew she craved adventure.

So, if the only thing holding her back was the lack of marriage—which he begrudgingly understood—then why was she so set against a flirtation with him? She acted as if she'd been deeply wounded by him in the past, as if he'd betrayed her somehow. But he'd not lied to her then, not promised her a wedding and then broken his word. He'd asked her to wait, that was all. There was no betrayal, no lack of choice...

His mind circled back like a dog chasing its tail.

He'd been so close to convincing her...he was sure of it. He'd seen the doubt, the desire and temptation in her eyes. Felt the exquisite bite of her teeth on her bottom lip as she'd remembered their pleasure together.

Everything he'd ever wanted had been in the palm of his hands, but then she'd fallen through his fingers once more. Something had stopped her from taking that leap of faith into his waiting arms. Before, he'd thought it was her feelings for Jorund, but, no, there was something else, another wall of defence in his way. Some shackle from the past he wasn't sure he could unlock.

What could it be? If he didn't understand it, how could he persuade her to ignore it?

Had his father threatened her or her family? It was possible, but that didn't make sense. Ulf had received his oath from Halfdan. What cause would he have to pressurise them further? And would they have buckled? Not without a fight.

He thought back to her criticisms of him. She'd called him disloyal more than once…as well as other offences.

Arrogant? Yes. Selfish? Possibly. But…disloyal?

While he worked, he brooded, the final slur rolling over and over in his mind as he ordered the ship's preparation for the forthcoming storm.

When had he been disloyal?

Because he'd wanted to leave his violent home and travel the world?

He'd *begged* her to join him and she'd been the one to reject his offer.

What else should he have done? Defied his father and married her?

He wished now he had. But there'd been his brother's life to consider. Would Ulf have allowed such an insultingly low match for his son and heir?

No, of course not, he would have demanded a divorce…or killed her, or, more likely, Erik. Even if they'd fought back, his brother still lived under his father's command and could have been slaughtered without penalty. Ulf knew that and he used it like a noose around both their necks, tightening it whenever one of them displeased him.

Halfdan sighed miserably. So much had been unspoken in Gotland—too much.

It was time to bring those chains out into the light, even if the idea of talking about that oppressive time made him apprehensive. Obviously, an arrow from the past was still lodged in Valda's heart and it could not be allowed to fester any longer if they were to ever move on.

They were meant to be together.

Why else would the Norns of fate weave their paths together for a second time?

Halfdan didn't bother to rest that day; he wouldn't be able to sleep anyway. Instead, he worked hard to match the speed of the wind, trying his best to not be distracted by Valda and her chastising glares.

As the day passed, the sky darkened to match Halfdan's foul mood and the waves began to roll under them with merciless fury. The boat's hull groaned against the increasing pace and the sail cracked like a whip against the unpredictable wind.

The sky and the sea were at war.

Chapter Ten

Valda didn't have long to ponder why Halfdan didn't go to bed at the changing of the watch as it became clear soon enough when the rain fell in increasing ferocity.

Before the storm the crew had worked hard to tie down everything that moved in preparation. She'd placed her sword, shield and cloak within her sea chest. She didn't need the extra bulk or weight—especially during a storm—when being lost over the side meant certain death. She'd pulled on her thick woollen tunic, the spare one she usually wore at night. Halfdan's tent had been dismantled and used to reinforce the current covers over the cargo. Everything was secured, or in some cases nailed to the deck.

Bori shouted to her over the deafening spray as they checked the ropes. 'We've used the storm winds to our advantage for as long as possible. But now it's time to head to the safety of the coast.' He pointed across the tilting horizon, but Valda couldn't see anything.

'We have to get there first!' said Svend grumpily as he and Odger baled buckets of water from the deck. 'Tostig will need you!'

She turned and headed towards Tostig, swaying with the ship and clinging on to anything within easy reach to keep her steady. The boat pitched suddenly, her stomach dropped and she nearly fell to the deck. Thankfully, she was able to grab Tostig for balance. He hauled her close and laughed at her panicked face, before giving her arm a comforting squeeze.

'Is this your first storm?' he asked.

She nodded, desperately trying to blink away the salt from her eyes. 'My first *bad* one.'

In truth, she'd done little sailing other than through the rivers of Francia. The longest journey she'd ever made on open sea was that time travelling to and from Halfdan's home. That had been many years ago during the height of summer when the seas were calm.

Tostig barked with laughter at her admission. 'This isn't a *bad* storm.'

She smiled with relief. 'Ahh, that's good to know.'

Tostig grinned cheerfully as he stared out at the cresting waves. The impressive ship now seemed small and vulnerable against the might of nature. 'We could still wreck and drown, of course. But I've survived worse.'

Valda winced. Drowning was not a death she longed for. An honourable death with a place in Valhalla would be nice. But she'd be just as happy in Freya's Hall, or even in Hel's with the rest of the ordinary souls, if that were her fate. She'd never imagined she'd end up deep beneath the waves with Rán and her husband, Aegir. But such was life and death. Unpredictable.

They'd kept up the sail for as long as they could, taking advantage of the wind. But eventually the decision had to be made.

'Reef the sail!' shouted Halfdan from the steering oar.

He looked magnificent as he gripped the huge oak beneath his arm, his legs planted wide to brace against the rolling deck.

'Good!' shouted Tostig with a bad-tempered grumble that was almost lost in the squall. 'If he left it much longer, even *his* sail would tear!'

Valda shivered. Even she knew that would be a disaster, especially in this weather. She was surprised Halfdan even risked it. Sails were precious. A huge cloth such as his took many months to make and so many bales of wool that the cost of it alone was staggering.

However, it had carried them with dizzying speed across the water and seemed worth every coin of silver it cost. No wonder Halfdan said he could make the journey to Miklagard in half the usual time.

Tostig made his way to the many cords of rope that made up the rigging. Valda followed, a little more cautiously. She still struggled to find her balance despite the hours they'd spent battling against the ferocious weather.

Rain poured down Tostig's ruddy cheeks and into his soaking wet beard, but he didn't seem concerned. Unlike her, he wore only a thin undertunic and woollen breeches with sturdy boots. Much like what Halfdan wore, although she had to admit she appreciated his physique far more. The men didn't seem to feel the cold as she did—she supposed their bodies were used to the harsh winds.

Valda, on the other hand, was miserable. She was soaked to the bone and wished her wool was better oiled and thicker, to keep away the chill. Her mother often joked that she'd lost the Norse ability to be hardy and healthy in any cold weather as she'd grown up in Francia and was used to a warmer climate.

They worked on the ropes. Big levers and blocks were

used to reel in the tough hemp, but even with several
men pulling on them they needed help to lower the sails.
No amount of clever pulleys and levers could match the
power of Thor. Any man not busy elsewhere was needed
to roll up the sail a section at a time. It was difficult work
and Valda's arms screamed with the strain of it, but she
ignored the discomfort and focused all her strength on
proving her place in front of the crew.

'Steady,' warned Tostig and Valda grunted in agreement as she and two other men strained against the
weight of the wind on the ropes. Across on the other
side of the ship a similar group of men laboured against
the elements. Each section of the ship had an even place-
ment of crew to help the distribution of weight, particularly important in rough seas such as this.

A large wave crashed against the prow of the ship,
flooding the deck with water and when the man in front
of her slipped all of them were jerked forward by the
rope.

'Steady!' reprimanded Tostig, but it was too late.
The sail had been unfurled in one section and raised
too tightly in another. They tried to rectify it, but a rope
had snagged along the cross-beam.

Valda was too much of a novice to know what needed
to be done to fix it on the pulleys below. But it seemed
a simple enough solution to climb up the mast and un-
snag it.

'I'll go,' she volunteered. 'It won't take me long.'

Tostig shook his head dismissively. 'Halfdan wouldn't
like it.' He turned his back on her as he began to loosen
a knot in another area of the rigging.

Anger and frustration clouded her vision with a rage
that rivalled the storm. She didn't care what Halfdan

thought. She already knew he only wanted her here to warm his bed, but she'd thought the crew still respected her in spite of that. Tostig's dismissal was like a slap in the face.

With renewed conviction and courage, she strode to the mast. Pegs were hammered into the wood as handholds and she resolutely began to climb them. If Tostig called for her to stop she didn't hear it as the wind quickly took her sense of hearing from her. The only sounds that remained were the whistling wind and the roaring sea, biting at her ears until they rang with cold. She didn't dare look down as she climbed; already the horizon sickened her with the way it boiled up to the sky and then crashed down with equal ferocity.

She gulped back a breath as the ship rocked to the side. She clung to the mast to keep herself from falling and waited for the swaying to ease.

A voice cut through the din. 'Get down!' it shouted. A quick glance below and she realised Halfdan was climbing up after her.

'I can do it!' she shouted back, although her stomach heaved at the distance between herself and the deck.

She shouldn't have looked! Raising her head, she saw it was only a few feet until the top of the sail. She could even see where the rope had snagged against another. It would only take a quick tug to fix it.

She gritted her teeth and climbed the remaining pegs.

The whole time the ship rocked from side to side and waves crashed upon the deck below. The rain whipped at her head and tugged the hair from her braid. Rain lashed her face with such force it stung her skin and made it difficult to see.

She reached for the rope. It was much thicker than

she'd imagined and the coarse hemp tore at her numb fingers as she clawed at it with the nails of her free hand, the other gripping tightly to the mast.

Frustrated, she leaned further across and gave it one sharp tug. The rope unfurled with a hiss that matched her own sigh of relief. As she swung her body back to the mast, the ship dipped and she lost her footing. Dangling precariously from a single peg, for one swallowed heartbeat she feared her arm would rip from its socket. Then a heavy palm thudded into her back and pushed her against the mast with a winding thud.

Even after she'd regained her footing the heavy palm remained. Halfdan climbed up against her, her body pressed between the mast and his chest. His hand snaked around her waist, quickly tying a rope between them with a clever one-handed knot.

'Climb down…carefully!' he grunted, easing to the side to let her pass. She moved quickly, half afraid he would fall himself, held up as he was by only the grip of one arm. She now knew how difficult that was.

The climb down felt as if it would never end, but eventually she reached the bottom.

When she saw Tostig's furious face she half wished she *had* fallen into the sea.

'No one,' he shouted, 'climbs the mast without *his* permission!' He spat on the deck with a snarl of disgust, before gesturing with a toss of his head to Halfdan who was climbing the last few feet to the ground. 'It's too dangerous. Only *he's* allowed and that's because it's *his* ship! Next time you do as I say, girl!'

The rest of the men were looking at her in horror and Valda was hit by a wall of shame. She'd presumed he'd not allowed her because he'd not thought her good enough and had dismissed her as Halfdan's woman, not because it was a rule everyone abided by. With sickening clarity, she realised her own pride had almost got her killed.

Or Halfdan...

She flinched, the cold wind stealing her breath as she shivered and rocked on unsteady feet.

'I'm sorry,' she said. Somehow, failing in Tostig's eyes was a worse punishment than anything Halfdan could think up.

When he dropped down beside her, she'd expected more tongue lashing. Instead, she was surprised by the concern in his stormy eyes. Pushing away the wet strands of her hair that had fallen from her braid, he tucked them behind her ear, his fingers brushing along her jaw as his hand dropped away, a caress that brought welcome heat and unwelcome feelings to the surface. Turning to Tostig, he said lightly, 'Valda was only trying to help, my friend. She won't do it again.' His voice deepened into a firm warning as he turned to face her. 'Will you?'

She shook her head miserably.

What had come over her?

'She best not! Stupid girl, thinking she knows better!' Tostig growled, before turning back to manage the rigging. The men leapt to work, afraid to receive a similar scolding.

She'd not been called a 'stupid girl' since her mother had caught her trying to juggle knives and she'd almost lost a finger.

'Don't worry,' whispered Halfdan in her ear, his breath hot against the miserable rain. 'He'll forgive you. *As will I.* We have much to discuss, you and I.'

He would forgive her? She stared at his back as he

walked away. A disturbingly wide and well-sculpted back, displayed too well by the wet linen against his skin.

Unsure if she were angry, ashamed or aroused, she was grateful for the distraction when a cry went out that land had been spotted and the crew focused their attention on sailing towards it.

Chapter Eleven

They made camp on a deserted shore, grateful to be out of the worst of the weather. They'd dragged the ship into the shallows of the bay, anchoring it in the sand by tying it down with heavy rocks. It wouldn't take much effort to get them back out to sea.

The deathly chill still hadn't left Halfdan's bones, despite him changing his wet clothes to dry. It wasn't the cold that disturbed him, but fear. The memory of Valda dangling desperately from the mast, her body swaying out into the empty air. She'd only been moments away from losing her grip and tumbling to her death.

He could have lost her. This time for ever.

He imagined the sight of it would torture him in his nightmares for years to come.

If Tostig hadn't berated her so hard, he might have lost his own temper. Shaken her until her teeth had rattled. Except he'd seen how pale and frightened she'd been, how ashamed Tostig's words had made her feel, and he couldn't face pouring salt on her wounds. Especially not in front of his men. She would have been humiliated and he could not bear to see her shrunken any further. He knew how awful that would have been for her.

A large fire was burning on the beach, covered by a makeshift shelter to keep out the rain. Clothing was laid out beside it either on rocks or sticks to dry out. There was still a little light left in the day and half of the men had gone out to hunt in the nearby forest, while the remainder, including himself, had set up camp.

Valda sat by the fire, brooding. She'd worked hard, but still looked despondent, like a kicked hound, and she sat a little away from the others as if afraid to face them.

It was time for them to talk and clear up whatever resentment from the past remained.

He walked over. 'Come with me.'

There was no point explaining why he wished for her to follow him—she would only argue. That's why he'd said it as an order, so she'd have no choice but to obey.

When he entered his tent, she followed, closing the flaps softly behind her. Probably expecting some form of reprimand by the way she stared at her feet glumly.

'You should change out of those wet clothes.'

'I'm fine, they'll dry.'

'Don't feel bad, it was a small lapse in judgement, nothing more.'

'How can you say that? I could have died, and…' She paused, looking wretched. 'You could have died, too. Mistakes like that cost lives.'

He shrugged. 'So? Every day onboard a ship is a risk.' It didn't seem to comfort her and he stepped closer. 'You can't begin to live until you realise you can die. When you understand that your *real* life begins.'

She stared at him, slack jawed for a moment, and then laughed with a shake of her head. 'You're a madman.'

'You made a mistake. We all make them.'

She looked up at him, her eyes pained with conflicted pride and shame.

'It's fine,' he added, reaching out to touch her arm. The wool was soaked through and cold to the touch.

'I'm not allowed to make mistakes,' she said, looking away from him and shrugging off his hand.

'Of course you are! Everyone is. It's what makes us human.'

Her eyes snapped to his, green and gold flecks alive with fire. 'In my experience, if a man makes a mistake, it's dismissed as youthful exuberance. If a woman makes a similar mistake, it only proves she's not good enough!'

'Not on my ship.' He bristled, knowing she spoke the truth and wanting to beat the senses out of any man who'd dared to question her worth.

'Really? How *nice*.' Her mouth twisted into a mocking smile and his mood soured further.

Was that what she'd thought when he'd refused to marry her? That she wasn't good enough?

He wanted to argue against it, but the truth was he couldn't have married her then for many reasons, including her status…because she *hadn't* been good enough in his father's eyes. He took a deep breath. 'In my eyes, there is no one better than you. No one.'

She stared at him, her eyes bright in the dim light of the tent. Rain pummelled the sides of the canvas like the rattling of glass beads and a flash of lightning illuminated the space between them, followed by a deep roll of thunder.

'Oh, I don't know about that,' she said grimly. 'You thought Olga better than me…and more than once, probably, and…were there others, too?'

'Olga?' He frowned. Again, he had the uncomfortable sensation that he'd missed something of great importance. 'Olaf's daughter?'

Valda snorted in disgust. Then she turned on him with hard eyes and a voice soured by bitterness. 'Yes, Olaf's daughter!' She shook her head with pity. 'That poor girl! She was *obsessed* with marrying you. Brynhild said she spoke of nothing else to anyone who would listen. You must have broken her heart when you cast her aside. Not to mention the *child.* I don't know why, but I thought you better than that. Leaving your child to be brought up by another...it's *despicable*!'

Confusion followed by a slow dawning of realisation flooded his senses. This must be the old arrow that plagued her still. Indignation reared with his pride.

How could she think such a thing of him?

'Cast her aside? I barely knew her! What are you talking about?'

Another flash of lightning illuminated Valda's face. Raw anguish burned across her beautiful face.

'Stop lying!' she shouted, her fists clenched at her sides.

Thunder boomed in the silence between them. She took a deep breath as if trying to calm herself. 'I saw you. The morning after we argued she was leaving your boat and you were lying there naked and peacefully asleep.' She laughed, the sound hollow and brittle, as if her voice might break at any moment. 'Don't pretend there is no one else in this world for you, Halfdan. It's insulting! You have already proved otherwise.'

'What do you mean? I have never been with Olga. Ever!'

She turned to leave and Halfdan grabbed her arm to

pull her back. Which was a mistake. She was a shield-maiden after all. He might have been physically stronger and bigger, but Valda was fast, highly skilled and battle hardened.

Before he could blink, she'd used a wrestling move to throw him to the ground. He landed flat on his back, winded and gasping like a fish on the sand. She stared down at him, enough fury in her eyes to rival the god of storms. 'Lies! You didn't care for me then and you don't care for me now.'

He tried to sit up and she landed a leathered boot firmly in the square of his chest to hold him down. If he'd thought he was struggling to breathe before, he was mistaken. The press of her boot made his ribs bow and his lungs scream for air.

'Enough!' she cried. 'The past is over! I do not want you! *Ever* again!'

He grabbed the back of her knee with one hand and forced it to bend forward with a jerk. She struggled with her footing and he took the opportunity to grab her tunic, twisting his body to sweep her off her feet. It wasn't a skilful manoeuvre, but it worked.

Sand spraying, she landed with a thud beside him. It was her turn to be winded and he used the opportunity to pin her down with both his arms and legs. She fought back, her limbs twisting and straining.

Odin's teeth! She was strong!

Frustrated, he thrust down with all his might to stop her bucking. 'I only ever cared for you!' he shouted, his voice rivalling the thunder outside his tent.

She glared back at him, but at least she was still. She spat words as if they were daggers. 'You are a deceitful, arrogant, unfaithful… Even after our argument you went straight to her, so our parting meant nothing to you! *I* meant nothing to you. Stop pretending I ever did!' The fight was gone in her muscles, but he continued to hold her down, determined to discover the truth. Afraid that if he let her go, she would walk away and never return.

He thought back to the night of their argument. 'I got drunk in my father's Hall…then I slept out on my boat. Olga did follow me that night. But I told her to leave me be. I must have fallen asleep. I thought she'd left… Believe me, I could not have made love to anyone that night! I could barely stand!'

At her disbelieving snort of disgust, he added, 'Olga did want to marry me. She even petitioned my father. Do you know what he did?'

Valda continued to glare at him, but reluctantly shook her head.

'He *laughed*! He'd heard from his spies in Olaf's retinue that she'd already been tumbled by one of her father's warriors. That's whose child she carried, not mine! Olaf had thought to trick him, but my father had suspected some kind of treachery. There was no way he would accept another man's bastard in his household. He threatened to beat Olga if she even dared to claim it was mine. But that was all after you left… I never realised she'd spoken to you, although I can see how she might have seen you as a threat to her plans.'

Shock dawned across Valda's face, denial and horror washing through her with equal force. 'I don't believe you.'

He let go of her wrists and placed his hands either side of her head, their bodies still close, his words quiet and sincere. 'Ask anyone in my father or Olaf's household and they will tell you the same.'

She sucked in a shaky breath, as if he'd punched her in the gut. 'Then you didn't...' Her voice cracked and her eyes shone with tears.

'Why did you not speak to me about it?'

'I...' She looked up and over his head, unable to meet his eyes. 'I was humiliated. Brynhild said it would be best to leave quickly. To act as if I didn't care. To not show you how much you'd hurt me. In my family we *never* show weakness. And I thought... It seemed so obvious that you'd...'

His own heart ached at the sight of her confusion and pain. He understood it now and it left a bitter taste in his mouth. 'I would *never* betray you.'

Why had the fates been so cruel? How could she believe such a thing of him? Did she not know him at all? But...why had he never spoken to her after their argument?

His youthful pride was as much at fault as hers for what had happened between them.

A thousand possibilities struck him like a volley of arrows. Of what could have been and what might have followed. Each one piercing his heart and breaking it all over again.

But what was the point in looking back?

He sighed. It was time for honesty. 'The truth is... there has only ever been you. No one else.'

A sob escaped her throat and she turned away. Cupping her face in the palms of his hands, he gently turned her back towards him.

Tears streamed down her cheeks. His beautiful, strong and fearless Valda was crying. It didn't seem possible and he couldn't bear it.

'I'm sorry,' she whispered. 'You must hate me.'

'Never.' He pressed his lips against hers. A desperately tender kiss, one he'd longed for since their last embrace. 'I wish things had been different, that much is true. But the past is done with, so we should look to the future. We can enjoy what time we do have left…together.'

The wasted years, the broken dreams, everything culminated in this fragile moment. As was his way, he took it tightly with both hands and refused to let go. He gathered her to him. Chest pressed against chest. With trembling hands, she wrapped her arms around his neck and pulled him closer…and all at once the kiss changed, from loving and gentle to fierce and passionate.

Their tongues and limbs tangled together like vines. Valda clung to him, breathless and confused, while his hands tugged at her tunic, desperate to remove the cold, rain-soaked wool from her body and touch the smooth heat beneath.

She moaned as his hand found her breast, the thin fabric of her bindings the only barrier between them, her thighs wrapping around his hips as he took the opportunity to lift her from the ground and deposit her on his bed covered in luxurious furs and soft woollen blankets.

Their bed, he corrected mentally. It had always been *their* bed, even before it had become one.

So much time had come between them and he was determined to remind her of their love.

Maybe then she might consider staying with him after their journey was over.

Halfdan peeled away the rest of her clothing, with the determination of a man who would not be thwarted a second time. He threw her undertunic to the ground with a wet slap of satisfaction, then his fingers got busy at her ties.

Valda shivered, although whether it was from the cold or the shock of the day's events she couldn't be sure. Her mind was still spinning.

For once, she didn't doubt him, and though there was a hundred people she could check regarding Olga, she didn't need to. The idea that his callous father would laugh in Olga's face and threaten to kill her child simply for lying sounded horribly true.

Besides, Halfdan's betrayal had never sat right with her and now she knew why. Even her own eyes had deceived her. All because she'd been ready to believe no one could love a fatherless shieldmaiden.

But she'd been so wrong and it was a hard truth to swallow. It meant that he had loved her and wanted her to sail away with him all those years ago. But she'd been too young and afraid.

In truth, he'd remained more loyal than she, who had set her sights on Jorund afterwards. Hoping—as he'd accused—for something better...or at least something more attainable.

She might have been happy with Halfdan. They could have travelled the world together, built a life together. Maybe in time they might have married. As Halfdan's success and independence grew away from his father, they could have broken away, had children of their own... Each thought only tormented her further, because there was nothing she could do to repair their broken past. Those opportunities were gone. Halfdan was right, they had to look to the future.

But was this a mistake? So much was still unsaid between them.

Would Halfdan still keep his promise to his father and marry another? He'd made no declarations and she was afraid to know the truth.

Could she accept even less than what was offered before?

Besides…could she even leave her family for another man…again? Things had always gone so badly in the past…

Was this just another lapse in judgement? Did she even care?

All concern and resolve melted away as she watched Halfdan methodically remove her boots and leg wraps, kissing the skin beneath with loving caresses as he revealed the flesh.

She wanted him. Desperately.

She didn't want to think any more. Halfdan was finally with her. Kissing and caressing her. Sitting up, she began to undo the ties that kept her breasts secure, tossing the strips of linen aside with renewed confidence.

Even if this was a mistake, she would treasure this moment of happiness for ever. Her hands flew to her hips as she peeled off the last of her clothing and threw her braes aside.

He moved away from the bed and she feared he would leave her. But when he started to remove his clothing, she breathed a sigh of relief, allowing herself to admire the man he'd become.

No longer a pale and slim youth, but a man weathered by the sea and kissed by the sun of distant lands. His bronze skin shone in the flashes of lightning that occasionally lit up the dim tent. Strong, lean muscle corded his arms like rope and his broad chest was heavily plated and dusted with gold. He might have been a merchant by trade, but he had a warrior's physique. A reflection of the strenuous and dangerous life he led.

'You can't begin to live until you realise you can die.'

Those words had rocked her soul. She'd thought herself brave. In battle, she'd had to take risks to succeed. Fearing death was natural and sensible. Was she a coward when it came to battles of the heart?

Her heart could be broken all over again. But the reward…the reward was as tantalising as a thousand pieces of silver.

He moved over her, immediately capturing her mouth and good sense with one of his hot, urgent kisses. She pulled him close, accepting his body against hers and allowing herself to risk it all for a dream.

Their naked passion collided like the wind and rain above, the fear and cold of earlier burned away by the heat of their desire. He pressed hot kisses against her neck, trailing them down her collarbone to her chest. She moaned and arched her back as his mouth closed over her nipple and lightly sucked.

Yearning mouths searched for one another, until they shared breath and mutual heat. She ran her nails down his back, squeezing him close, delighted by the rolling muscle beneath her fingertips. Hot honey pooled between her thighs and she opened her legs, eagerly cradling his rock-hard abdomen and sighing with pleasure as he rubbed against her. It was as though they were once more in the boat of his youth. Both confident and eager to meet each other's needs.

Reaching down between them, she gripped his hard length in her hand, revelling in the silky feel of him. Knowing exactly what he liked, she stroked him firmly, causing him to moan against her neck. The sensation of his breath against her pulse caused butterflies to shiver across her skin and she bit her lip with a triumphant cry of her own.

'I've…missed this so much… I've missed *you*,' he gasped between more kisses, his fingers finding the sensitive flesh between her legs and caressing it with a possessive touch.

'Then let us make up for what we have missed. If I cannot have a future with you, then I want what we should have had, for a while at least. For now, I am yours. Take me.' She opened her legs wider for him and he groaned.

Gathering her hips in his hands, he pressed forward, his manhood piercing and filling her with rigid heat until she cried out with a whimper of satisfaction. Nothing had ever felt as right, or as good, as him inside her.

She needed more.

Gripping his hips, she urged him into a steady rhythm. His thrusts were smooth and hard and she clung to his waist as he slid in and out, their carnal pleasure overpowering their minds and leaving behind only searing pleasure. Her heels dug into the pallet as her body rocked against his with an increasing pace. She bit her lip and moaned with frustration, sensing her release was only moments away. Relentlessly, he rode her body hard, taking her up to the highest pleasure she'd ever known, focused solely on fulfilling her needs above his own.

Halfdan rained urgent kisses against her face and neck, as if he were a man drowning and she his only air, and his rhythm became more erratic as he fought to control his climax.

The thunder and lightning continued to rage outside

the tent, covering the sounds of their keening moans and cries.

'Come with me,' he gasped, his voice hoarse. 'I need you.'

Exquisite waves of pleasure rushed through her and she cried out with delight.

He followed shortly after, unable to contain himself a moment longer. He jerked away, spilling his seed over her belly and hip, his head thrown back and his neck strained.

After, Halfdan flopped on to the space beside her with a deeply appreciative sigh and she shifted on her side to allow him more room on the narrow pallet. Gathering her close, Halfdan curved his body into hers, cupping her breast possessively, as he always used to do when they'd slept together in his boat.

It felt both familiar and strange, as if they were living in one of their idle memories from the past. Valda was afraid that once the storm of their passion eventually faded away, nothing real would remain and she'd be left alone once more.

Chapter Twelve

After the storm had broken, they spent a few days waiting for more favourable winds. Halfdan didn't mind. They were safe on this part of the coast and it was a welcome break after travelling a great distance in a relatively short space of time.

The lull in their journey was pleasant and rejuvenating. He and Valda spent their days hunting, or they worked with the crew making minor repairs to the ship. At night they made love in their tent beneath the stars. It felt as if they were reliving that summer, their desire and passion for each other as insatiable as it had always been. It was such a joy to be with her again, he could almost forget the insurmountable problems that loomed in the distance.

He could sense Valda's hesitation.

They'd not spoken of the future. It was a crack in their newfound happiness they both deliberately ignored. Uncertainty held their tongues captive, afraid to speak of the inevitable in case it shattered the fragile bliss of their reunion.

Maybe it was for the best? They'd only just found each

other again. Their relationship needed time to breathe and settle before facing the challenges ahead. *Better to take advantage of fair winds when you had them.*

So, instead, they'd got to know one another again. Talking about the years they'd missed and how they'd grown as people since that summer. Valda had battle scars on her skin and in her mind, but she dealt with them well. He was beginning to understand why she might long for peace and quiet after some of what she'd seen. But it still didn't feel right to him—she had too adventurous a spirit and he thought he could see it in the glimmer of excitement in her eyes when he told her of his travels…unless it was only his wishful thinking?

Maybe, when this voyage was over, she would still walk away from him, regardless of whether he could offer her more or not? The question made him uncomfortable and he pushed it from his mind. They had many days left together, many sights to see, and he was determined to show Valda how exhilarating a life by his side could be.

As much as he had wished they could stay on this shore a little longer, the winds eventually changed and started to blow north-eastwards. A sign for them to push onwards.

Fully stocked with fresh water and supplies, they pulled up the anchoring stones and left the shelter of the bay.

Valda sat beside Tostig on one of the benches as she rowed. Halfdan could see she had the rhythm mastered. Strength and stamina were obvious requirements, but it was the synchronised pace of the rowers that ensured a swift journey. She caught him staring at her in admiration and she rolled her eyes with a half-smile.

'We'll be back in Jorvik if he doesn't pay attention to where we're going!' shouted a bad-tempered Tostig and Valda laughed.

Halfdan focused back on his steering oar and directed them eastwards. There was no point worrying about the future, he decided. He could not live like that.

They sailed for two days, the weather getting colder as they headed further north. Then they reached the River Neva that led to Lake Ladoga, and they had to switch to oars, fighting the current of the river with each roll of their arms.

They passed the trading post of Staraya Ladoga, stopping only for more supplies, and entered the river that flowed down into the land of the Rus, a kingdom of fortresses. They sailed past many heavily defended settlements but no one was concerned by their fleeting and familiar presence.

The next two weeks passed without incident as they flowed with the Neva River through dense forests. Occasionally, they stopped to hunt, but mostly the crew stayed aboard, taking turns to rest or navigate the river. Halfdan and Valda now slept together in his tent and as he'd expected the crew had barely blinked at the change in circumstance.

At times, the river became unpassable, the water too shallow to navigate without the danger of becoming stuck in the riverbed. Before this could happen, he took the precaution of hauling his ship on to dry land, dragging it by ropes, the oars used beneath to help it roll across the earth. Then they would reach a deeper part of the river and launch it back into the water with weary relief.

It was amusing how shocked by the process Valda was, which revealed how little portaging she'd done in Rouen. It was strenuous work, but he reassured Valda it was perfectly normal and a way of life on the eastern trade routes. Settlements had sprung up around these portage areas, so there were always plenty of helpers—for a silver coin or two.

He rather enjoyed giving her these new experiences. He hoped it showed her that no matter the challenges faced there was always a solution—you just had to think a little differently.

They arrived in Novgorod at the beginning of the summer. The Rus city was nestled in among the thick forest, a mighty wooden palisade built on a mountain of earth protected the inhabitants like cupped hands around a jug. The spout of the city, a huge wooden harbour, poured out into the river, connecting all who passed with the opportunity to trade.

As soon as they were spotted, sentries rowed out to meet them. The Rus controlled this region and they observed closely who passed on their rivers, demanding tribute and respect from all.

Halfdan greeted them like old friends, welcoming them aboard with warm smiles, and generous refreshments. It was always wise to remember their names, likes and dislikes. His seal, given to him by their ruler, Igor, ensured he could pass through without issue. But the sentries could delay them, or even overlook excess cargo if it suited them, which Halfdan always ensured it did. Gifts of walrus tusk and ermine pelts were handed over as tribute and the sentries left as quickly as they'd arrived, with pleasant farewells.

After they'd gone, Valda came to stand beside him, watching in astonishment as they sailed away from the city without even stopping to replenish their supplies. 'You paid them so little. I thought the taxes to the Rus were higher than that?'

He shrugged. 'Usually. But I am a distant kinsman to their rulers. The Rus were once Norse themselves, although it is long ago, and almost forgotten. But we still have some familial links…it makes for good business. The only thing I'm grateful to my father for.'

Valda chuckled. 'I would have thought you'd be grateful for this ship!' The laughter died in her throat when she saw the offence on his face.

'This is *my* ship.'

Her eyes widened and she looked around, as if she might see his name engraved on the wood—the way he'd done to his first ship. 'Oh, but…' She paused, as if searching for the words.

'It is mine. The first ship was my father's. He expected me to return from my first trading voyage in debt and begging for help. I came back with two boats. The next year, I'd trebled the amount of silver his boat had cost him and owed him nothing more. I still take cargo for him—it's part of our agreement—to allow Erik to join with me in trade.'

'But then you're…free of him…' She stared at him in shock and he realised there was still much more they needed to discuss. They couldn't avoid the future for ever.

'No, we're not free. Not yet.' He smiled, trying to reassure her, but he could tell she was more worried than before. 'It won't be long until we reach my settlement. We'll talk about it there.'

'*Your* settlement?'

He shrugged, more than a little pleased by the surprise in her eyes. He was proud of his accomplishments and the settlement was his greatest achievement so far. 'More of a trading post really, although the local Slavic tribes have begun to settle around it. That's another reason why I pay so little tribute here. Igor gets his silver from me further down the river.'

When they reached Halfdan's settlement, Valda was surprised to discover he had been more than a little humble in his description of his 'trading post'. There was a well-fortified fort up on a hill overlooking the surrounding plains.

The forests had slowly receded down the river from Novgorod and now the horizon was filled with a sea of grassy plains and the shadow of a mountain range far off in the distance. The world suddenly seemed endless to Valda and she wasn't sure if she ever wanted to return to muddy Jorvik.

Halfdan's people greeted them with cheers as they sailed in to dock and many of the crew jumped off the ship and waded through the shallow waters to greet lovers and children. The people wore similar clothing to those back in Gotland, but with more of a Slavic influence. They wore fur-trimmed caps, sometimes with jewellery strung along the front or topped with decorative silver cones, and their dresses and tunics were brightly coloured and heavily embroidered, sometimes embellished with the occasional scrap of silk.

It was clear that this village, rather than Gotland, or any port in the east, was the crew's true home.

Two richly dressed women rushed towards the ship, fussing over Tostig mercilessly as he jumped down on to the wooden jetty.

Tostig quickly confirmed who they were. 'My daughters, Lada and Marzanna,' he said and they gave her a warm nod of greeting before berating their father in a rush of prodding hands and scrutinising eyes.

Valda laughed at Tostig's dark scowls as he was pushed around by his two daughters, who admonished him in a language she couldn't understand, while he grumbled back an exasperated response in the same tongue. Despite his ill humour, Tostig eventually hugged each woman in a fiercely tight embrace, before walking with them back up towards the fort, his arms draped around each one's shoulders.

Halfdan's shadow fell beside her. She turned to him with a teasing smile and a hushed voice. 'Now I understand why he longs for death.'

He threw back his head and laughed. When he laughed like that it rose from deep within and burst out with bellowing glee. It was both masculine and boyish, a pleasure to her senses.

She would miss it.

They passed workshops, tanners and family homes along the way. It reminded her of Jorvik, but on a smaller and more manageable scale. Halfdan nodded in approval at a craftsman who held up an elaborate beaded necklace with a proud smile as they passed. The people seemed happy and well fed, which was an improvement on some of the places she'd lived. It made for a cheerful and bustling home.

The fort was large and securely defended—her warrior's eye couldn't help but notice the well-armed men on its walls and the quality of steel they carried. The longhouse in its centre was large and sturdy. There were also a couple of barns, a smithy, a well and a stable all within the walls of the fort, suggesting a thriving community with plenty of food, and substantial protection. They entered the Hall, and Valda gasped at the fine tapestries, and weapons displayed on its walls. A central fire bathed the timber in a welcoming glow. People rushed around them with merry smiles as they prepared a homecoming feast.

Halfdan was more than a jarl's son. He was a ruler in his own right.

'It's a fine home, you should be very proud,' Valda said, as she stared in awe around her.

'I am,' he said. 'It could be your home, too, if you'd like?'

Chapter Thirteen

Tostig's daughters, Lada and Marzanna, were in charge of the feast, directing the serfs with dazzlingly swift competence. Huge quantities of rye bread, stews and fruits were consumed, as well as goat and mutton joints, roasted over the fire until tender and succulent. Large casks of a beverage called *kvass* were poured out into bone cups. Everyone was cheerful and lively, eager to celebrate Halfdan's return and the prospective trip onwards to Miklagard.

After eating their fill, she and Halfdan moved to a small table away from the boisterous crowd. They sat opposite each other in high backed chairs and played a game of Tafl together.

It was a beautiful set, the pieces made from a dark blue glass and etched with a white swirling pattern. The board was a beautifully polished piece of oak, gleaming in the firelight. In their first match, Valda had captured the king in a handful of moves, winning with ease. It was a warrior's game after all, and she'd played it many times over the years.

However, Halfdan seemed determined to win the

next match, and was taking a long time to decide his next move.

She sipped from her cup of kvass while she waited. The drink reminded her of mead with its sweet, light taste. However, there was a distinctive tang of some fruit or herb that she didn't recognise, setting it apart from anything else she'd tasted before. Not in an unpleasant way, it was still delicious and refreshing.

A bit like Halfdan's Hall in many ways. Familiar comforts of home mixed with the flavours of the east.

Here, the food tasted warmer and richer. The tapestries were familiar in style, but decorated with far more silk than anyone would dare use back home. The people, too, were different, slightly darker in colouring than the Norse and believing in a mixture of pagan and Christian religions, judging by the crosses and charms displayed around their necks, their lives built around the animals they bred and herded across their wide, endless plains.

They had a different language, music and culture to the warriors that ruled the fort, yet those differences didn't bother them and they seemed happy and at peace with Halfdan's men. After all, these men weren't oppressors, they were fathers, husbands and uncles. Family.

Could she live here permanently? As Halfdan had asked?

It would potentially mean accepting a married man as her mate, something they both knew she would never do. No, this could never be her home, as pleasant as it was. Valda didn't feel at home anywhere, never had. Strange, considering how much she longed for one. A place of security.

When she'd not answered him, he'd suggested she

could bring her family here. But this wasn't the land and farm her mother had dreamed of. This was a trading post.

She'd answered him honestly. *'My family wouldn't be happy here.'* They wouldn't want this for her, to watch her waiting on the whims of a married man. It lacked honour and pride. Two things she needed in life, as much as food or water.

It didn't feel right, but neither did leaving Halfdan.

She sighed, confused by her conflicting thoughts.

Halfdan wanted her to take a risk on him, but how could she trust her judgement—when she'd *repeatedly* failed so thoroughly in the past?

Finally, Halfdan moved his piece. She could see his strategy, and she immediately moved to deflect it. At least she knew what to do when it came to war.

He frowned at the board and she smiled.

'You're too good at this,' he grumbled, scratching his chin thoughtfully. Hesitantly he touched a piece with his fingertips, but then, thinking better of it, removed his hand with a huff.

'So are you...' she shrugged '...when you finally make a decision.'

He gave a dry, unamused laugh and she eased back into the cushions of her chair with a sigh of contentment. It was fun playing Halfdan—despite his lack of wins, she could tell he was an excellent player. She suspected she'd struggle against him in the future—once he'd learned her habits.

Biting his lip, he made the fatal mistake she'd been expecting all along. Her eyes flew to his mouth. She tried to ignore the flutter of excitement the sensual gesture caused her and concentrated her attention back to the board. A flurry of moves quickly followed as they battled for dominance, but in the end his king fell.

He cursed, but it was in a good-humoured way, not bitter or petulant.

'Would you like some advice?' she asked lightly.

He began to reset the board. 'Please! I have never lost so badly before—you are a master of this game.' He wagged an indignant finger at her. 'I must learn your clever tricks.'

She inclined her head with a modest shrug, before answering him. 'Your problem is that you are unwilling to make any sacrifices. You are so busy trying to defend everything that you leave yourself with no option to escape or attack.'

He gave her a devastatingly bright and teasing smile. 'But I don't want to lose a single piece... I want to keep them all.'

A cold, desolate, gloom swept through her and she had the feeling they were no longer talking about the game. 'You can't have everything, Halfdan.'

His smile dropped. 'Why not?'

'The object of the game is to save the king. Nothing more.'

He shrugged, then moved a piece with a resolute clink of glass on wood. 'Let's keep playing. I'll find a way.' Determination filled his handsome face. So hopeful and unwavering, his optimism was usually infectious, but at this moment, it only made her sad.

It must have destroyed him when she'd left without saying a word, believing her unwilling to make any sacrifices of her own, and now it was too late.

'No,' she replied softly. 'No more games tonight. What

did you mean earlier, about your brother? Is his freedom dependent on your marriage?'

As he looked up from the Tafl board, his eyes locked with hers. He must have seen the torment behind her gaze because he pushed the board aside and reached for her hand. 'Come, let us go to our chamber. There's a lot I have to explain.'

Halfdan's bedchamber was separated from the main hall by a wooden partition covered in tapestries. A large bed filled the space, a few chests, and a lit brazier gave enough light to see by. It was simple and comfortable, but lacked any personality, unlike his tent on his ship, which reflected him so perfectly, with its navigation tools and engraved bed.

'Is this where you propose to keep me then? If I did stay,' she asked, her heart heavy as she looked around the chamber.

'You don't like it?'

She sighed. 'I prefer the ship…' Quietly she added, 'I prefer being with you.'

Smiling broadly, he said, 'Then you will always be with me. If that's what you wish.'

She tried to smile, but found she couldn't. She needed to know. 'Will you still be married? When you return to your father.'

His smile dropped. 'I don't know.'

She nodded and sat on the bed, looking down at her boots. He hadn't decided, then, if she was worth it…

'It is not just my word. I have Erik's future to consider.'

Kicking off her boots, she made herself more comfortable, looking up at Halfdan as he paced the room.

'Do you not have enough silver to pay for his freedom? Is that why you agreed to this marriage?'

'I have enough,' Halfdan said quietly and it was a blow to her pride. *If he had enough, why would he still agree to it?* He stopped pacing and stripped off his extravagant silk tunic, tossing it into a basket by the door. Then he kicked off his boots and joined her on the bed, wearing just his braes and undertunic.

Focusing on his face, she tried to ignore the enticing flex of his muscles beneath the thin linen, or the way her insides turned to warm honey at the sight. 'But?' she asked. There was something else holding him back. He'd hinted as much earlier.

He took her hands in his, as if pleading with her to understand. 'My brother's freedom is assured. I am wealthy, but it will cost nearly all of the silver I have saved over the years to pay my father for Erik. But it will be worth it. Soon, he will have no hold on either of us.' He paused. 'I'm not sure how to explain… You see, we never spoke of it in the past. You didn't know he was a slave, only that he was an outcast… What had you heard?'

Valda frowned as she tried to remember the rumours that had been muttered all those years ago. 'Only…that he was an outcast, that your father was displeased with him and had therefore not acknowledged him. That's why he didn't eat or sleep in the Hall and why no one spoke with him. Although my family thought that nonsense, as you know…' She thought of Brynhild, who'd been determined to speak with him, and how she'd come back pale and quiet. They'd all avoided him after that. 'There was talk he wasn't even your father's child.'

'He is,' Halfdan replied firmly. 'His mother, Anahita, was still almost a child herself when she was captured by

Ulf. He enslaved her after he raided her father's lands, apparently a revenge attack for some *slight...*' He said the last word bitterly. They both knew Ulf took offence easily and sometimes without reason. 'Erik is older than me, by two years. If Ulf had acknowledged him, then he would have been the rightful heir, not I.'

'That's not your fault.'

'I know...but Ulf used it constantly against us. Forcing us to compete against each other in all kinds of challenges. Running, swimming, rowing, climbing, and of course, fighting. I...' He stopped, guilt washing across his face. 'After my mother died, I tried to win my father's approval. I tried hard to beat Erik, not realising that most of the time he was letting me win.'

'You were children. We did the same—it's how you learn to fight, sparring against a partner, being competitive,' she said, trying to reassure him.

Halfdan looked at her with raw pain in his eyes. 'Did you carry on? After your opponent was down? Did you keep striking them because your parent told you to do so? Until they bled? Until they passed out?'

Horror and shock rushed through her and she shook her head.

'My father encouraged it. But Erik always refused to hurt me badly. Only enough to prove that he was trying, because if he didn't, he'd be punished anyway—for not trying hard enough. My father asked me to pick an ultimate challenge. I was an excellent swimmer and decided that would be the easiest way for me to win—because Erik is the better swordsman.

'But my father thought that too easy, so he decided we should swim across one of the lakes, not in summer as I presumed, but the next day. It was winter and they had to break the ice with axes to clear a path for us. I was not prepared. I struggled and lost my strength quickly in the cold—too used to the comforts of a warm hall. Erik saw me failing and he could have let me die. But he didn't, he swam to me and pulled me back to shore. Afterwards, I asked him why he saved me and he said he "didn't know", but I knew. My brother is a good man—better than me. I will give him the birthright he is owed.'

There were tears in Halfdan's eyes after he stopped speaking and Valda wrapped her arms around him. 'I understand. Maybe we should end it now, before it becomes too hard to say goodbye...' she said.

'No. Stay with me, please, at least for this journey... I will try to find a way for us...'

His hands dropped to her crossed legs and stroked up her thighs. Then he leaned forward, pressing a tender kiss against the side of her neck in the place he knew she loved. A silent question.

But could she leave her mother and sisters behind? Again?

To be with a man that could never truly be hers? Not completely, at least. Not as she wanted him to be... Because her feelings for Halfdan were as strong as they ever were.

But did that mean she should give up on her principles?

She wanted a home, a family. The security and consistency she'd never had as a child. Could she have that here? In this distant land. It would be a pampered life, that much was certain, but did she want it?

No. She didn't. But she did want him.

'Halfdan,' she murmured in both denial and affection.

He slipped his hands beneath her tunic, then smoothly lifted it up and over her head.

Sensing her doubt, he pushed forward and she laid down on the bed, his big body arching over hers. Smoothing his palm from her waist to her breast, he cupped the curve of her flesh with a possessive hand. His golden head lowered to press his lips against the swell of her chest, just visible above the band of linen that secured her breasts.

Glittering like jewels his eyes locked with hers above the band and then his fingers curved into the linen, sliding between her skin and the cloth. With a hard tug he pulled it down and under the breast, immediately capturing her nipple in his hot mouth as soon as it was free. She let out a low whimper as searing heat flooded her veins and he sucked gently on the tight bud.

'I can make you happy,' he whispered, his lips brushing against her wet skin, causing her to gasp.

She shook her head in denial, even as her back arched to meet his tongue.

Taking his dagger from his belt, he sliced through the linen, using the blade carefully so as not to cut her. She bit her lip, her body already hot and needy for him. Tossing aside his knife and belt, he pulled off his under-tunic and arched over her once more, this time capturing her mouth in a kiss, his tongue urgent and demanding.

In reverence her hands caressed his back and shoulders, pulling him closer.

His whole body appeared focused on one thing and one thing alone, her pleasure. 'Give me the chance to prove it to you. That's all I ask.'

The moment changed from sweet to erotic in a hand-

ful of breaths and their eyes locked with insatiable desire
as they both knew what would surely follow.

Gasping for air against his lips, she began to tug at the
knot around his waist, defiantly refusing to answer him.
With a savage curse he turned her on to her front and
she was more than happy to be beneath him in this way
and wouldn't have fought it for all the silver in the world.

She raised herself up on to her elbows and knees to
look back at him over her shoulder. Her hair fell out of
her braid in rippling waves of flame—he must have loos-
ened the leather tie—and she had to toss it a little to see
him better. He watched the movement with thirsty eyes
and she smiled in triumph.

'I swear I can make you happy!' he vowed, leaning
forward, his breathing laboured against her back. 'You
will have everything you could ever want. You'll see...'
He trailed kisses down her shoulder, their naked skin
pressed close.

Wantonly she raised her hips, pressing her backside
firmly into his erection, murmuring with a husky tease,
'You can try...'

He hissed, one hand plunging down the front of her
braes to cup the mound of her sex. 'You want me...say
it!' She was wet and slippery in his palm and his finger
began to circle her sensitive bud with ease.

She moaned, but refused to answer him, enjoying the
teasing battle of wills far more than she'd like to admit.
Both of them guaranteed to win. She rubbed her bottom
against his hard member, wishing there was no cloth between them.

Gathering her close, he held her tightly pinned beneath him, her aching sex in one hand as he pleasured
her, while the other held her hip tightly as he ground his

hips helplessly against her backside. Spiralling sensation began to build within her and her breathing became more urgent and ragged.

'Please…' she gasped, her need to have him inside her so desperate that she tried to pull her own braes down to offer herself to him. 'Please.'

The sweep of his fingers became faster and faster until she was thrusting herself against him with pitiful whimpers. 'Yes…yes… I want you!' she finally cried.

A triumphant grunt followed by the tugging down of his own braes was the only notice she had before his hard length impaled her with glorious heat. She shattered instantly and it took only a few thrusts before he joined her, their panting cries filling the room and muffled only slightly by the sounds of feasting and music from beyond the partition.

With a blissful sigh she collapsed forward, exhausted. Nothing equalled the pleasure she felt in Halfdan's arms. She'd had no lover before or after him, and she knew he'd spoiled her for anyone else. His needs and desires matched her own—he understood what she wanted and when.

Kicking off the last of their clothes, they curled up under the covers together, the sweat drying from their sated skin.

Maybe she should focus on enjoying these last few weeks together rather than worrying about the heartache to come. The pain was inevitable—her heart had already thrown itself into the fight without her even realising it. But at least she could be happy for a while.

Then, when she went back to her family, she'd be left with some memories to treasure. Wasn't that the worst thing about their love before? How short that summer had been. Now, she had a chance to savour the time she had with Halfdan.

Yes, that was what she would do—enjoy the short time they had left together...before this exciting life ended and her new one began.

As she fell into a deep sleep, she was vaguely aware that he might have spilt some of his seed inside her by mistake.

Only a small amount, though, surely nothing to worry about.

Chapter Fourteen

The next morning, they rose early and had a tub brought to their chamber, where they bathed quickly before dressing for the day.

Valda enjoyed her favourite pastime—watching Halfdan—while she combed out her wet hair and began to braid it. She was already dressed, but he was not, and as he moved around the room she couldn't help but admire him.

'I have something for you,' he said, still distractingly naked, as he opened a chest by the bed. He removed a large parcel wrapped in cloth and placed it on the pallet beside her.

'For me?' She frowned. 'I don't need anything.'

'You might need this.' When she didn't reach for the parcel, he added, 'It's armour.' He laughed with the eager way she jumped for it.

Valda tore open the cloth to reveal a helmet and a chainmail shirt. The helmet was smooth and solid, with curved protection around the eyes and a plate over the nose. The kind she'd worn in battle, before she'd had to sell everything apart from her sword and shield. Her hand glided over the intricate iron rivets and rings in awe. 'It's magnificent. But I can't accept… It's…too much.'

'Why would you let perfectly good iron gather dust in a chest? That is no place for it; it needs to be worn and used. Otherwise, it is an insult to the smithy who made it.' After his speech, he smiled with self-satisfaction and Valda scowled at him. She couldn't argue with that logic.

'Why don't you wear it, then?'

'It does not fit me. My mother had it made for me when I was still a child, when she thought I would follow her family in likeness. Unfortunately, I grew bigger than she imagined.' With a grin he puffed up his chest and flexed his bicep for effect. Valda laughed at his nonsense and he grinned. 'My armour is always aboard my ship, although there's usually no need to wear it. Please take it, Valda, my mother would be glad to know it protected the woman I…' he paused '…I care for.'

The significance of the gift burned brightly in her chest and she blinked, tenderness and affection threatening to overwhelm her. She swallowed it down and looked up into his handsome face. She sensed a deep vulnerability below the surface when he'd spoken of his mother. One he refused to think about, let alone talk about, but who was she to judge when it came to a reluctance in discussing feelings?

However, it was disturbing that his mother had equipped him for battle before he'd even been broad enough to wear it. Not a sword either, but armour. She'd wanted to protect him. With a man like Ulf as her husband, maybe she known better than anyone what her son might need.

'Thank you,' she finally said and he gave a pleased

nod, walking away as naked as the day he was born and just as unbothered.

He opened another chest by the wall, ignoring the fine clothes he'd thrown in a basket the night before. To Valda's surprise the bundle of clothing he pulled out was nothing like the grand clothing he usually wore. They were well made and practical, but in a sturdy and enduring way—without any scrap of wealth adorning them.

Next, he took off his jewellery, ring by ring, even the gold at his neck, and placed it all in the chest before closing the lid and locking it. Everything was put away except for his mother's bronze arm ring.

Valda was already dressed and braiding her hair, but she paused as she watched him, confused by his actions.

Amused, he answered her silent question. 'Why don't I wear my grand clothes to Miklagard?'

'Is it because you don't wish to draw attention to your wealth in an unfamiliar territory? That would make sense.'

'It would. But that's not the reason.'

She rolled her eyes as she waited for him to explain further and when he didn't her patience snapped. 'Well?'

He ignored her glare and began to dress. 'I wear the silks for my customers, not for myself. I am a merchant and must show them what they are buying. I don't tend to wear them when we sail. I'm sure you've noticed I tend to only wear an undertunic at sea…'

The smug smile on his lips suggested he'd seen her admiring stares and she rolled her eyes.

As they left the Hall, she couldn't help but wonder: *was anything real with Halfdan?* Or was it all a game, a strategy? A way for him to always get his way.

If she did agree to stay with him, would he put her

away in a locked box until he had need of her, or toss her aside when he was done? She still didn't trust him, she was ashamed to admit. But then when had she trusted anyone except her family? Only Jorund…and that had been a disaster.

She'd agreed that Halfdan could try to tempt her to stay while they enjoyed their last few weeks together. But she doubted he would succeed in changing her mind. She wasn't a fine silk to show off to a jarl and neither would she accept a life in a locked box.

After breaking their fast, they walked out into the fresh morning light and headed towards the jetty. The settlement was already buzzing with activity like a large beehive, everyone busy with their work.

'We have to leave the longship here,' Halfdan said as they clattered down the wooden walkways towards the ship.

Valda looked up at him in surprise. 'I don't understand. Are there not more rivers…? And I thought there was another sea to cross?'

'There are. That's why we're changing to those.'

He pointed towards three shallow-hulled boats. They swayed beside the beautifully carved dragon ship, looking like poor cousins in comparison.

Valda was a little disheartened to see no tent on any of them. 'But…why?'

Halfdan laughed loudly at the look on her face. 'Will you miss *our* bed?' he teased.

She shrugged, a little embarrassed. Yes, she would miss *their* bed.

He sighed. 'As will I, but the next part of the journey is the most gruelling and my ship is far too big, and there are places not suitable for it…even for portage. Too noticeable.'

That caught her interest. 'Dangerous?'

He nodded. 'Yes, nomads wander the grasslands and they are our biggest threat. They trade in horses and meat from their herds, but will happily raid travellers for their wealth. You may need your sword at some point. I hope not, but keep your weapons and armour close just in case.' She noticed then that he wore several daggers in addition to his Saracen blade.

She bristled, her hand resting on the hilt of her sword. 'I am not afraid.'

'I know you're not.' He chuckled, the sound warming her from the tips of her toes to the top of her head. 'Still… I avoid strife when I can. Which is why we have three unassuming boats for our cargo and our crew will be split between the three. It helps, especially when we reach the difficult passes and have to carry the boats up hill on the return.'

The crew were already loading the cargo from the ship into the three boats and they began to help, though it didn't take long, most of it consisting of pelts and ivory from the north as the luxury goods had been sold or traded along the way.

Once the cargo was aboard, she realised how little room was left for the twenty men in each boat. They would be wedged together tightly, only enough room to sit at the oars, or rest their backs against the sides of the ship. No lavish tent. Only a few small, oiled cloths to use as shelter on the riverbanks, as well as a few camping supplies. Miserable conditions, and on top of that they would need to be on their guard against nomadic raiders.

'Why are you smiling?' asked Halfdan curiously, as he hopped on to the deck beside her.

She looked up at him and grinned. 'This is going to be fun.'

He laughed and passed her an oar. 'You've spent too much time with Tostig.'

'How long until we reach Miklagard?' Valda asked Halfdan as they used their oars to navigate a particularly shallow stretch of the river, probing with the wood to check the depth, to ensure they didn't get stuck on the rocky riverbed.

It wasn't fun any more.

She didn't want to seem ungrateful, but her clothes reeked and were covered in dust. She'd slept on rough ground for weeks, although she'd stopped counting days and couldn't be sure how exactly long they'd been travelling any more. The endless, sun-drenched days all seemed to bleed into one another and only seemed to get hotter and longer as they sailed the never-ending Dnieper River.

None of that she minded. But there was no privacy and Halfdan had not made love to her since they'd left his fort. Understandable, considering they slept side by side with another twenty men on the boat, or were huddled around a campfire on the riverbanks, their eyes always searching the horizon for potential threats.

'Soon.' Halfdan smiled as he stood beside her at the prow of the boat. He dipped the oar into the water, then pushed against the riverbed to manoeuvre their boat around some rocks. She joined the other men on her side of the ship to balance the movement, pressing their oars into the riverbank to ensure they didn't stray too close to the shallows.

Their boat was at the head of their party, Tostig, in charge of the boat immediately behind and Aarne commanding the remaining one.

'Will we need to carry the boats at some point?' she asked, frowning at the rocky river up ahead. As they'd moved further south, they'd experienced every type of land Valda could have imagined, passing through swamps, towering hills, marshlands and expansive plains. Now, the river was narrowing and rushing over rocks with increasing ferocity and it made her nervous.

Halfdan shook his head with a knowing smile and that only worried her further.

'Halfdan?' she said sharply.

He laughed. 'You might want to prepare yourself.'

'I *would* prepare myself—if I knew what was coming!' she growled, finding Halfdan's humour less and less tolerable with every laboured breath. Her hair was escaping her braid and her muscles ached from constantly pushing the boat in the right direction.

'There is some rough water coming up,' Halfdan explained. 'That's why we couldn't bring my ship. This area is too rocky to transport boats over land, especially on the way back, while small ships can mostly make it through.'

'*Mostly?*' Valda glared at him as she straightened up, finally able to take a moment to gather her breath as the river seemed to idle along on a wider section. 'Was this why you insisted I join you on your boat?'

'I just prefer your company!' shouted Halfdan with a smile and she realised then that the sound of the river was getting louder. She cocked her head and in the distance she could hear a powerful din of crashing water. Her mouth became dry and she gulped down a nervous knot in the back of her throat, the significance of the sound slowly dawning on her.

Rapids!

She'd rather face an army.

The boat rounded the sweeping bend in the river and she saw it. The water narrowed, surrounded by large stone banks on either side, and in the middle stood an island of huge grey rocks. The water crashed against them and then rushed down either side into destinations she couldn't yet see.

She glanced behind her and realised Tostig's boat and the one behind were slowing, creating a distance between them, no doubt allowing each boat time to navigate the rapids before the next one attempted it.

'This way!' shouted Halfdan, giving the boat a mighty push with his pole towards the left-hand side. Valda quickly adjusted her feet to feel more secure, then used her oar with the others to help steady their course.

'Get low!' shouted Halfdan and the crew of the boat pulled in their oars and crouched down in what little space was available in the hull of the little boat. Valda did the same, gripping the side with white knuckles.

The only person who remained standing was Halfdan. When it looked as if their boat were about to crash into the island of rocks, he used his pole to push their vessel out of the way. In a rush they followed the sweeping water down into the rapids. Only then did Halfdan drop to sit beside her, excitement lighting up the blue of his eyes.

'Doesn't this make you glad to be alive?' he shouted

over the roaring of the water, as their boat pitched forwards.

Cold foam splashed Valda in the face and she wiped
it away. 'Alive? I just hope we stay that way!' she replied
sourly and Halfdan laughed.

A moment later he said, 'Now for the big one!'

Valda sucked in a deep lungful of air as her eyes
searched the river up ahead. But she couldn't see anything of concern.

The deafening fury of water crashing against rocks
began to approach, yet the river calmed as if holding its
breath. If anything, the stillness of the water only terrified her more.

A twist in the river became visible, followed by a
drop. A waterfall. An incredibly high one considering
the size of the boat.

However, the height of the drop wasn't the most terrifying aspect of it. Below, shards of rock littered the
river's path, like the jaws of a terrible monster closing
tight, and the water crashed from side to side in the narrow snaking path, like ale sloshed inside a tiny cup. There
were more, smaller waterfalls after, as well as whirlpools
of swirling, boiling foam, eventually spitting out again
into a wider, more meandering river.

Her heart hammered in her chest and she looked to
Halfdan, hoping his expression might give her some answer to what she might expect.

To her surprise he was watching her. 'It will be fine,'
he said gently.

She nodded, but she didn't believe him.

*Was this to be her fate? To die in strange waters,
in a strange land. What would become of her sisters
and mother? Would they be forced to marry? How long*

would her sisters wait before they raised a rune stone in her memory?

So many questions raced through her mind and she reached for the hilt of her sword.

A firm hand covered hers and brought it up to the side of the boat. She gripped the wood, his hand on top of hers, golden against her bone-white skin. Sky-blue eyes stared with concern into her own and she almost drowned in the purity of their colour.

'Trust me,' he said. 'I give you my word, everything will be fine.' Then, louder, he shouted to the other men behind them, 'Hold!'

Valda's grip tightened painfully, as the boat dropped over the edge and her stomach with it. She closed her eyes as the frigid air pulled at her, begging her to let go against the unnatural pull. Her mouth clamped tight against the urge to scream.

The boat hit the water below with a jarring thud, water erupting around them in a mighty wave. She gasped, grateful for the icy water that soaked her skin. Elated to find herself alive and still within the boat, unharmed. But most of all, she was glad that Halfdan's hand had not left hers.

'See,' he said, with an easy smile made even more handsome by her appreciation to still be among the living.

'Yes.' She laughed and could tell by the cheers behind her that everyone else on the boat felt the same way.

His eyes brightened and then his lips crushed against hers. The kiss was powerful with its intensity, but as quick as lightning he broke away. 'For luck!' He grinned and she laughed, because it felt right.

She wouldn't have wanted to be on this voyage with anyone other than Halfdan.

They didn't have long to savour it, however, as the river was already gliding into the rapids below. Halfdan gave her hand a gentle squeeze before releasing it.

'Oars!' he shouted and everyone jumped to their feet, poles at the ready for the challenge ahead.

They worked together tirelessly, every man following Halfdan's shouted orders with careful precision, using their oars to push away from the rocks or beat away from whirlpools.

At least Valda no longer had time to be afraid. She could cope with her fate being dictated to by her own actions. But allowing herself to fall like that had been terrifying and she was glad not to suffer it again.

As the river calmed and widened, they pulled up their boat under a shade of trees and waited for the others. When each boat appeared, the crews cheered with exultant relief.

All her friends were safe.

Valda had never felt happier.

She'd lived among all of these men for so long she knew each of them well. Knew their loves and hates, their petty grievances and their dreams for the future. She loved each of them like brothers and would be sorry to part with them once this journey was over.

Soon they were on their way once more, not wanting to linger too long in the land of the Pechenegs tribe, notorious nomads. They sailed tightly together following the widening river towards the Black Sea and the glittering treasure of Miklagard just beyond the horizon.

Chapter Fifteen

After the rapids, the journey became almost leisurely, the boats flowing downstream with the pace of the current. As they approached the mouth of the river, they reached an island—a well-used, final stopping point for travellers before sailing out into the Black Sea.

They pulled the boats on to the shore and made camp for the night. The island had many birds and a small, friendly settlement, and it wasn't long until they had fresh supplies and several birds roasting on spits over their campfires.

It was good to eat well again. Their supplies had been dwindling daily and, although there was plenty of fish to catch, Valda was getting tired of stale biscuits and fish stew for every meal.

They didn't need much for the journey on to Mikla-gard, but Halfdan had arranged a large haul of supplies to be collected on their way back upriver. After Valda finished eating her fill, she sat beside Halfdan and watched the sun sink into the water.

The journey here depended heavily on connections and local knowledge, something Halfdan seemed to excel at, treating everyone he met with respect and good humour, and a scattering of silver in his wake.

So different from how his father ruled with fear and violence.

His father. Her mother and sisters. They all felt so far away. As if she had travelled through Yggdrasil, the world tree, and left the land of mortal men behind, so distant felt that life and those people. Had she unknowingly travelled through the nine realms and was now moments away from entering the land of the gods?

She sighed as the sun burned the sky with a hundred colours of fire.

Could she go back to her old life?

Live without him?

Her love and trust in Halfdan were building day by day, while the life waiting for her back home seemed less and less real. A distant land like Miklagard had always seemed in her mind, except, less inviting...

She didn't want to become a farmer.

Admitting it, even to herself, felt like a crime against her mother and sisters.

Neither did she want Halfdan to marry another.

But what choice did she have? And that's what worried her the most—the lack of choice. She was a warrior. A shieldmaiden who could hold her honour and courage like a sword and shield in battle, even when Loki's luck was not on her side. However, that was when she was fighting, when her destiny was dependent on the skill of her blade and the swiftness of her wits, not on her weak heart.

A life with Halfdan, even if he could somehow change his oath to his father, was a life dependent on another soul. Trusting in that person completely...and that, she was slowly realising, was the main thing that frightened her. Loving Halfdan felt like dropping from that waterfall. Holding on to the side of a flimsy boat, and the hand of your lover, hoping they'll save you.

Grim thoughts plagued her despite the beauty of the sunset and she looked around her at the other men for a distraction. Odger and Borin were arguing over who'd brought down the most birds, while Arne snored loudly in front of the fire.

Living with them had been an unexpected joy on her trip. She'd never realised how much she'd missed the camaraderie of Jorund's army until now.

'Where are they going?' she asked Halfdan, as she noticed another three members of their crew walking out into the woods. Several others had gone and returned shortly afterwards. At first, she'd thought they were relieving themselves, but it seemed like all of the crew were taking it in turns to go out into the woods.

'There's an old oak tree in the wood. They're making offerings,' replied Halfdan, tossing a bone into the fire, and sitting back on his elbows with a contented sigh.

The fright of the waterfall had affected her far more than she'd realised, because she found herself saying, 'I should make an offering.'

She had a lot to be thankful to the gods for. Her safe passage, the positive turn in her family's fortune, and… Halfdan. She was still unsure of how long it would last, but she was grateful for the truth, and the joy.

There was only one thing she could give.

Her hand dropped to the hilt of her sword.

It was time.

She needed to let go of the bitterness and pain of the past. Allow her fate to fall as the gods wished. Let go of

Jorund and all the bitter disappointment he represented. It would make a worthy gift, with its elaborate decorations. And it was Frankish steel—highly prized for its quality.

Halfdan rose, brushing the sand and dirt from his clothes with heavy slaps before offering her his hand. 'Come, I'll grab a bow and take you to it. We'll bring down another bird and bury some silver with it to appease the gods.'

She laid her hand in his and he pulled her to her feet. How things had changed between them. Once she'd have ignored his hand, now she took it. Not because she needed his help, but because it felt good to have someone offer it.

'No. I'll make the sacrifice. I want to give it to Aegir and Rán—I owe the gods of the sea a gift,' she said, unsheathing her sword and holding it up to the red and gold fading light. Deliberately ignoring Halfdan's curious stare, she admired it.

'Are you sure?' he asked, obviously surprised by her choice.

She shrugged. 'We have plenty of weapons with us.'

'But they are not as fine as yours… Offer one of those instead.'

'But the gods will know I have tricked them,' she answered with a teasing smile. 'No…better to offer them something with meaning and value. They will be pleased with it, I think.'

He nodded, and they walked away from their camp along the winding shingle of the riverbank. They reached a small inlet, out of sight from either the settlement or the crew and facing south-East.

She tossed the weapon lightly from hand to hand, then held it up, revering the weight and balance of it. 'It was a gift from Jorund. To thank me for my service as his second-in-command.'

Halfdan stared at the weapon as she held it up to the sunset, fire flashed along its deadly blade. 'It's beautiful,' he said.

'But those days are behind me now.' She returned it to its scabbard with a sharp thrust. 'No matter what happens…that life is behind me. Better I ensure our safe and profitable return with it… I must look to the future. I can no longer live in the past.'

She handed Halfdan the sword as she stripped off her clothes and untied her braid. When she was done, he laid it down into her open palms, his eyes bright with understanding. She strode forward into the river, her spine straight as the water enveloped her like a lover's embrace.

The cold water shocked her skin and the pebbles bit into the soles of her feet. But she gritted her teeth and moved forward without hesitation. The dying sun was reflected in the water around her and the rocks petered out into soft and forgiving sand. She raised the sword above her head and said a prayer to Aegir and his wild mistress Rán.

Sucking in a deep breath, she dropped beneath the surface, placing the sword on the riverbed below and covering it with a wide sweep of sand, her hair swirling around her like scarlet seaweed.

When she broke the surface, she gasped in the cool air as if it were a healing balm. Then she turned and walked away. Feeling lighter in spirit as she met Halfdan by the water's edge, she smiled.

She didn't know what the future held, but she hoped

her past was finally buried, so that she could enjoy the time they had left without fear.

Valda emerged from the water and walked back towards him. A true goddess of the sea, her flaming hair mirroring the blazing sunset that rippled through the river as it flowed out to sea. Her body, sleek and powerful, but also femininely soft and gloriously curved. His throat tightened painfully at the sight.

'I have let go of my past,' she said happily, as she stood dripping with water and shivering.

Watching Valda make her offering had felt as if a fist had tightly gripped his heart. The sword was the last symbol of her old life and her old love. The fact that she was willing to give it away stole the air from his lungs.

There was hope for them—this was proof of it.

He reached for her, wrapping her in his embrace and kissing her hard with all of his heart. 'And what of your future?' he asked, breathless with need.

She bit her lip, uncertain. 'I am willing to see…'

Relief and joy flooded through him with equal measure. He unclasped his cloak and lay it on the ground. Silently, she followed and he shrugged out of his clothing, his eyes never leaving hers.

Then he covered her with the warmth of his body and she sighed with contentment, wrapping her arms around his neck and arching up to kiss his mouth. He stroked her body, his hands following her curves with reverent longing.

'Let's enjoy every last moment,' she whispered and he could barely see her face in the twilight. 'Together.'

Her confession pierced his heart, flooding bitter-sweet heat through his veins. Kissing her neck and then her breasts with increasing need, he whispered, 'Together.'

Chapter Sixteen

The sea was a beautiful turquoise—it reminded her of Halfdan's eyes—but rowing through it was a little tricky. The winds were low and the boats bobbed lightly on the surface of the Black Sea as they meandered through the waters with less speed than she was used to. Even so, they made decent time, crossing it within two days.

Her frustration was probably due to her eagerness to reach their destination. She was not disappointed when they came within sight of the Great City of Miklagard.

It was everything she'd hoped for.

The city was nestled on a peninsula stretching like clasped hands between the east and west. A focal point of all that was grand and mysterious from both kingdoms.

At the crest of the largest hill was the centre of the city. Upon it stood a huge marble-clad building that dominated the landscape. A curved dome for a roof, it shone in the hot sun like a golden shield. She had never seen anything like it and knew with certainty that nothing would rival it in her lifetime.

'It is their holy building,' whispered Halfdan in her ear. 'Built long ago and expanded many times. There—'

he pointed to a stone curved wall a short distance from the church '—is the Hippodrome. It is even older...truly ancient.'

She stared at the sights in front of her, unable to believe that such things could exist even now, let alone many years before. Yet, here was the proof!

'It's...beautiful. I always imagined...that Asgard might look something like this...' She noticed Halfdan was no longer staring at the impressive city, but at her, and she blushed, feeling ignorant for suggesting such a thing.

He smiled. 'So did I. But they are not gods who live here. Just ordinary men and women, same as us.'

They sailed past a large harbour set before the city and swung around to the north.

Halfdan caught the look of confusion on her face, and quickly explained. 'There is only one dock allowed to the Rus and Norse. After Oleg's—Igor's father's—last attack, there were strict rules put in place that we must all abide by. We can only reside in one area, just outside of the gates, called The Golden Horn.'

She eyed the substantial defences that hinted at the magnificent treasures protected within.

Not only was there a moat with its own smaller walls, but also two huge stone walls running parallel to each other, encircling the city. They were so thick and tall that they appeared impassable in their own right, but they also had guard towers and parapets. She could not imagine how many backs had been broken in the building of it. Too many to count.

'Oleg must have had a substantial number of men to dare attack this,' Valda said thoughtfully.

'Two thousand boats. Although, I, personally, was more interested in the trade agreements than the looting.'

'You were there?' she asked in astonishment. She'd never thought of Halfdan as a warrior until now.

'In a small capacity…' He shrugged. 'I only had a few ships to offer. We ransacked and looted the outer areas. At least, until the Emperor agreed to our terms. He saw reason and allowed us better trading rights. However, now, when we enter the city, we must not bear arms. They're nervous of us still.'

Valda frowned at that; she didn't like the idea of entering a strange city without a weapon to defend herself with.

'It's worth the benefits,' he reassured.

'I'm sure it is…especially if you helped write them,' she teased.

He gave a humble incline of his head. 'We are exempt from the local custom payments, receive free board and lodgings—as well as an allowance for other expenses—and, of course, some supplies for the return journey.'

Valda laughed. 'No wonder these trips are so profitable for you! I was beginning to wonder, considering how much you spend getting here.'

'I told you… I want it all. I'm never happy unless I get my way.'

His words sobered her a little, and she looked back at the towering city, wondering if she were another treasure he'd become obsessed with possessing.

After securing their cargo and lodgings the crew were eager to head out into the city. The day was still early and they'd spent too long cramped in a boat's hull.

They wanted to stretch their legs, explore the markets and enjoy the Byzantine baths.

First, they crossed the wooden bridge over the moat. Then they made their way through the outer gates, eventually arriving at the final entrance into the city. This gate was lavishly decorated with white marble. Golden sculptures sat above its arched doorway, while flanked on both sides were huge towers manned by guards.

It was an intimidating welcome.

Even before they reached the doorway, they were met by a team of guards. Valda smiled coldly at the nervous man who eyed her suspiciously as he approached. She opened her arms wide to show that she carried no weapons, but he reached for her anyway, presumably to pat her down, as he'd done to the other men. Halfdan's solid palm stopped the man in his tracks before he took another step.

The man spoke in the Byzantine tongue and Halfdan answered. She couldn't understand what was said, but Halfdan's tone was pleasant yet firm and the man backed away with a nod.

Halfdan seemed to speak their language smoothly, without a moment's hesitancy. She couldn't help but admire him for it. He was clearly born to travel.

They passed through the gates without further incident. They didn't carry much with them today. Halfdan had explained that he would meet with his usual buyers first, before the men were given leave to sell their own goods. As such, the packs they carried were samples to demonstrate the quality of Halfdan's cargo.

She tugged at her woollen tunic to allow the air to reach her skin. Halfdan had said to wear her poorest set of clothing on their trip into the city. She presumed he wanted to downplay their presence to discourage robbers.

Unfortunately, her most threadbare clothing was also her warmest woollens. Since they'd journeyed south, the sun had grown warmer and brighter in the sky, lightly browning her skin and scattering even more freckles across her arms and chest. No doubt across her face, too—although she had no polished plate to check.

Usually, she preferred balmy heat, disliking the cold and wet of Jorvik, for example, but today the thick fabric was too much and she was already sweating profusely.

She walked through the magnificent stone gates decorated with strange figures of another world and was immediately overwhelmed by the sights, sounds and smells within.

There was the usual stench of a city. The filth and sweat.

But coating it was a heavy cloud of exotic scent, almost making it palatable. Spice, incense and flowers filled the air and different languages buzzed and flew around the market like birds. Skins of all shades, from dark brown to pale ivory, walked the streets, the people clothed in everything from simple tunics—much like the one she wore—to elaborate, long silks that even a king in the west would struggle to afford. Here many wore them, the precious fabric an easy commodity to own.

The bazaar was filled with all manner of delights, including several food stalls that made her mouth water. Sweet, honeyed fruit, creamy nuts and spiced meat were offered as they passed and she tried to hide the rumble of her stomach.

'So, what do you think?' asked Halfdan, moving to her side.

'It's so strange, but also…familiar.'

He smiled at her words and she wondered if he thought

her a simpleton. She certainly felt as though she sounded like an idiot. 'All people like to trade. It's just the goods that change,' he said and her shoulders relaxed. Halfdan always put her at ease.

As they moved deeper into the city, the streets became choked with people, carts and all manner of goods. Valda wished many times that she could stop and look at the stalls, but Halfdan largely ignored the traders who called out to him.

Unable to help herself, she finally stopped at a stall that caught her wandering eye. A small, bear-like creature leapt from a trader's shoulder to the canopy of his stall and back again. The man beamed at her with a broad smile and broken teeth, offering her a small, corked vial and speaking in a language that had a soft melody to it. He seemed pleasant and well meaning, pleading for her to take his merchandise with a cheerful smile.

However, she was far more fascinated by the small animal that hopped around his stall.

'It's called a monkey,' explained Halfdan softly. 'This man sells Arabian perfume. Would you like to try some?'

'No...' She shook her head, but then felt a little self-conscious. 'Although it's been a while since I bathed.'

He laughed and shook his head at the trader, who promptly offered her something else. A string of colourful beads. 'We'll be visiting the bathhouse soon. We like to go at the start and end of our visit. It's become a tradition.'

Valda nodded, distracted. 'Maybe I should get Helga some beads...when I'm ready to sell my furs...'

The monkey jumped on to her shoulder and she gasped in surprise. It lifted a lock of her hair, fingered and sniffed it curiously, before leaping back to his master. It screamed at her angrily as if she offended him.

'I don't think he likes my hair.'

She laughed as Halfdan took her gently by the arm and guided her away, murmuring quietly in her ear, 'It's lucky you have nothing to rob as you are an easy target for thieves. Such animals, and even children, can be used as a distraction to lighten your purse. Did you learn nothing wintering in Jorvik?' he teased.

'Jorvik feels like a lifetime ago.'

The laughter died in her throat. *They were waiting for her.* Expecting her to return with enough silver for their farm. *Focus, Valda!*

She doubted her family's furs would sell for many dirhams, but she had to try to get as much as she could for them. Her share as part of the crew would be enough to pay for the farm, but they would need more for supplies and tools. Even with Brynhild's income she doubted her mother and sisters would earn much in her absence.

Turning to Halfdan she said, 'I would welcome your advice on where to trade my furs…when the times comes.'

Halfdan winced. 'About that…'

Valda's eyes snapped to his and narrowed. She was always so fiercely attractive when she was angry. Then again, she had looked just as beautiful laughing in wonder at a disease-riddled monkey, too.

'Your furs… I'm afraid they've gone missing from the boats…' It wasn't a lie. They had gone missing. It was because he'd left them at his trading post and supplemented them with better stock.

At Valda's horrified face he was quick to make

amends. 'It's my mistake. I should have checked the cargo more thoroughly. Don't worry, I've put aside an equal weight of my own furs for you. Your sisters will still be paid for them. And I can even sell them for you to the Emperor's court with my own. I'll get a good price for you and it will save you the effort of selling them yourself.'

Valda slowly looked away, a small twitch of amusement and more than a little exasperation teasing at the corners of her mouth. 'Hmmm, I think I will benefit more from the loss of my furs than you will.'

Halfdan forced a deep sigh of regret. 'As Tostig says, I am *"reckless and irresponsible"*. But I could not face your mother and sisters again without compensating them for my terrible mistake.'

Valda took his hand and squeezed it. 'You are a *good* man, Halfdan.'

He'd never felt prouder for doing so little. He'd never thought of himself in that way. Cunning, manipulative and adventurous, *yes*, but never *good*. The fact Valda believed it only wanted him to be even better…if that were possible.

They continued on through the bazaars and winding streets, Halfdan leading the way with Valda at his side, the men he had kept with him flanking either side of them like an arrowhead. Most of the houses in the city were small buildings built of timber and crowded together, sometimes with a communal oven at the end of the street. But in other areas the homes were further apart and palatial. Majestic buildings of stone decorated with elaborate sculptures and bright mosaics, some even had private courtyards and lush gardens, and behind the elegant high walls covered in vines they heard the sweet laughter of children playing.

Eventually, they entered the main square that lay between the ancient Hippodrome and the Hagia Sophia—the spectacular domed church that watched over the many hills of the city. Valda's steps slowed as she stared in wonder at the entrance to the Hippodrome and the huge monuments at the centre of its old chariot track.

She peered curiously through the arched columns and he didn't have the heart to pull her away.

He took Aarne aside, handing him some coins. 'Go to the bathhouse with the others. We'll see you back at the lodgings later.'

The men left, eager to relax and wash the dust from their bodies, and he turned back to Valda.

'They used to race chariots here. But now it's used for festivals and the Emperor's speeches. Would you like to go in?' he asked.

Bright hazel eyes filled with hope looked up at him. 'Can we?'

'Of course, we have plenty of time.' *At least, he hoped they did.* His heart ached; he had everything he wanted, but only for a short time. If he couldn't think of a way to change his oath with his father, their relationship was doomed to end here.

Their stay in the city would be short—much shorter than normal—and it had only been an excuse, anyway. A temptation for Valda and an opportunity for them both. But it would end soon. Word had been sent to his brother. They would meet again at his settlement in a few weeks' time, which meant they had to begin their return journey in only a few days. Especially if he was to ensure a swift return to Jorvik before the autumn.

'Come,' he said, taking her hand in his.

The Hippodrome was largely empty—a few stalls and some locals sitting on the old worn benches to eat fruit and talk with companions in the sunshine.

As if Valda had read his thoughts, she said, 'It's so quiet here, compared to the rest of the city…and big!'

'It looks as if there is nothing happening here today. I'll ask if there are any events taking place during our visit.'

'I don't mind if there's not,' Valda said cheerfully as she walked towards the line of gigantic monuments in the centre of the oval arena. The sand was a little bare in places, untidy weeds growing up through the earth. Its time of glory was also at an end.

She walked past men who openly stared at her presence as if she were one of the wild animals that used to be displayed here. Halfdan smiled at them and followed her, impressed and proud of her confidence. She was as unique as the stone obelisk she stood beneath. A shieldmaiden from the icy north. A beautiful woman with flaming red hair and the stance of a powerful warrior.

'They look like runes,' she said, as Halfdan came to stand beside her. 'But different… Is that a bird?' She pointed to a symbol above their heads.

'I think so.'

She smiled and then pointed at the square rock below. 'But this looks more like the Christian sculptures and it has their language on it.'

'Yes.' He pointed to the soaring needle above the base. 'That part is older. I've heard it was brought here from an old kingdom from further south. They worship cats and favour triangular buildings.' She raised an eyebrow of disbelief at that and he raised his hands with a laugh. 'It is what I have heard.'

They spent a couple of hours admiring the sculptures and monuments, pointing out the similarities and differences to things in the west. But mainly just enjoying each other's company. It felt right to explore these places with Valda, as if they were making up for the lost years, when they should have been exploring this city together.

Eventually the heat became too much and he had noticed Valda tug at her woollen tunic more than once. 'We should move on.'

'Are we going to the bathhouse now?' she asked hopefully, her face flushed, small curls of soft hair unravelling from her braid around her face.

'We need to meet with someone first, but it won't take long.'

'Who are we meeting? I thought you were trading with the palace tonight?'

'Yes, but we need to meet with a friend of mine first. A tailor from the imperial court. They'll fit us with silks for the feast.'

'Is that why I'm wearing this?' she said with a bad-tempered scowl. 'So you could force me to accept new clothing from you? There is no need for it, Halfdan, I don't have to go with you.'

He knew she would grumble about it, but he didn't want to leave her side, even if it was only for a moment. 'It makes sense to do this. The emperor only allows a certain amount of silk out of the city. Personal clothing does not count. All of us wear our worst clothes in and new out. I have an arrangement with the silk craftsmen of the city. As soon as they heard of our arrival, they will have delivered silk tunics to all the men at the bath-house. I prefer mine to be well fitted by my friend, as I wear mine to trade, which is why we must visit them personally.'

'But I can't pay for silk! Everything I earn must be in silver for my family,' Valda cried.

'Consider it a gift. Silk is one of the most luxurious goods in the west. And, later, your family can always sell it if they need the coin.'

'I can't accept your furs *and* your silk!'

'Then you will look very strange at the meeting.'

'Then I won't go!' she said, crossing her arms. 'You don't need me there, anyway.'

'But I do!' he said, not realising until this moment how true his statement was. He did need her, always had. Without her he'd always felt as if he were missing a part of his soul.

Startled by the realisation, he quickly smothered the thought, describing in detail how helpful her presence was to his business, rather than to his heart. 'As a Norse woman your presence would be an exciting spectacle for the Emperor. Very few of our women have journeyed here. Seeing you draped in one of our fur mantles might even drive up the price of our cargo... Maybe I should put you in the fox trim, add some amber beads, and feathers to your hair? A beautiful shieldmaiden wearing Byzantine silk and decorated with the trinkets of our homeland? Yes, that will drive up the price of our cargo very well.' She frowned in disbelief, until he added softly, 'Valda, you are considered *exotic* here.'

Her eyes blinked and then narrowed. She obviously wasn't as enthused about his scheme as he was. 'And you want to show me off? Like some prize!' she growled.

He sighed, reminding himself that nothing worthy of its salt was easily won. 'Don't help then. I just thought you wanted as much silver as possible for your family.'

It was a manipulative statement that was not lost on Valda, and she thumped his arm with her fist. He gladly took the bruise; it was deserved.

'Unfair!' she retorted. But her resolve to thwart him had buckled and she laughed.

Chapter Seventeen

They arrived at a magnificent stone building a short while later. To Valda, it looked more like a palace than a craftsman's home. Nothing like the little workshops they had in the west. This person's work must be highly valued.

The house was tall and narrow and had a private garden surrounding it.

Inside, they were taken towards the back, to a single-storey structure where large windows allowed in plenty of fresh air and light. Instead of a central firepit there was a marble fountain, the sweet melody of the water adding a calming serenity to the room. Golden light flooded in from an opening above and bathed the blue-tiled fountain below, causing it to shimmer prettily. The room was filled with mosaics, sculptures and lush potted plants, making the space almost cluttered with its huge swathe of decoration. Fine silk furnishings and heavy curtains covered the arched doorways into the other rooms of the house, allowing a cool breeze to flow through while maintaining the owner's privacy.

Four large day beds surrounded the pool and on two

of them lay an extravagantly dressed Byzantine couple. As Valda and Halfdan entered they both cried out in welcome and got quickly to their feet in a rustle of silk.

The woman spoke to Halfdan in the language Valda didn't understand, but it was obviously a friendly greeting. Then the man stepped forward and greeted him with warmth. They were quite old, with wide girths and plain faces. Unremarkable in all ways except for the richness of their clothes.

The matronly woman clasped Halfdan's hands tightly within her own, and he obligingly leaned down to kiss her cheek.

Valda rolled her eyes at the now-familiar reception Halfdan received wherever he went and was surprised to see the older woman beaming up at her with equal delight.

Halfdan translated for the woman as she began to talk to Valda. 'She wants to know who the angel is that I brought with me.'

Valda glared at him, wondering if he was elaborating on the woman's words to placate her earlier disgruntlement at coming here.

He laughed. 'I promise! I'm only repeating her words.'

Valda huffed in response and when he replied to the woman, she heard her name being said. Then Halfdan turned back to her. 'This is Theodora and Lukas Stauricius. They are influential in the court's clothing and silk trade.'

Valda looked at the cheerful couple with renewed respect and inclined her head. Anyone who held power in such a luxurious commodity must be important and demand respect, despite their appearance to the contrary. Neither of them looked as if they'd ever held a sword.

Then again, they didn't look as if they needed to. Gold and jewels could be used equally to defend oneself and they were dripping in those.

They wore strange hats on their heads that were encrusted with jewels and gold thread. Their dark hair was oiled and styled away from their face, delicate strings of pearls hanging down from their caps to frame their faces.

Their tunics were made entirely of silk in an almost gratuitous display of wealth, although she supposed if it were their trade, maybe they demonstrated it, as Halfdan did in the west. Despite their soft, round bodies, their eyes were quick and intelligent, watching her with unnerving excitement and anticipation.

She felt a sudden kinship with that monkey in the bazaar as they stared up at her in fascination.

'Theodora is excited to hear you are a shieldmaiden. She begs to be able to dress you for the court's banquet tonight.'

'Isn't that why we're here?' Valda hissed back, although she gave the couple a friendly smile, not wanting to appear rude.

Halfdan grinned in response. 'Yes, but now it's their idea and will cost considerably less.' He spoke some more in the Byzantine tongue and the couple seemed genuinely elated by his words.

Theodora clapped her hands with surprising ferocity and a sea of servants emerged from the billowing curtains. Valda jumped at the sudden movement and reached for her sword. Belatedly, she realised she no longer carried any weapons, due to her offering at the river and the rules they must follow within the city walls.

Halfdan's hand reached for hers and gave it a reassuring squeeze. 'They are good people and will treat you well. They wish only to bathe and dress you. A beautiful woman like you in their latest silk designs will cause a stir among the nobles at court.'

Valda shrugged. 'I am different, that's all. I don't think I've seen any woman with my height or colouring since leaving Gotland.'

Halfdan smiled. 'There is no one like you anywhere in the world. Believe me, I've looked.'

Before she could think of a response, she was quickly taken by the arm and led out by a crowd of chattering women, Theodora firmly at the helm.

The time passed by in a blur.

Valda couldn't understand a single word anyone said to her. It didn't seem to stop them from trying, however. At least after Halfdan's reassurance, she was no longer worried about their intentions. She let them buzz around her, allowing her body to relax and enjoy the pampering.

Soon she'd have to face the forthcoming court banquet and whatever new experiences that entailed.

They stripped her naked and measured her limbs with cord. Placed a linen tunic on her, pinched it tight with clasps, then marked it with charcoal. The linen was then quickly whipped off her body and squirrelled away to be used as a template, Valda suspected.

Then she was ushered into yet another room—this one was dominated by a metal steaming tub in its centre and she sank into it gratefully.

However, before she could enjoy the experience for long, several hands went to work scrubbing at her hair and body.

She tried to argue with them, demonstrate that she could wash herself. In fact, the Norse prided themselves on their cleanliness and bathed once a week compared to the Christians in the west who barely bathed at all.

But…she had to admit it had been more than three days since she'd last bathed in the river and she'd done lots of rowing since. So maybe she did look as if she needed a good bath and who was she to argue with the Byzantine method of hospitality?

After her bath, they massaged her body with fragrant oils that smelled of flowers and spice. Then they gently pushed her down into a soft chair to begin drying her long hair with linen and oils.

They brushed it for so long she wondered if she would have any hair left in her scalp, but she felt too relaxed to care.

It was as if she were floating on a delicious cloud of indulgence. One she'd never had the fortune to experience before. She suspected it would frustrate and annoy her if she were treated like this every day, but after such a long and emotional journey a bit of indulgence was gladly received.

'Do your worst,' she whispered with a blissful sigh.

The sun framed by the window began to set, causing the light in the room to fade. Bells began to ring in the distance, calling the Christians to prayer, and Theodora came bustling back into the room, her arms laden with the most beautiful emerald silk Valda had ever seen.

However, when Theodora held out one of their strange headdresses, Valda shook her head vehemently. 'I'm not married. I can wear it loose.'

'It's breathtaking!' Valda gasped as she stared in wonder at the interior of the Hagia Sophia.

Normally Halfdan would have agreed with her.

The Byzantine cathedral was magnificent, both in its sheer size and grandeur. Its domes and arches defied nature and were covered in white marble.

Inside were mosaics and paintings, shrines and sculptures, all of which shone as if with an inner light—the walls laden with so much silver, gold and precious jewels that it was almost blinding. Even in the twilight, with hundreds of candles burning, it was incredible, the walls shifting and moving as if the people and creatures depicted on them were alive and watching the occupants of the room from the shadows. Under his feet the marble appeared to shimmer like a frozen lake.

But there was only one breathtaking beauty that truly enthralled him this night.

Valda.

Tall, strong and beautiful.

In her green and gold silks, she outshone even the ancient and holy church in its splendour.

Valda's red hair shone like liquid fire. Most women covered their head with a cap or bound their hair with a length of silk. But not Valda—she let it flow down her back freely, as any Norse maiden would, proud of her heritage and feminine power. There was no one quite like her in the whole world, which made her, in his mind, as unique and as wonderful as the Hagia Sophia itself.

Distracted by the new sights before her she was oblivious not only to his own admiration, but also to the stares from the Byzantines as they passed. They were not Christian, so they could not fully enter for the ceremony, but he'd wanted her to see the inside of it at least. If they went in much further, they'd have to be segregated into the male and female sections. Even now, a few of the priests frowned at him for breaking the rules by standing with her.

He'd gladly break every law in Miklagard if it meant he could stand by her side for ever. Grimly, he thought of his own vow to his father. Could he break that?

'Is that the Emperor?' whispered Valda, nodding towards the young boy wrapped in purple silk and surrounded by both guards and noblemen. He sat devoutly praying by the silver and gold altar.

The brush of her perfumed scent against his senses was enough to have him gasping for air. He leaned forward a little, pretending to take great interest in the sight of the Byzantine rulers.

'Not yet, he is the son of Leo the Wise, the last Emperor, and will likely succeed him when he is old enough. His Uncle Alexander ruled for a time, but died recently. He was…unpopular at court.' There were even rumours he'd been poisoned, but Halfdan wouldn't speak of it, not even in the Norse tongue. Diplomacy in this pit of vipers was the only thing that kept a man in business. 'Nicholas Mystikos rules as regent now. The older man, over there, in the priest's robes.'

He lowered his voice so that only Valda could hear him, partly to be discreet and partly so that he could take a deep inhale of her alluring neck. 'But things change quickly in the Byzantine court. The Empress and several other nobles all fight for dominion at court.'

The Empress caught his gaze just then and he inclined his head respectfully. He'd always been on good terms with her. She was intelligent and cunning, regularly playing the ambitions of men against each other and still managing to maintain her position somehow.

'She's very beautiful,' murmured Valda and he wondered if he'd provoked her jealousy by accident. If he had, he could not see it by her expression; she seemed only curious. Oddly, that disappointed him.

'She was his mistress, before she became Empress. He married her after the birth of their son…to legitimise him, I suppose.'

Immediately, Halfdan cursed his stupidity.

What had possessed him to reveal that? As if showing her how highly the Empress had risen by being a concubine might somehow encourage Valda to do the same?

It was a *very* poor choice of words, as Valda's next insight proved. 'And yet she cannot rule in her husband's place? Also…why does she wear the robes of a nun?'

He squirmed like a fish on a hook. 'I believe Nicholas forced her into a convent. He does not wish to legitimise her claim to power. The Empress agreed to ensure her son's welfare and position.'

Valda turned to him, her eyes bright and sharp, a dark smile on her lush lips. 'So the selfish man, who is no relation to the original Emperor, rules instead? Why am I not surprised?'

He had no response to that. She was right and he was an idiot for bringing up the topic—he blamed it on her dazzling beauty tonight, it had addled his brain.

The cathedral began to fill with music and song, the sound reverberating through the building and capturing the hearts of all those who listened. Valda watched with interest, her eyes shining with unshed tears as she listened to words she could not understand, but was moved by regardless. She did not need to understand something to appreciate it.

Maybe she felt that way about him? Because at this moment he could not understand himself either.

While Halfdan felt the censure of Valda's point in the marrow of his bones, he also wondered if he could ever free himself from the conflicting desires that pressed down on him.

What else could he offer to keep her with him?

Possibly marriage…if his little scheme worked out, although the chances of that were slim and he'd not build up her hopes only to disappoint her. She'd been disappointed before.

At the end of the service, they were invited to a feast by one of the nobles who dealt with the taxation of trade in and out of the city. It was a man familiar to Halfdan, one who wisely planted his feet firmly on both sides of the warring court. Usually, he would have been invited to dine with this man at some point during his stay. But he suspected Valda's presence at his side had caught the curious attention of many influential people, speeding up proceedings, which was good, considering they had very little time to spare.

'Your angel has them all clamouring to show their appreciation,' said Theodora, as she joined them with a triumphant smile. 'I can't wait to tell that ridiculous Prudentia Zonara who dressed her! She will turn as putrid as those awful tunics she inflicts upon the court!'

Lukas laughed and patted his wife's hand gently. 'She will indeed, my dearest.'

Halfdan quickly explained what was happening and Valda took it in her usual confident stride. Theodora and Lukas climbed into their litter and Valda followed without hesitation.

For a woman who claimed to lack a desire for new experiences, she adapted surprisingly well to them, gliding serenely from one moment to the next. A she-wolf surrounded by lambs.

Always sure of herself.

Unlike him.

Halfdan was determined to show Valda all the delights Miklagard had to offer while also conducting his business as swiftly as possible. Determined to have everything he wanted by his return to Jorvik.

After all, a profitable trip hadn't been the main goal of this voyage.

His goal, if he were honest with himself, had been to dazzle and seduce Valda into wanting him again, or at least realising what she'd lost by walking away from him.

But so much had changed since they'd left Jorvik.

Firstly, they'd realised the cruel trick fate had played on them by Olga's deception and they'd realised how much they still meant to one another. Now, he felt like a poor craftsman trying to broker a bad deal.

What did he *really* have to offer except a lifetime of empty promises? At least his mother had known Ulf could be a devious and cruel bastard when she'd married him. She'd hoped to change him, or at least that's what Tostig said.

She'd learned a bitter truth.

You could not change a person by will alone. He knew that better than most.

If Valda could not be happy as his concubine, then what choice did that leave him? He could not be happy without her, nor could he cast aside his brother, as his father had.

'Be the man he should have been,' said his mother's voice in his head.

Chapter Eighteen

Valda stood in the Hippodrome and stared up at the monument as she waited for Halfdan. He was in one of the many palaces of the Emperor, agreeing prices for their returning cargo. He'd sold the goods from the north that first night to the many artisans and traders at the feast, exchanging coin or silk for them.

That coin he now spent widely, ensuring he acquired enough precious silk, beads, glass and jewels to make the trip worthwhile. She'd also realised why three ships were better than one. Each Norse ship was allowed its own quota of silk. The trade was heavily regulated by the Emperor, but Halfdan slithered through the rules with the ease of an eel, taking three times the amount usually granted. She couldn't help but admire his intellect.

She squinted up at the stone column piercing the sky like the blade of a sword. It defied nature, like many of the buildings here.

Everything about the city was overwhelming to the senses, from the clash of cultures to the conflicting religions and languages. Even the clothing varied in style and richness with every twist in the road. Christianity was everywhere, unsurprising considering it had been a Byzantian stronghold for so long. And yet, the city was also very different to what she'd expected. Older, somehow, as if the icons of religion were an adornment for a much older place. Ancient ruins of a long-dead people still remained. Crumbling…but present, as if to remind Valda that this was not a new city, even if it were new to her. It wasn't even called Miklagard here, but Constantinople, and it had been many other names before that.

Three days ago, she'd been in awe of it, wondering if she were about to sail into the land of the gods.

But there were no Æsir walking these stone streets—much to Valda's disappointment. Only people, not so very different from those back home. They fought among themselves like dogs with a bone and indulged in exotic trinkets, just the same as the Kings and Jarls in the west.

Halfdan had been right when he'd said she was *exotic* to them. The first night, at the feast with silk traders, he'd told stories about her, like the tales he'd told of endless sands. She couldn't understand what he'd said, but she'd been sure it was about her life as a shieldmaiden. He'd said her name several times, sometimes pretending to slash the air with an imaginary sword.

They'd listened to him, enthralled, eyes bright with excitement and purses open, watching her as if she were a mythical serpent. Both beautiful and deadly. She didn't mind that so much. After all, she was both a warrior and a woman, as happy in armour as she was in her beautiful green and gold gown. She did not care what some pampered citizens thought of her. She knew her worth.

However, she'd become intensely irritated when a few of the guests had turned a little too brave for their own good. One man had even tried to cut a lock of her hair from her head. She'd almost broken his wrist.

Oddly, the man didn't seem to mind—if anything, he seemed pleased by her reaction, crowing to his fellow traders in that strange musical language of theirs.

Halfdan hadn't been happy about it either and had said some harsh words to him. It was good to know that he didn't expect her to be treated like an object—even if he was taking advantage of her looks. At least she and her family would also benefit from the sales, otherwise she'd never have agreed.

The second day had been spent in a flurry of meetings, extravagant entertainment and meals. It had felt like an endless parade of all the best things the city had to offer, until she'd become grateful to retire to their lodgings to sleep.

Today was their last day as the winds had turned in their favour and it was important they catch them—as this was always meant to be a swift trip. When Halfdan had announced their imminent departure, she could tell by the weary expressions of the men that this was not normal. They sighed grimly, but nodded in agreement.

Valda dreaded leaving. She could sense a shift within her. The seasons were changing and she along with them. Natural and inevitable, as if she were slowly waking from a lovely dream, one so blissful and pleasant that like a child she refused to remove the blanket from her head. But she could not ignore what was coming for ever.

It was the peak of summer and their voyage. Soon, they would dive into the long journey back, returning to Jorvik before the leaves fell. A cool breeze whipped across the arena, blowing sand and grit in her face, as if reminding her of the threat of autumn despite the blazing sun.

Turning away with a heavy heart, she headed back to the entrance where she'd promised Halfdan she'd meet him at noon. Most of the crew were with her as they'd walked together into the city, all of them planning to visit the hot baths for a final time before they left.

'You well, girl?' asked Tostig with a frown of concern as she joined them. He'd taken to calling her 'girl' ever since her idiocy during the storm. It had annoyed her at first, but over the many weeks it had become a kind of endearment, and as Tostig was the only person who dared to call her that, it was easily forgiven.

She gave a weak smile and rubbed her belly. She wore her usual attire today—although the clothes were new, yet another gift from Halfdan. 'It's all the rich food,' she explained, although really she was tied up in knots with indecision.

Tostig laughed. 'Looking forward to my biscuits again, are you?'

'Can't wait,' she said drily and several of the men laughed. The pan-baked bread travelled well, but was always burnt or badly seasoned when Tostig made it.

Halfdan arrived then, resplendent in his latest silks. These ones were blue with silver trim and complemented his good looks like the spice added to the Byzantine food. Perfectly balanced.

'All done?' asked Tostig conversationally.

Halfdan nodded. 'Yes. The last of it's on its way to Aarne now.' His smile tightened a little as he looked at her. 'We're free to leave.'

The air tightened in her lungs as if she were breathing

in ice-cold air. She looked away from him, unable to face his unspoken question. Their time in Miklagard was over.

I need more time.

'Come, I've arranged a private room for us at the bathhouse,' Halfdan said, taking her hand in his own. 'Usually, men and women are separate. But some make exceptions for private customers.'

Upon arrival at the old stone bathhouse, they were met by a small group of cheerful women. Two of the women ushered Halfdan and Valda down one corridor, while the rest of the crew followed the others down another.

The stone building was beautifully carved, with high arched windows letting in light from above. It was a warren of corridors and separate rooms, out of which steam billowed as they passed. A general hum of heat and conversation ran behind the marble walls.

Eventually, they entered a small stone room tiled with elaborate mosaics depicting either naked people artfully draped in cloth, or mystical creatures that reminded her of some of the tales from the motherlands.

One of the women spoke to Halfdan with an eager smile as she opened a chest to reveal bundles of linen and vials of perfumed oil. The other lifted a lid on a huge urn, demonstrating the clean water inside and the cup they could use to drink from it. There were several jugs and buckets dotted around, all beautifully painted.

Then the women began to undress them, folding their clothing carefully and placing them inside another chest. Valda blushed—it felt strange being naked with Halfdan in front of others.

'It's normal here,' Halfdan muttered in explanation, although he looked a little embarrassed himself and was deliberately staring at the ceiling above her head in deep concentration.

The two women giggled and waved them forward through another set of doors. Valda had always thought Christians more prudish than the Norse, but it appeared that wasn't the case here.

As soon as they entered the next room they were hit by a cloud of hot steam. Valda flapped her hand in front of her face to clear the air a little. The floor was warm under her feet, and the heat reminded her of Norse saunas, except the room was much larger. Her skin beaded with sweat immediately and she stood still for a moment as her eyes adjusted to the gloom.

The room was divided into two spaces, a hot area in which they stood, with benches along the walls, and then further in there was a turquoise pool set into the floor. The water sparkled in the light of the torches surrounding it, a light steam rising from its surface, and bright sunshine streaming in from an opening in the domed roof above.

It was beautiful and tranquil. A perfect end to their stay.

Valda sighed with pleasure as she sank into the warm water. Halfdan followed soon after with an appreciative groan of his own.

'Will they be coming in here?' she asked, gesturing with her head towards the closed doors of the dressing chamber.

'No, but we only have to call for them if we need them.'

'Good,' replied Valda. There was something about the two women that made her uneasy. Not their manner—they seemed friendly enough—but something…in their style of dress, maybe? They weren't like the rest of the women she'd met so far.

'It will be a long time until I can wash my hair properly again. I might as well do it now.' There was a tray of soaps and combs as well as a large jug on the opposite side of the pool and she swam lazily over to it.

She spent some time combing out and thoroughly washing her hair, savouring the use of the precious soaps and oils that would cost a fortune back home.

With a splash Halfdan dropped below the surface, emerging with a mischievous smile beside her.

'Will you do mine?' he asked, turning his back to her.

'If you wish.' Pushing up with her arms, she sat up on the edge of the pool, her knees level with his shoulders and her feet dangling in the water. Lathering the soap with her hands, she tugged him closer. He stepped backwards and she opened her thighs so that he could stand between them. A sensual flutter of excitement ran down her spine as it always did when he was close.

'It's got long,' she murmured as she tugged on the leather tie wrapped around his hair. 'It will take me a while.'

'Then I'll cut it off. Shall I call them for a knife?'

'No, don't do that. I was starting to forget they were there.' She laughed as she began to wash and comb out his hair. It reached down past his shoulders, dark gold and as straight as an arrow. As she worked, she smiled at the happy moans and blissful sighs Halfdan made.

'You really do like being pampered, don't you?' she teased.

'Only when you do it,' he said, stroking his hands down her calves. Then he turned around slowly, his eyes level with her breasts, which he happily stared at without a flicker of shame.

Unable to resist him she leaned down to taste his mouth. Their tongues glided against each other in a gentle caress, as if they both sensed there were going to be tough days ahead and wanted to enjoy the peace while it lasted.

She wiggled forward, intending to drop down into the water in front of him.

'Stay there,' he said softy, his mouth already trailing tender kisses down her breasts and belly. Knowing what he was about to do, she leaned back on to her elbows and released a blissful sigh of pleasure.

His head dipped between her thighs, his lush mouth pressing against her centre and causing her to groan. He worked her body with relentless kisses, his lips and tongue bringing her to a hard and fast climax that left her reeling with waves of delight.

After she managed to get her breath back, she slipped down into the water, boneless and content. Wrapping her arms around his shoulders and her legs around his hips, she encouraged him to take his own satisfaction in return.

The water splashed around them as he rocked into her with leisurely thrusts, the sounds of their lovemaking echoing around the tiled room, until they both cried out with ecstatic delight.

They found a tiled ledge within the side of the pool and sat on it to rest.

'See how wonderful our life could be together,' he murmured as he pressed a kiss to her collarbone that made her shiver despite the heat of the water.

A masculine shout of laughter came from one of the

other rooms beyond the wall, followed by the sound of giggling women. Valda's back stiffened, as she realised what had unsettled her before.

'Is this…? Are there…*whores* here?' she whispered in shock.

Halfdan sighed. 'Yes, but men and women are segregated in the normal baths, and I wanted us to spend as much time together as possible before we left.'

Valda frowned, but nodded. It made sense. But she couldn't shake the discomforting thought that somehow, by being here, she was branded in the same way, at least in Halfdan's eyes. After living with her mother for so long, she would be the last to condemn a woman for satisfying her desires outside of marriage. But the fact he would bring here…to a place where men *bought* their pleasure…soured her view on their relationship.

Moving to stand in front of him within the water, she took a deep breath and gathered her strength for what was to come.

She nodded to the doorway. 'Do you want me to become like one of them? Your mistress, like their Empress was?'

'No!' Halfdan denied. 'But—'

'Because to do so would ruin a young woman's married life before it's even begun and would dishonour me as well.'

Frustration gathered like a storm between them.

'You can have anything you want from me. All I ask is that you give me the time to find a solution.'

The suspicions and doubts she'd had before rose to the surface. 'Is that why you brought me here? To show me what I *could* have had…if only I'd trusted you more?'

'No,' he replied weakly, but she could tell he was lying.

'That's what it feels like.' Her voice was soft and tarnished by sadness, but it grew louder with every word that followed. 'With every day that passes, I feel as if you are silently telling me—Look! Look at this! Look at what you have missed! I was willing to forget the past, but it seems you are not. I made a mistake and now you are punishing me for it.'

He hissed a curse. 'That was not my intention! I only wanted you to see what could have been, what still could be... I love you. Is that not enough for you?'

His declaration was a blow to her resolve and she gritted her teeth against it. She paused a long time before answering. She could not return his words, not because she did not feel them, but because the risk of humiliation was too great. 'You should marry your lady from the Western Mountains and keep your word.'

Disappointment and hurt washed across his face. He sat up straighter, all earlier relaxation forgotten. 'Valda, give me time...'

If he truly loved her, he would throw aside his vow and choose her instead. But once again she was a *second choice* and it burned through her with vicious fury. A volley of memories struck like arrows, each one harder and deeper than the last.

Her mother's muffled tears in the blankets as she cried herself to sleep every night after Bjorn's betrayal. The countless men who'd asked her to call them 'father' but who had walked away without ever saying farewell. Finally, she thought of her sad declaration of love to Jorund. How he'd kindly told her she wasn't the woman for him. How she'd openly wept in front of him, like a pathetic beggar at his table.

Never again.

'No,' she said firmly. 'I also have honour and a family that need me, too.' She was proud of the conviction in her voice, even if her head was pounding fiercely. 'I understand why you feel the need to do it. But if I were Erik, I would not wish for you to sacrifice your happiness for mine.' Suddenly exhausted she stepped from the heated pool. Her stomach was churning and she had a sour taste in the back of her throat. 'I do not want to be a jarl's wife, or to have silks or jewels…and, although I have loved travelling with you, it is not enough. I want a *home* and I do not think I can have that with you. I will join my sisters on their farm. That is where I belong.'

Halfdan thrust one arm through the water in frustration, causing a spray of water to rush across its surface. '*Coward!* I have told you that I love you, but you have *never* returned my words. I will never be enough for you! It is your pride and fear that keeps us apart and not my oath!'

She didn't have the strength to argue. It would only lead to more heartache. The fight in her had gone out, like fire in the rain.

'Maybe I am…' she whispered. She spoke a little louder as she walked away. 'I will see you back at the dock, I'll sail with Tostig or Aarne. It's probably best we go in separate ships.'

Halfdan's only response was to scowl, then look away, his jaw clenched tight.

The oppressive heat was suffocating her and her stomach rolled as if she'd swallowed a live snake. She hurried towards the doors.

Bursting through them, she entered the first chamber, letting them swing closed behind her. Thankfully Halfdan did not follow.

The two women jumped from the bench in surprise. Valda barely looked at them, her head was spinning terribly. She slumped on top of one of the chests, and gulped in air, but it didn't help.

One of the women shoved an empty bucket under her nose, just in time, as the entire contents of her stomach was suddenly heaved up in an awful rush. After she was done, she dropped her head back against the mosaic tiles in exhaustion, her heart hammering in her chest wildly and the taste of burnt metal on her tongue.

The women hurried around her, taking away the mess, and dabbing her face with a wet linen cloth. They hushed her in soothing voices, although she couldn't understand a word they said. Valda gave the one closest to her a weak smile. The woman clucked her tongue at her in sympathy and called to the other, as if she were giving out instructions.

A cup of cool water was brought to her and she gulped it down greedily, letting the water calm the fire at the back of her throat. Sweat poured over her skin and she sucked in a shaky breath before allowing the woman to help her stand.

They wrapped her in linens and took out her clothing. One said something to the other and they both laughed.

'The heat…' she tried to explain by fanning herself. 'It was just the heat.'

The woman reached across and tapped Valda's naked belly lightly with a knowing chuckle, before helping her to dress.

'No… I was just hot…' But the words died in her

throat, as one of the women urged her to eat some fruit. She took it with numb fingers.

How long had it been since she last bled? Too long.

The sooner she was back with her sisters the better.

Chapter Nineteen

Thankfully, she managed to ease the sickness by eating nuts and fruits as often as she could, keeping a bag of them tied around her waist and hoping Halfdan wouldn't notice.

She needn't have worried. Halfdan had taken easily to avoiding her company. He'd not even spoken to her since the bathhouse and they'd travelled in different boats as she'd suggested. It was truly over between them.

Which was what she wanted, wasn't it?

Other than the silk, the luxurious cargo was much smaller and lighter than all the fur, bone and swords they'd brought with them to trade…but far more precious. They flowed with the wind, across the sea to the mouth of the Dnieper River.

But the rest of the journey back to Halfdan's trading settlement was not as easy. They had to row against the current and made slow progress over land around the rapids and waterfall.

There was always the threat of the nomadic tribes who preyed on travellers. Each night they made camp and took turns to keep watch.

Halfdan deliberately chose to sleep when it was her turn to guard. She couldn't criticise him for it, it made life more bearable. But they were both miserable and silent, when before the trip had been fun.

They weren't the only sullen ones.

All the men seemed worse tempered than before and anxious to return home. Tostig had cursed their slow progress more than once and had looked at both her and Halfdan with bitter and accusing frustration. She always ignored him.

Today, the light of dawn bathed the steppe's grassland with an amber glow. But Valda noticed a low smudge of dust on the horizon. She went to Tostig, who was sitting beside the fire preparing the morning meal. She told him about it and he took one look at the distant cloud and smiled.

'You were right to tell me,' he said, then he poured the morning's stew over the flames.

Banging the pot loudly with his ladle, 'Pechenegs!' he bellowed, stomping through the sleeping men and kicking those not leaping to their feet quick enough.

The camp burst into action. Men cursed and knocked into each other in their haste. But Valda had seen many battles and she allowed her mind to sink into old habits. She took deep, calming breaths as she focused on her tasks ahead.

Halfdan had already given clear instructions as to what to do in the event of an attack. On the Dnieper they were safer in their boats. The nomads would be on horseback and, on this wide stretch of the river, they would be out of reach from their spears and bows if they sailed down its centre. They'd passed the seven waterfalls at least, so all they had to do was break camp and launch their boats.

Each boat's crew worked furiously to load and push out their boats. It was their only chance of escape. As the thunder of hooves rumbled closer, and the dust cloud grew nearer, they manage to get the first ship into the water.

Valda was part of the second boat's crew and she dragged the heavily laden ship with the other men to the riverbank, using the oars beneath to help roll it. Aarne ran between the prow and the stern, taking the oars two at a time from the back and positioning them at the front. But as Aarne ran past her, an arrow thudded into his shoulder and he let out a scream of pain, dropping the poles.

Valda grabbed her shield from the side to cover him and three more arrows hit the wood with deadly force. 'Keep going!' Valda shouted and Aarne threw the oars in front of the ship despite the yellow of his tunic turning to crimson with blood.

The ship rolled on to the oars and continued out into the water, the men pushing with all their might to launch it. As it bobbed and jerked in the shallow water, the men followed it, grabbing their oars from the ground as they ran and jumped into the ship.

Valda grabbed Aarne, ignoring his grunt of pain and covering them both with her shield as she dragged him through the waters to the ship. More arrows slammed into the side of the ship with a hiss and she glanced back.

The nomadic raiders were so close. Nearly a hundred of them by her calculations, all racing towards them with bows and spears raised. Even as their horses galloped, they let loose their arrows. They wore long tunics down to their knees, loose trousers and leather boots. Rather than looking like poor, opportunist raiders, as she'd presumed, their clothing was vibrantly embroidered and dyed and coned hats or helmets adorned the heads—sometimes with silk ribbons tied to their armour and weapons. They carried spears, bows and swords and they were built for warfare.

Valda looked at Halfdan's ship. His was the last to launch because it contained most of the camp supplies. But it was fully loaded and only a short distance from the shore. Two of the crew were dead on the bank, arrows protruding from their bodies.

It was Bori and Frode, men she considered friends, but it wasn't the time to mourn them.

'Valda! Get in!' shouted Tostig from above, offering her his arm from inside the boat.

She should think of the babe in her belly. Climb in and row with the others as fast she could. The first boat had passed the bend in the river and was already out of sight.

A few of the swiftest riders had already reached the river bank and were charging towards the launching ship. Halfdan grabbed a sword and shield from the boat and charged towards them with a fierce battle cry that she felt deep in her bones.

She had to answer. How could she face their child if she'd allowed its father to die?

'Go!' she shouted to Tostig, thumping the wooden side. Turning, she ran through the water to the remaining ship.

Halfdan had brought down two of the five Pechenegs, and Odger had joined him in battle. They stood back to back as the raiders, still on horseback, circled them, thrusting spears at their raised shields.

The boat breached the water with a heavy scrape against the shingle, and she knew the best help she could give would be in defeating the remaining Pechenegs, so that all the men could return to the task of making their escape.

She ran forward on to the river bank and took her dagger in her hand, throwing it at one of the riders as soon as he came into range. It struck true and the rider slumped to the ground in a tangle of limbs and weaponry. The remaining three riders noticed her then and one broke away to charge her, his shield and spear raised.

She ducked and rolled to the side, allowing her instincts to take control. The spear thudded into the ground where she'd once stood. Halfdan's bellow of outrage filled the air and she heard a horse scream as both raiders were taken down.

Halfdan ran to her, grabbing her by the arm, dragging her to her feet, as the three of them ran back towards the boat.

Odger stopped dead and cried out with grief when he saw Bori's body. 'I can't leave him!' He fell on to his knees and tried to drag Bori's body to him.

Holding her shield above them both, she gripped him by the arm, her voice low but firm. 'He's already gone.'

Odger nodded grimly, took Bori's arm ring and Halfdan took Frode's with a pained expression, then they ran. The rings would be given to their families and rune stones raised in their honour.

The remaining crew were leaping aboard, pushing out with their oars to catch the current and move away from shore.

'Get in!' Halfdan shouted, thrusting her towards the ship, lifting her off her feet with the force of it. An arrow thudded beside her and she rolled into the ship without any argument. Attaching her shield to the side of the boat to cover her, she grabbed the nearest oar and began to row with all her might.

She breathed a sigh of relief as she saw Halfdan and Odger board also, but she would not relax until they were far away from their attackers. Arrows flew at them from the riverbank, but none struck home and eventually their attackers gave up and rode away. She doubted anyone would want to sleep or make camp again until they'd reached Halfdan's settlement.

'You shouldn't have done that,' snapped Halfdan behind her, leaning forward so that only she could hear him. His breath was hot and ragged on her neck and she shivered.

She spoke quietly, her face turned slightly so that only he could hear, as she rolled backwards with the pull of the oar. 'You said you needed another sword.'

Silence, as he waited for the next pull of the oar, so that they could be close once again. 'Your duty was to stay with your boat. Never do that again!'

She turned her head, and glared at him, but refused to miss the beat of the oar. 'My duty is to go where I am needed! At least I have proved myself as a hired sword… worthy of my weight in silver.'

He rocked forward as the oars lifted from the water. They were so close, his lips brushed against the side of her neck as he spoke. 'There is not enough silver in this world to pay me for your loss.'

The weight of his words felt like a boulder on her chest.

'Then it is lucky I am not owned by you,' she snapped and they went back to ignoring each other.

Chapter Twenty

'Brother!' cried Halfdan, as he embraced Erik with thunderous slaps to his back and a fierce hug. They had met a short distance from his settlement's fort, Halfdan walking up from his arrival at the dock and his brother walking out to join him.

As usual, Erik greeted him warmly, but only called him by his name. A habit drilled into him by their father. 'Halfdan, good to see you. I got your message to stay here until your return. Is something amiss?'

'Nothing's wrong, but let us talk inside.' They turned and walked into the Hall.

Hopefully, Erik's presence would help with his doubts. Valda's words still plagued him.

I understand why you feel the need to do it. But if I were Erik, I would not wish for you to sacrifice your happiness for mine.

Her accusation had kept him awake every night since leaving Miklagard because he'd *not* thought to ask Erik what he wanted for his future. Halfdan had presumed that he wanted the life that Halfdan was destined to have. To own land and rule.

But...should he have asked him what he wanted?

Of course, then he might have refused Halfdan's help if he had—in fact, he knew he would. At least this way it would come from their father and might even seem like the apology Erik was surely owed from him.

Which was why he'd made the bargain in secret.

Besides, it had been almost a year since he'd last seen Erik; he wouldn't have been able to ask his opinion anyway.

Erik travelled up and down the Volga and well into the heart of the Islamic caliphate's lands. A treacherous path that could lead to great riches, or a mysterious death, but Erik didn't seem to mind it. He had his mother's tongue and colouring and so he fared much better than most Norse merchants in such territories. Without Erik's hard work, Halfdan would not have accumulated so much wealth, or have been able to afford the ridiculous price Ulf had set for his half-brother's freedom. In Halfdan's mind, half of his silver belonged to his brother, even if the laws of the land said otherwise.

Even so, Halfdan worried for him while he was away, as he knew he was not happy. Erik did not have the same adventurous spirit as he did and the trips were not an experience he treasured. He preferred to be back here, building and managing the settlement.

They sat at the gaming table and Halfdan tried to ignore the twist in his gut when he saw the Tafl set untouched from the last time he'd played with Valda. 'Your trip was successful?' he asked instead.

Two horns of ale were passed to them by a servant, and he drank it greedily.

Erik smiled. 'Ulf will be pleased.'

'And what I gave you to trade?'

He grinned. 'I have enough to buy my freedom—no matter his price this time.'

Halfdan slapped his brother's bicep again with a loud cheer. 'Well done, my brother!' Ulf had raised the price of Erik's freedom each time Halfdan had gone to pay it. 'And don't worry, he cannot raise the price again. I have made him swear before his warriors that the price is now set. We pay him this autumn in Jorvik.'

Erik gave a weary smile. 'I'll believe it when he gives me an arm ring of my own…not before.' His smile faded to a frown as his dark eyes caught something behind Halfdan's shoulder. 'Is that…?' His eyes widened with recognition and then he stared at him as if he were mad. 'What is *she* doing with you?'

He didn't need to turn around to know that Valda had walked in with the rest of the men. 'She asked to join me…it's only for one trip.'

'I have never understood why you do half the things you do…but accepting a woman into your crew who broke your heart seems a little odd—even for you. Are you punishing her?'

Halfdan stared at his brother in horror. 'Punishing her? No! Why would you think that?'

Erik shrugged.

'Her family need silver.'

That caused Erik's head to snap up. 'Why?'

'Her mother and sisters want a farm. Their wealth was stolen from them, and they wish to bribe another jarl into giving them land.'

'I take it she'll have enough now to secure a farm for her family?' Erik asked mildly, taking a sip of ale.

'Yes.'

'So, you're just helping out an old…*friend*?'

'Of course.'

'And you feel nothing more for her?' Erik's dark eyes caught his and held them.

Halfdan made a gruff sound of agreement and looked away to take another long drink of his ale.

'And you haven't had sex with her?'

Halfdan choked on the ale as he struggled for moment to gather his wits.

'Not…*recently.*'

Erik rolled his eyes to the oak timbers with a curse.

'She ended it this time. She's not happy with me,' Halfdan added, not quite sure why he had to explain himself, but feeling compelled to do so anyway.

'So…it *was* for revenge,' Erik said slowly, his head tilted as if in deep concentration. He was watching her, Halfdan was sure of it. It took all of his sanity not to give in and turn to look.

'No, it was not!' he replied, with a hiss of disgust.

Erik shook his head in disbelief. 'I still don't understand.'

'She wants marriage.'

Erik stared at him. 'Again?' Then he shrugged. 'Maybe you should marry her. Ulf would have killed her before, but now I doubt he could manage such a thing.'

'I don't want to.' Halfdan had decided not to tell Erik about the deal, so he allowed Erik to presume that he didn't want to marry Valda for the same reason he'd always given for never marrying—his freedom.

His brother sighed, but nodded, accepting his answer without question. 'Then you must accept a life without her. Porunn's daughters are too stubborn to accept anything less than full devotion.'

Halfdan spat on the rushes, the ale suddenly tasting

like vinegar on his tongue. 'Indeed, well…she will not be with me for long. When we arrive in Jorvik, I will return her to her mother and sisters. I'm sure Brynhild and Helga will have missed her greatly. They will probably hear of our arrival before our cargo is even unloaded and come to take her straight away…' Halfdan watched his brother's expression with interest.

The only indication that the news affected him was a slight clenching of his jaw.

At least he wasn't the only man troubled by Porunn's fierce daughters.

Valda unrolled her bedding in a corner of the Hall and laid down to sleep with weary bones. Exhausted, her shoulders and arms ached from the long days carrying or rowing the boats. She would be grateful for a night's rest before they prepared Halfdan's larger ship in the morning.

The next half of the journey would still involve lots of rowing upstream, but it would be safer at least. Soon they would reach the sea and the late summer winds would carry them back to Jorvik… To her family…her home.

Swiftly, she hoped, touching her belly beneath the blanket and realising it was already beginning to swell. She would need to loosen her belt and billow out her tunic more to hide it.

A large, dark figure walked close by her bed roll and stopped beside her. She rose up on to her elbows to see his face better in the firelight.

'Erik?' she whispered, not wishing to disturb the other men who slept on benches and bed rolls around the Hall. They needed their sleep especially poor Odger, Svend and Aarne, who'd lost kinsmen.

Erik hunched down into a squat to face her. 'Valda... how are your sisters and mother?'

Valda blinked in surprise.

Erik wanted to ask about her family? In the middle of the night? 'They are well. We hope to acquire a farm.'

He nodded. 'Yes, Halfdan told me.'

A strange silence descended between them and she almost wished him goodnight. But then Erik took a deep breath and asked her suddenly, 'That's what you want... a farm?'

Anger flared within her. 'Yes. Do you have a problem with that, Erik?'

He shook his head. 'No, it just surprised me. None of you struck me as the farming type...except, maybe Brynhild. She always liked animals.'

Valda stared at Erik, bewildered. She'd always thought him strange, but this odd conversation confirmed it. At least now she had a better understanding of why he was the way he was, although she still couldn't forgive him for hurting Brynhild. 'Depends on the animal.'

Erik ignored her tart reply, his voice slow and thoughtful. 'Porunn... I suppose she could eventually turn her hand to farming, especially if she can't fight any more?' He glanced at Valda for confirmation and she gave a sharp nod. 'Helga... Well, she's more of an elf than a farmer, but being in nature would appeal to her far more than a city like Jorvik... But you... I can't imagine you on a farm...ever.'

'Well, thank you for that insight, Erik,' she retorted, although she was a little shocked a man she'd barely known nine years ago could read her family so well. 'But as I haven't seen you for many years, I doubt you know what I...or *any* of my sisters want in life.' She flicked her blanket sharply and settled down for the night, deliberately turning her back on him.

'I always thought you wanted my brother,' Erik said in a hushed voice. Valda's back stiffened, his next words cutting like a knife across her. 'Is his heart not enough for you? Must you take his freedom as well?'

Rage and frustration boiled within her and she reared up to face him like a serpent striking. 'I want respect and peace! I would have thought you of *all men* would understand that!'

To her surprise, Erik laughed. 'Oh, I do. But if you can have only *one* thing… Take my advice…choose wisely.'

Valda sank back on to her elbows, defeated. 'And you think I should give up my honour for him?'

Erik shrugged and stood. 'I think…that no one likes to be someone's second choice. Why does the absence of wedding ring matter anyway?'

She laughed, realising that Halfdan had not told his brother about the betrothal agreement. *Well, it was not her place to confess it.*

'Goodnight, Erik,' she replied, sinking on to her thin bedding with a heavy sigh and turning towards the wall. He couldn't understand what he was asking of her.

Her hand skated to her stomach. Even if she could accept Halfdan marrying another, she would not accept her child being treated any less than his legitimate children.

For once her mother had been right.

It was better for a child never to know their father than live as an embarrassment in his eyes.

Chapter Twenty-One

A shout went out across the deck as the Northumbria coastline came into sight. They steered towards it, pulling on the ropes to adjust the sail accordingly. Valda breathed in a heavy sigh of relief as she worked on untangling some old rope.

She'd never been happier to see England, even if it were through a cloud of miserable drizzle. Depending on their current location they could be within Jorvik by nightfall. She searched the cliffs and found what she was looking for: the mouth of the river that would lead them straight into the heart of the city.

She should have known Halfdan would bring them so close to the right position. He was the best helmsman she'd ever met, instinct and skill his finest tools. Their journey from his settlement to here had been relentless, landing only for the most urgent of supplies and never stopping anywhere for long, either to rest or trade, and keeping all their luxury goods for sale in Jorvik.

Tostig sat with a heavy grunt on the sea chest beside her. 'When will you tell him?'

A cold shiver ran down her spine at his perceptive gaze.

Did he know?

She looked around them, but the rest of the crew worked on oblivious. No one close enough to hear them.

'Tell him what?' she said, her hands clumsy as she tried to pull the knot out of the thick hemp.

He gave a snort of disgust and leaned in, his voice deliberately hushed. 'I have been married for many years, girl. I know when a woman is with child—even if that idiot does not.' He jerked his head in Halfdan's direction.

Halfdan stood at the steering oar talking with Erik, thankfully oblivious to their conversation at the prow. She'd not spoken a word to him since the nomad's ambush and he'd not sought her out either. They behaved as if the other did not exist and somehow they'd managed to get through the endless journey back, even if they were both wretchedly despondent the whole time.

She turned in her seat to face Tostig, her voice low with menace. 'If you say *anything* I will gut you like a fish, *old man*! Don't think that I won't!' Her hand rested on her blade. It was an ordinary sword, plain and simple. But she did not regret sacrificing her old weapon, it had paid the gods for their safe return at least.

Tostig chuckled at her scowl. 'I'm sure you would and it would be no dishonour for me to die by your hand… but I would prefer a more noble cause of death than idle talk. I swear I will not speak of it if you wish. But I will tell you this… I think you are making a terrible mistake. One I urge you to reconsider.'

'Really?' She laughed darkly. 'You *do* know he is the one that has refused to marry me, don't you?'

Tostig frowned. 'That is a deal he should not have made and will quickly regret. If he knew of the child…'

She was a little surprised Tostig knew of the deal for

Erik's future. But then she remembered how like a real father he was to Halfdan. Closer to him, she suspected, than even his own brother.

'Then I would definitely not accept him,' she said through gritted teeth as she thumped the rope with a snap of her wrist, finally loosening the tangle.

'Why not?'

She looked at Tostig with hard resolve. 'I will not force a man to marry me. If he wishes to be free of me, then let him be free of me.'

'You are both idiots.'

'Possibly. But I would not be happy if he only wanted me for the sake of the child.'

Tostig huffed angrily at her agreement. 'Take this, then.'

Valda stared at the bag he offered. 'What is it?'

'What do you think it is? My silver.'

Valda stared at the heavy purse in horror. Halfdan had estimated the profits of their venture last night and had immediately paid the crew their share in silver, herself included. Erik had earned enough dirhams from his voyage in the east to allow it and huge chests sat in the cargo hold overflowing with Halfdan's own wealth. She was sure he'd deliberately paid them early. Eager to get rid of her as soon as possible. At least this way she wouldn't have to wait for the goods to be sold. She shook her head vehemently at Tostig's offer. 'No, I can't! Besides, I've plenty already.'

'I promised you my silver if I lived and sadly I have.'

'I never thought you actually meant it! If it's because…' She glanced around to double-check no one was listening. 'My sisters and mother will look after me. You don't need to worry, Tostig. I'll be fine.'

He rolled his eyes and dropped the silver by her feet. 'It is not for you, you stupid girl. It is for the child who is blameless and also a member of my kin… Halfdan's mother would never forgive me if I didn't offer my help. She may never forgive me anyway for not telling her son about it, but I am a man of my word.' He cleared his throat loudly and Valda tried not to laugh at the bad-tempered scowl on his face. He was the kindest and grumpiest man she'd ever met. 'I will miss you, Valda Þorunndóttir…you are a good oarsman, as well as an impressive warrior, and I wish you well,' he said gruffly and she thought she saw the mist of tears in his eyes, but he blinked them furiously away and shrugged. 'But I have too large a hoard as it is. The gods will punish me for my lack of generosity if I don't give it away. Think yourself fortunate and just accept it…before I ram it down your miserable throat.'

'For the child, then.' Valda smiled gently, unbothered by his harsh words, realising the true emotion behind them and struggling to find her own words. 'I will miss you, too, Tostig… I never had a father, but if I did, I would want someone like you.'

Colour flushed his leathery face and he gave a brisk nod of acknowledgement. 'If you ever need me, I will come.' He walked away without another word, shouting curses that someone had not tightened the rigging well enough.

Humbled, Valda picked the bag up at her feet and put it away with the rest of her belongings.

The bustle and chaos of Jorvik filled the air as the ship was strapped to the jetty and the crew gathered around

Valda to say their goodbyes. All of them would be staying with Halfdan, but it was an unspoken understanding that she would not.

Like her goodbye with Tostig, it was a gruff, yet touchingly emotional farewell. Many of the crew she now considered close friends, after having spent so much time together. She gave Aarne, Odger and Svend the tightest hugs, wishing that Frode and Bori were still with them. But as even they said, sailing was dangerous work.

But eventually they were done and she headed towards the wooden ramp, not daring to look at the steering oar, or the man who stood beside it.

'Valda,' called Halfdan and she turned to face him, more than a little surprised that he would break his silence with her after all these weeks. She held her sack of belongings across her front, thankful the curve of her belly wasn't too obvious, especially with her tunic worn so loosely around her waist. A few more weeks and she would have been unable to hide the truth of her condition.

She wasn't sure what he would do if he found out. As a jarl's son he could demand to acknowledge the child, or even take it from her. She doubted Halfdan would do such a terrible thing...but if his father learned of it? It was possible. Halfdan had said Ulf was determined to continue his legitimate line—hadn't Erik's cruel childhood been proof of the man's lack of decency, and what about the time he'd threatened to beat Olga's child from her belly if she continued to claim it was Halfdan's? She shivered, another good reason to keep the babe a secret from everyone. Tostig wouldn't tell, but she would need to a secure a farm for her family quickly.

'Yes?' she answered, trying to hide all of her emotions behind a shield wall of cool indifference.

Would this be the last time?

In spite of herself she found her eyes soaking up the image of him. The fall of his blond hair, the sapphire eyes surrounded by dark kohl, the handsome jaw. Would their child take after him? Or would she be forced to describe him to their curious child? Unlike her own mother, she knew she would tell them everything.

'You forgot something.'

She stared at him in confusion. *Was he asking her to stay?* But that made no sense.

'Your silk,' he said and she noticed the parcel he carried. Opening her sack, he pushed in the bundle of green and gold cloth.

'But it's yours; you paid for it!' she gasped.

'It was made for your body, not mine. What use is it to me?'

She looked away. She didn't have the strength to argue. 'Goodbye, Halfdan.'

He stared at her with cold eyes and then gave a sharp nod before walking away. 'As you wish.'

She paused on the ramp, her spine stiff, the temptation to turn and scream at him almost overwhelming. But with a roll of her shoulders, she put one foot in front of the other and continued like that all the way to her family home.

Halfdan watched her leave and felt his heart pull with longing, as if a great rope were wrapped around it and Valda held the end. When she'd paused on the ramp, he'd hoped for a moment she would turn back. Profess her love and cast aside her stubborn hopes for him to break his oath and marry her.

Love him without conditions or price.

If he were honest, that was what hurt the most. She'd never said she loved him and he couldn't shake the feeling that, without marriage, he wasn't enough for her.

If she'd said she loved him, he would have done everything in his power to avoid the marriage, but why should he sacrifice Erik's happiness on a woman that did not love him back?

'I have not spoken to you before now, because I'd hoped you would see sense. But it seems I must intervene,' Tostig said with a scowl, as he moved beside him. 'You're going to let her go, just like that?'

'She does not want this life, or me.'

'Oh? I thought she didn't want to watch you marry another... Seems reasonable to me.'

Halfdan glared at him. 'My marriage means nothing. A deal. Nothing more.' He gestured to his ship. 'I offered Valda a life of freedom, I even offered to find a way to stop it, if she gave me time. She was the one who chose not to accept me.'

Tostig rolled his eyes. 'Your ship has become your cage and Ulf your master. You claim you want freedom, but then bind yourself to your father without thought of the consequences.'

'I know the consequences,' Halfdan retorted, looking towards his brother meaningfully. Erik was helping to sort the loading of the silver on to mules. Soon they would deliver it to their father.

Tostig shrugged. 'Does *he*? All he wanted was his freedom. You did not need to buy him more.'

'He doesn't need to know. It will seem as if my father finally saw sense. It's what he deserves.'

'Hmmm, and your sudden marriage won't be at all

suspicious? Especially after Valda has left you for no apparent reason.'

Halfdan looked at his friend sharply. 'I told you. She does not love me; she has never even said she loves me. Why should I give up my brother's future happiness, to appease one woman's desire to own me?'

Tostig sighed. 'You are like me in so many ways. When I was young, I used to be afraid that marriage would take me away from my first love, the sea. Rán's salt sang in my veins and filled my heart with joy.' He paused, fixing him with a hard look. 'But when I am gone, and nothing remains of me but my old, grey bones, do you know where I wish to be buried? Beside my *wife*. The sea is exciting and vast, but it does not ease her loss. You think that love can live without responsibility? An endless horizon with no anchor? That is not love, that is loneliness. The sea calls to our blood, but it does not own our bones. I loved my wife deeply. She owns my bones and you will return them to her after I am dead. I think Valda owns your bones, too, whether you like it or not.'

Halfdan's throat closed painfully and he swallowed hard to clear the emotion.

But Tostig was not finished, he had one more axe to throw. 'Ask yourself this: can you live without her?'

'I have done it before,' he answered through gritted teeth.

Tostig surprised him by laughing. 'Of course you can! As I live without my heart every day...' His eyes narrowed, all mirth gone. 'But do you *want* to? Why do you think I long for death? It is not for adventure or glory—it is to meet my love once again in the afterlife. To stroke her beautiful hair with my rough hands and tell her about our daughters and grandchildren. To feel her hand in mine and know with certainty... I am home.'

Halfdan jaw tightened. 'I have given my word.'

'You are as hard and as stubborn as granite!' Tostig snapped, walking away with a thousand curses.

The hut was still in the same pitiful condition as it had been when she'd left. Guilt churned in her stomach as she realised how they must have suffered in her absence. But the water barrel was full and the plot of land seemed surprisingly full of herbs and maturing vegetables. All of which boded well for their health.

There was smoke coming from the doorway, so she knew someone was home, although she couldn't see who until she was closer.

She paused in the garden, uncertain. It might scare them if she burst in unannounced, and would they welcome her...when they realised what she'd done?

At a loss as to what to say, she called out, 'I'm back!'

There was a gasp and a squeal from inside, followed by a flurry of movement, and even a few curses, as someone tripped over something, or someone. Valda stepped back a few paces in the hopes she wouldn't be trampled to death by their enthusiasm.

Her mother rushed through the doorway first, followed quickly by Brynhild and Helga. Porunn grabbed her in a fierce embrace, cupping her face and kissing each of her cheeks. Her sisters wrapped their arms around her, too, and she was smothered in their love.

Valda's tears threatened to fall at their welcome, but she clenched her jaw tight and stared at the grey sky above their heads, until the aching tenderness eased.

She took a deep breath and pulled away from their smiling embraces.

'Well… I have enough to bribe even the most resistant of Jarls into a granting us a farm!' She dropped her sack and it made a metallic crunch as it hit the ground. All three women grinned broadly at it. Brynhild slapped her on the back with a proud grin, while Helga stared at her with a curious look in her eyes.

'Was it exciting?' asked Porunn cheerfully.

'Dangerous?' asked Brynhild with equal glee.

How could she tell them?

As if Helga knew the struggle inside her mind, she reached across the space between them and touched the slight rounding of her belly. 'I'd wager it's a girl.'

Brynhild frowned at Helga's odd words and then her mouth dropped open in shock.

'Are you with child?' cried Porunn, her face creased with worry.

Valda couldn't speak. Shame clawed at her throat and tears burned the backs of her eyes. She nodded.

As if waking from a dream, Porunn smiled reassuringly. 'All will be well,' she said, gently covering Helga's hand with her own.

'Of course it will,' Helga reassured, as if the addition of an illegitimate child were a minor issue.

Valda looked to Brynhild. The sister she was closest to and whose judgement she feared the most. *How many times had they cursed their mother's reckless behaviour when it came to men?* And now she'd failed them all, in exactly the same way. When she opened her mouth to speak, her voice was raw with anguish and fear of rejection. 'I'm *sorry*—'

Brynhild strode forward and wrapped her long, powerful arms around her in a bear hug that squeezed the air from her lungs.

'I'll look after you,' Brynhild whispered in her ear and Valda's tears finally began to fall.

Chapter Twenty-Two

The Hall was quiet and tense, as if it were waiting for some terrible sacrifice.

Ulf stood before Erik, the hoard of silver in an obscenely high pile on the table behind him. With cold, unsmiling eyes he held up a coarse iron arm ring for all to see.

Everything about the ceremony was full of spite.

The ring was made from a cheap metal and lacking adornment, apart from the stamp of freedom. It appeared Erik would not be granted anything of equal or higher value than the bronze Halfdan wore.

Erik was on his knees, subjugated even in the last moments of his enslavement. But it would all be worth it. *It had to be.*

'Erik the Black,' said Ulf, his voice as hard as stone.

Halfdan scowled. His father would *still* not acknowledge him. Even now, after he'd received a king's ransom from the back of his children.

'I grant you…'

Halfdan waited, his breath held tight. The whole room

seemed to lean forward as if to press Ulf into finishing his speech.

'Your…freedom.' A sigh went round the room, but Ulf ignored it. 'You are no longer my thrall, but a freeman. As will be all those of your line who follow you.'

As soon as Ulf had stopped speaking, Erik stood to face him. Their eyes locked and Erik took the arm band from his father, taking it from his clasp with an angry tug. Ulf's lips twisted in amusement, but he said nothing.

He couldn't.

Erik was finally free.

Halfdan cheered the loudest. Thrusting a horn of ale into his brother's hand, he embraced him, whispering closely in his ear, 'Have *one* drink…to avoid any later feud. Then we will be free to leave.'

Erik nodded and walked back to Halfdan's table. Their men waited with wide grins to toast his well-earned status.

Halfdan should be celebrating with them.

But Tostig's words still tormented him, although he'd refused to speak of it since.

Had he been right? Would he regret his decision to secure land for his brother, instead of offering Valda marriage?

He'd been restless ever since she had left that morning. The last weeks of the journey had been unbearable. He'd been counting down the days until he was free of her. But now she was gone, he felt even more pained by her absence than by her presence.

It was madness.

She didn't love him. If she did, she would have said… wouldn't she?

Except, Valda was fiercely proud and afraid to trust

anyone but herself. Why would she risk telling him she loved him when he was bound to another? Hadn't she told Jorund she'd loved him and he'd *still* rejected her.

'How was your voyage? Eventful?' Ulf asked. His tone was mild, but his eyes were calculating. Halfdan straightened, focusing his mind on the present.

'I lost two men,' Halfdan replied.

'So your shieldmaiden wasn't worth her steel then?' Ulf smiled, his teeth as sharp as a wolf's.

'Without her, I would have lost more. Perhaps even my own life.' Halfdan met Ulf's eyes with unwavering conviction. Every word he spoke was true and at least he didn't have to guard his tongue any more, no longer fearful of Ulf retaliating against his brother. It was a relief he'd not appreciated fully until now.

'I hope it was worth the *dalliance*. Still…two men. That's a lot of wergild to pay out from your profits.'

He gritted his teeth against the urge to spit in his father's face. 'I paid the families the compensation they were owed.'

'If you used thralls—'

Halfdan had had enough.

Suddenly, all became clear, as if the sun had emerged from a sky of dark clouds. He could never please his father or make up for Erik's mistreatment at his father's hands. There was no reason to seek any more from Ulf because he would never give them anything of worth. Not only that, but Valda had been right, Erik wanted nothing more to do with their father.

Why had he ever thought otherwise?

Unable to stop himself, he asked about it anyway. 'Have you land for my brother?'

Ulf's eyes narrowed. 'Yes…but you must marry first.'

Halfdan nodded. 'And where is she? My bride?'

The bride and her representative had been here when they'd arrived, but he'd given them a message that there were horses waiting for them if they wished to run. Only they needed to do it during Erik's ceremony if they had any hope of escaping.

It looked as if his instincts had been right and they'd decided to run.

Good luck to them both.

A pulse in Ulf's jaw jumped as he looked around the room. 'Where is she? *Find them!*' he roared and several warriors leapt to their feet.

This was his chance to escape the deal honourably. But he found he no longer cared. He didn't want to have *everything* any more. He didn't need to win this contest with his father.

'I think they're gone. It's probably for the best.' He took a step closer to his father and smelt the sour ale on his breath. 'The deal is done.'

Ulf laughed, the sound as bitter as bile. 'You think yourself so *clever*. When I find her—which I *will*—you will marry her! And…does Erik know about this deal you've made on his behalf? If you wish to argue the details, then feel free. We'll discuss it…*openly.*' He snapped his fingers at a nearby thrall who rushed to serve him a cup of ale. He took a long sip, before lowering it with a smug smile. 'You should also know… Erik's settlement will be the one closest to the Briton lord, your soon-to-be brother-in-law. There is a battle for power in the area and, after some persuasion, we agreed to terms for peace— including your marriage. Erik's land, and its safety, will be closely reliant on your bride's happiness. They call her brother the Dragon in the Mountains…and he's considered quite *ruthless*. But don't worry, your bride—once she returns—will be safe in my hands, as will Erik. You can even still go trading if you wish…'

Halfdan stared at his father with distaste.

The land was a bargaining tool. The Welsh Lord and Ulf probably held members of each side captive and the marriage alliance would release them. He felt bad for those nameless strangers, but if his father had anything to do with it, they were probably already as good as dead.

And what did that mean for Erik? If his bride were ever harmed in his father's care, would that mean immediate death for his brother at the hands of the Welsh Lord? Were they both, once again, trapped under their father's control?

The deal had been rotten from the start. Halfdan could keep his honour intact, wait around to see if the lovers were ever found, or he could walk away now and be an oath-breaker.

He suspected that if he waited he could win in this scheme or at least squirm out of it with some concession for his brother's future.

But for once, Halfdan didn't want *everything*.

He just wanted one thing… Valda.

'No,' he said, watching with interest the surprise and anger flare in his father's cold blue eyes.

Had he ever said no to his father before? Or had it always been deals and negotiations?

'Don't you dare!' snarled Ulf, his fists clenching at his sides.

'What are you talking about?' shouted Erik from his seat.

'My gift to you,' Ulf said with a snide smile and then fixed Halfdan with a pointed look. 'I am making you

Chieftain of one of my settlements, Erik. Would you like that? A land and title of your own?' It was Halfdan's last chance to do as his father wished.

A silence descended over the feasting Hall, but then Erik spoke, his voice loud and clear. 'Under *you*? Never.'

If anything, the silence deepened, the weight of Erik's insult striking a death blow to the already pitiful festivities.

'I see you still have *no respect*!' shouted Ulf and the thrall beside him flinched and shuffled a few steps back.

Erik ignored their father and looked at Halfdan in silent question. Ulf was no longer his master to obey.

How could he be so blind! Of course Erik would want nothing from his father. He might deserve land and a title, but he'd probably rather crawl on his hands and knees out of this Hall than ever be ruled by their father again.

Ulf's cup sailed through the air, striking Erik on his shoulder. Tostig immediately grabbed Erik by the forearm to stop him rising to attack their father in retaliation, urging him in a hushed voice to wait.

Halfdan turned on Ulf, no longer willing to accept his schemes or his cruelty. 'The deal is off. Keep your land. I pray the gods are kind and you never find her.'

Ulf grabbed his arm, pinching it in a punishing grip. 'You swore an *oath*, Halfdan!' Spittle flew from his mouth and he began to scream in outrage. 'You cannot go back on your word, otherwise... I will disown you! You will become a man without a name, without honour, and *all* will know of it! Oath-breaker!'

Halfdan pushed his father away from him and Ulf stumbled into the table behind. The hoard of silver rattled, some pieces falling to the ground with a hollow clatter.

Halfdan looked to Erik and the two brothers shrugged. 'So be it,' Halfdan replied, already walking towards the door.

'All the Jarls will learn of your treachery! No one will trade with you!' screamed Ulf, his voice hoarse. 'No one!'

The Hall watched with unsympathetic eyes as the man struggled to stand, the alcohol he'd imbibed finally getting the better of him.

The two brothers left, their loyal men following, and even a couple of warriors from Ulf's command joined with them. Ulf's power had truly crumbled.

Chapter Twenty-Three

Valda waited in Jarl Ivar's Hall for their turn to speak. The room was thick with people as Ivar was a powerful and influential jarl, and many wished to approach him with requests and neighbourly complaints.

Helga and Brynhild stood, while Porunn and Valda sat on a bench. Her sisters had taken to treating her as if she were an invalid, but at least it gave Porunn an excuse to sit with her.

'Does your leg ail you?' asked Valda, concerned by the tight frown on her mother's face.

Porunn rubbed at her old wound with a smile. 'It's the changing of the season. It makes it ache a little.'

'It will be better when we have our farmstead, and you're no longer sleeping in that hovel.'

Porunn chuckled. 'Watch your tongue. I've grown rather fond of that *hovel* since you left.'

'Was it very bad—while I was gone?' Valda asked quietly, her guilt gnawing at her insides. She'd seen the amount of silver they'd put aside for the farm in her absence and they couldn't have managed that amount without starving themselves. She'd felt too guilty to pry earlier, but now the curiosity was eating her alive.

'It's not been easy. Gunnar was spiteful and halved Brynhild's pay after you left. She tried to find work with Ivar, but he was away for much of the summer. But… we did have plenty of food…' Porunn paused, as if unsure whether to continue or not. Then with a sigh, she added, 'Halfdan sent us supplies every week. He didn't tell you, did he?'

Valda shook her head in disbelief. 'No, he never said.'

Porunn gave her a shrewd look. 'It is a pity you do not love him. I always thought you suited one another, both of you so adventurous, and now that we know the truth about Olga… Well, it seems he is loyal, too. Could you not…grow to love him?'

Valda stared glumly at her feet. She'd wished she'd not told her about that. But then she'd felt compelled to explain why she'd fallen so easily in bed with a man who'd betrayed her so badly in the past. Unfortunately, it had only given them more questions.

Her mother was still waiting patiently for her to answer.

'I never said I didn't…care for him…but he's to marry another woman.'

Porunn shrugged as if such a thing were a minor problem and anger whipped down Valda's spine. 'You might not care about the dishonour, but I do!'

Porunn raised an eyebrow. 'If it bothers you, then demand he not marry her.'

Valda glared back. 'He made a deal with his father and he chose to keep it.'

Porunn frowned. 'He chose his father? Over his own

child? That can't be right. Ulf is not the type of man to earn such loyalty, even over his own kin.'

'The deal was for his brother, Erik…so that he could have land of his own.' Her mother's confusion didn't seem to ease and she added quietly, 'And… Halfdan does not know of the child.'

'He doesn't *know*?' cried Porunn and several people including her sisters looked round to stare at them.

Valda turned on her mother with a hiss. 'When has that ever stopped you in the past?'

Porunn moved closer and her voice hushed. 'I have *always* told the father. Two out of three of them…they didn't *want* to know.'

That took some of the wind out of Valda's sail and her shoulders slumped. Only Helga's father had acknowledged her, which meant Brynhild and Valda's had been the ones to walk away. She'd suspected they'd not cared enough to stay, but she'd always thought Porunn had chosen her own independence first. Although that might be the case, it still hurt that their fathers would reject them so thoroughly.

'Halfdan might do the same,' she said in a weak voice.

'He might.' Her mother nodded with brutal directness. 'Or…he might realise that your love, and that of your child's, is worth more than whatever deal he made for his brother.'

Valda's stomach twisted and for once it wasn't because of the babe. 'I haven't told him…that I love him. *Ouch!*'

Porunn's slap to her arm came with lightning speed and she scowled at her mother more in outrage than in any real pain.

'Are you stupid?' barked her mother.

Brynhild leaned back with gritted teeth. 'Will you two *stop it*? We're the next to be seen!'

Jarl Ivar's voice carried over the heads of the four women, filling the room with barely concealed irritation. 'Shieldmaidens, did you wish to speak with me or not?'

Porunn and Valda jumped to their feet at the commanding tone of the Jarl. He stared at them from across his table with grey shrewd eyes, his pale blond hair cut short around his head. He was a little younger than Porunn, but not by much, and he still had the air of a powerful warrior.

He had a reputation for being honourable and fair to women under his rule and it was why they'd chosen him as the Jarl to petition. But he also had a reputation for being impatient.

Brynhild spoke first, giving them both a hard look for putting them immediately in such a poor light with the Jarl. She quickly introduced them and listed their exploits and victories before going on to offer him a heavy payment of silver for the 'opportunity' to farm his land.

'And none of you is married?' he asked, his expression giving nothing away.

Their mother shook her head. 'No, my lord.'

'Then who will inherit your farm when you die?'

'My daughters.'

'And after they are gone?'

'Their children…if they have any. Otherwise, the land will revert to you, my lord.'

Ivar frowned and all four women held their breath. 'I have many farms and settlements sworn to me through blood as well as oaths.'

'We will, of course, swear allegiance to you, my lord,' said Brynhild.

'But if you all marry. I will have to accept four men not of my choosing. It could become…complicated.'

'If we marry, it will only be with your permission, my lord.'

He rocked back into his seat with a deep exhale, as if he were weighing up their offer on a pair of trading scales. Valda was worried they were not tipping in their favour. Should she speak of her pregnancy or would that only make matters worse?

'What if we never marry?' asked Helga softly.

Ivar frowned. 'I have other men. Men with families who could farm the land and offer me a warrior's service when required. They will be loyal because their children's inheritance depends upon it. So far, you have only offered me silver and an uncertain future.'

'I am a warrior in Gunnar's guard. I will answer the call if you need me,' said Brynhild, her eyes meeting his with conviction burning bright.

Ivar nodded, but still looked uncertain. 'Your reputations in battle are impressive.' He glanced at Valda as he spoke. 'I heard you fought nomads on your journey to Miklagard?'

Valda nodded. 'I did, my lord. Two men died, but we were able to escape.'

He paused again, then said, 'I will help you.'

All four women sighed with relief, but the Jarl was not finished.

'Leif!' he called and a young, strong man with brown hair and blue eyes stepped forward. 'Leif is a fine warrior and has done well in my guard. If one of your daughters marries him, Porunn, then I will grant you a farm.' All four women slumped with defeat and Ivar leaned forward to add, 'Just one of them, it doesn't matter which…and you can keep your silver.'

The women stared at each other, indecision rushing through them in a silent wave.

'Valda…' It was Leif's voice that carried to them, strong and kind. She looked at him and he smiled. 'I would be grateful if you considered me first…'

'Typical!' grumbled Brynhild.

'He seems nice,' whispered Helga. 'He has kind eyes…'

'I am already with child,' Valda said. He blinked in surprise, but nodded.

'If the father is no longer around, then I will accept both you and the child as you are.'

Valda stared at Leif in shock. Here was a man offering her security and a home for all her family…and she did not want him.

Brynhild locked eyes with her. 'Only do this for you. Not for us. Life is too short to waste it on regrets.'

Valda sucked in a deep breath, her mind spinning with indecision.

'I want… Halfdan.' Everyone, except Porunn, stared at Valda in surprise.

'Who is Halfdan?' muttered Leif and Ivar shrugged.

'Then go to him!' Porunn urged, before she turned to the Jarl and began to explain. 'Thank you for your kind offer, Jarl Ivar, but my daughters are shieldmaidens and must follow their hearts first.'

Helga clasped Valda's hand in her own and squeezed it, as Halfdan had done so many times before. 'Go, Valda. Sail away with him.'

For once in her life, she'd decided to tackle her problems of the heart with the same directness she would have used in battle.

Valda flew from the Hall as fast as her feet could carry her, Brynhild helping by shoving anyone and everyone out of their way.

As they skidded into the muddy square, the sun shone, as if welcoming her decision. She raised her hand to cover her eyes, so that she could see better. 'Which is Jarl Ulf's Hall? I can't remember!' she cried, flustered now that she'd finally come to her senses.

'It's the one over here,' said a rich, deep voice from several feet away.

Valda turned towards Halfdan, her face suddenly numb. He stood with Tostig and Erik, as well as a large number of his crew. They all stared at her with an odd mixture of surprise, pleasure and amusement.

'Were you…looking for me?' he asked incredulously, as if he'd not expected to stumble on her again so soon… which was fair, she supposed.

'Yes!' she replied with more bite than she'd intended.

'Why?' he asked, but Tostig elbowed him sharply in the ribs, and he added, 'I mean, I was also looking for you… Although, I did not expect to see you as soon as I stepped foot outside my father's Hall…'

'And why would you need to look for me?' she asked and she heard her mother mutter a curse under her breath, so she added, 'Are you married yet?'

'No… I broke the deal with my father.'

She gasped, her eyes flicking to Erik who gave a nonchalant shrug. As she'd suspected, he was unbothered by the loss. Gathering up as much pride as she could muster, she said, 'Then I insist you marry me. Not only do I love you…but I am—'

'You love me?' he asked, such a smile on his face that it had some of the men rolling their eyes in disgust.

'Yes,' she said, her eyes narrowing into a glare. 'Of course I love you. I'm sorry I didn't tell you before. I was afraid. Love has always gone so badly for me in the past, but I do love you. You are clever, kind and generous. I have met no man better than you in my entire life…and I am—'

'I broke the deal with my father because I can't lose you a second time. I was just being stubborn, wanting to have it all. That was wrong, and I'm sorry!' he said in a great rush, as if he were afraid to let the moment pass without confessing it to her. His blue eyes were clear with honesty and something else—nerves? But that was impossible, Halfdan was never uncertain. But then he stepped forward and reached for her hand. She gave it without hesitation. 'I do want to marry you, Valda, if you'll have me…if it's not too late. I love you and if you wish to stay here and farm land with your family, then I will give up the sea.'

'You could never give up your ship,' she whispered, horrified.

'If you are not on it, then I will never be happy. My bones would miss you too much.'

She frowned. 'Your bones?'

'It was something Tostig said…' Tostig nodded enthusiastically at her confused face, while Halfdan continued. 'But I mean it. I need to be with you…more than anything else in the world…'

A thought intruded on her happiness and she broke away from his mouth with a sharp inhale. 'If it's because of the child—'

He frowned. 'What child?'

Valda stared at him, unsure if she were dreaming. There was no deceit in his eyes; he meant every heart-wrenching word. The breath left her body in one long exhale, taking with it all her doubts and fears.

Slowly, understanding dawned on his face and he grinned from ear to ear. She jumped into his arms and he caught her, holding her fiercely to his chest as their lips met in a searing kiss.

The muddy square erupted into cheers and hoots of laughter.

Chapter Twenty-Four

'Freya will be jealous in her hall tonight,' said Porunn with a teasing smile.

'Mother.' Valda sighed with a roll of her eyes. 'Don't anger the goddess of love on my wedding day. I want her to bless this union! Not curse it.'

Porunn chuckled. 'Why would she curse it? She had a hand in this—I am certain. You are already blessed by her! I knew there was a reason she gave me three such beautiful daughters.'

Brynhild snorted from the bed where she lay sprawled. Unable to find a comfortable place to stand inside the tent, she'd quickly decided to flop on the bed instead.

'You are! Beautiful and strong, and clever!' Porunn repeated with a reproachful glare at the bad-tempered Brynhild. Then she smoothed a hand down the green and gold Byzantine silk. 'It's a pity I have no *kransen* to give you.' She sighed before picking up a comb to brush out Valda's hair. 'And I wish I were better at this sort of thing.'

Valda winced as the comb snagged on a knot. She turned and took it from her mother with a reassuring smile. 'Leave it. It only matters that you are here.' Then she touched the slight curve of her belly with a smile. 'I can hardly wear a virginal crown in my condition!'

Helga burst into the tent then, her face flushed, but triumphant. A basket full of flowers swung from her elbow, scattering a few petals on the floor. 'I found some!' she cried, thrusting them forward with a grin. 'I knew there would be some by the river bank if I walked a little further down.'

'Is that where you went? To get flowers!' Brynhild laughed. 'I thought you were finding a Gothi to perform the ceremony. Do we have flowers for a wedding, but no one to perform it?'

'Oh, I got him, too!' Helga said at Valda's alarmed look. Quickly she took the comb from Valda and began running it through with a far gentler hand than their mother's.

Porunn took a seat on a nearby stool, gratefully relinquishing the task of dressing Valda's hair to an expert.

'It's like I always said…we'll all be married with flowers in our hair.'

Valda took Helga's hand in her own, touched that her sister would do such a thing. After all, it was autumn and flowers were hard to find in muddy Jorvik, especially so many! 'Thank you.'

'Hardly a prophecy!' Brynhild snorted and Helga smiled mischievously.

'I will do your hair next, Sister!'

Brynhild rolled her eyes and Helga's hands flew to her hips. 'You promised, Brynhild, and you never break a promise!'

'I never thought it would actually happen!' Brynhild

groaned, then thumped her head against the bed frame, causing all of them to laugh.

'We will all marry and you'll be next!' Helga pointed an accusing finger at Brynhild who grabbed the bedding as if it were a shield.

'Odin's teeth! Don't curse me, woman!'

The four women emerged from the tent a short time later, flowers in all their hair. All of them radiant and beautiful in their own way, even if Brynhild looked bad tempered and surly, with the barest of all the flower crowns on her head.

The wedding was conducted by a Christian priest, and then by a Gothi as Halfdan wanted no one to ever question the legitimacy of their marriage. The ceremony was short as they both had no land, title or family swords to exchange. But to Valda and Halfdan, it was perfect.

They had no Jarl's Hall to feast in so they feasted on Halfdan's ship, cooking the meat in a nearby black-smith's—they'd paid handsomely for the use of his furnace.

Ale and food were passed around and music filled the air above Halfdan's magnificent ship as the crew talked, danced and sang all night in celebration. Torches and braziers were lit upon the deck and everyone was merry and cheerful. Even Brynhild and Erik seemed to be less brooding than normal.

Tostig came to sit beside Valda as the first light of morning began to splash across the deck, grinning as if he were a cat with a bowl of cream. 'I am pleased you both saw sense in the end.'

'Me?' Valda gasped with mock outrage. 'What did I do wrong?'

'You were too honourable. A terrible flaw in any man…worse in a woman!'

'Really?' Valda laughed.

'Really…but the gods appear to love you regardless.'

Valda smiled happily as she looked to her husband where he was talking with his brother. There seemed an easy peace between them now that they no longer feared for each other's future and it was lovely to see. 'You're right. I am very lucky.'

Tostig spat out a curse with a twinkle of mischief in his eyes. 'Two lucky souls on this ship! Will I never die?'

'I hope not,' Valda said with a grin. 'Who else will guard our child with their life? Oh, that reminds me—I should give you back your silver. Now that I'm with Halfdan, I'll have no need of it for the babe.'

Tostig choked on his mead and stared at her with horror. 'Don't you dare! Give it to your sisters or your mother—anyone! I don't care what you do with it, just accept the damn gift!'

Valda held up her hands in defeat. 'Fine, I will give it to my sisters!'

'Good. Besides, you've made me sixty dirhams anyway… Damn you!'

'How?'

'The men made a wager and unfortunately I won.'

'What wager?'

'That Halfdan would marry you.'

Valda blinked in surprise. 'When did you make this wager?' She'd not seen or heard anything regarding this supposed bet and she'd been living among these men for months.

'The day you first stepped aboard this ship. We were playing dice in the corner and I recognised you. I knew what you'd meant to him in the past. Then when he showed you onboard, all puffed up with pride, I knew his feelings hadn't changed. I just never imagined you'd feel the same, otherwise I never would have made this foul wager!'

Touched by Tostig's insight, she wrapped an arm around the man's shoulders and tugged him close, and for once he didn't grumble. She grabbed the cap off his head and kissed the bald skin beneath, then returned it quickly, patting it back into place. 'Remind me to introduce you to my mother, Tostig.'

She laughed as Tostig muttered another bad-tempered curse. 'Are you sure you won't come with us on this trip?'

He shook his head. 'I will be back with you soon enough. Once I've sold Halfdan's goods, you can pick me up again in the spring with Erik.'

Halfdan walked over to them. 'It's time,' he said, his expression full of remorse.

She rose and squeezed his hand to let him know that she was fine. Saying goodbye to her family was hard, but it was for the best.

They made their way over to her mother and sisters and they rose from their seats.

Porunn hugged her tightly first. 'I will miss you so much!'

'You could come with us!' Valda said, her voice tight with emotion as she looked at her sisters. 'You all could.'

Porunn laughed. 'I am not good at sea. Besides, I still wish to farm. Erik says that he knows a jarl who might help us.' She glanced towards Erik with a smile and he gave an awkward nod of his head, not quite comfortable joining the group of women, but loitering like a shadow only a few steps away with Tostig.

He'd sworn to Halfdan that he would look after her mother and sisters while they were away. 'Good. Thank you, Erik.'

He inclined his head with the slightest of nods and Brynhild looked personally offended by it. With a huff she moved forward and gave Valda a fierce hug. 'We'll be fine! There's no point in you staying in Jorvik. Not with Halfdan's father, and potentially a Welsh warlord, raging for his blood. It's best you disappear for the winter. I'm sure by the time you return in the spring, all will be forgotten.'

Erik made a snorting noise of disbelief and Brynhild gave him another disapproving glare.

Helga stepped up last and hugged her tightly. 'All will be well.' Then she placed a hand on Valda's stomach and smiled serenely. 'See you soon, little one!'

Valda grinned. 'Are you sure about your guess?'

Helga chuckled. 'I never guess…and it is a girl.'

Their eyes locked and then with a tearful smile they embraced for one last hug, Brynhild and Porunn joining them almost immediately. Then they each embraced Halfdan, kissing his cheek and hugging him tight.

Valda laughed at the bemused look on his face. 'You have two sisters and a mother-in-law now.'

He grinned. 'Lucky me!' But she knew he meant it.

They waved them off, and then made their way to the back of the ship as the crew began to untie the ropes attaching them to the dock.

They sat on a pile of furs at the steering oar—their latest cargo, gathered in only a couple of days. Halfdan had been wrong about the other Jarls rejecting him—they'd embraced his break from his father with open arms.

Halfdan wrapped a pelt around her shoulders to keep her warm. Immediately she threw it across his shoulder, too, and tucked herself beneath his arm.

Pulling her close he kissed her neck. 'Where shall we go? The silk road? Miklagard? The land of the Moors? Name it and I will take us there.' The sun began to rise, lighting the river with rippling flames.

Valda smiled, her eyes filled with happiness and hope. 'I don't care where we go, as long as I'm with you.'

He pulled her close, an arm slung around her shoulders as he steered the boat with his other. They left Jorvik without looking back, their future spread out before them. A golden winding path, full of possibility, adventure and love.

* * * * *

If you enjoyed this story, be sure to read the other books in the Shieldmaiden Sisters miniseries, coming soon!

And whilst you're waiting for the next book, why not check out these other great reads?

A Nun for the Viking Warrior
The Viking Chief's Marriage Alliance

Read on for a sneak peek of Brynhild's story in
Tempted by Her Outcast Viking
Coming soon!

'Brynhild, may I speak with you?' Erik asked quietly, moving to her side. She tried to hide the surprise in her expression. He wanted to *speak* with her? Why? Was he determined to goad her into a fight? Like the one they'd had in their youth. She hoped not, something told her she would behave just as badly as she had then…if provoked.

She groaned, her eyes locking with those merciless dark pools. Erik was ridiculously handsome. Unlike his brother Halfdan—who was all golden and cheerful in his appealing looks—Erik was all darkness. Even his skin was a darker shade, inherited from his Persian mother. Maybe if he'd looked a little more like his younger brother he'd have been treated better by his father? Although, she doubted it. Brynhild loathed Ulf far more than even Erik because Ulf was where Erik had learned his cruelty first hand.

Sucking in a deep breath, she tried to appear unshaken, despite feeling lightheaded and jittery in his presence. She shrugged. 'Speak, then.'

He glanced at Helga, who was still busy paying for her purchases, and began walking ahead, creating some distance between them. Brynhild followed, knowing that her sister would be able to catch up easily.

'I wanted to apologise to you, Brynhild.' His words were soft and uncharacteristically hesitant.

'What?'

Well, she'd not expected that!

If he'd admonished her for making assumptions earlier, or worse, offered his aid to her family in his usual smug way, she could have believed it.

But to say he was sorry?

She stumbled a little in the muddy earth and his scarred hand snapped around her forearm to steady her. The hairs on her arm rose as if in expectation of a storm and she shrugged it off quickly.

He frowned at that, as if she'd insulted him by avoiding his touch. When she had every right to remove his hand!

'I've been meaning to say it since we met again, but I never seemed to find the opportunity.'

She turned and strode forward, flustered and unsure how to respond. Then she stopped for a moment and stared at the ground. He'd seemed sincere. His shadow fell across her and she knew he stood close by. 'There is nothing to apologise for,' she said quietly and, to her surprise she meant it. She didn't like him, that much was true, but she'd also said things that were unkind and she'd humiliated him, too…in her own way.

She moved forward, hoping he would leave it at that. But of course, he didn't.

'I think there is.' His long stride matched her own and she felt an odd excitement rush through her veins. They were forced closer together as the twisting path between the buildings became narrower. 'I was young and still trying to prove myself to my father. A waste of time, as I later learned… But, regardless, I shouldn't have taken my rage and frustration out on you. I was wrong.'

How many times had she dreamt of him saying such words? She'd always imagined them meeting again. But on the battlefield. In her fantasy he'd fallen beneath her expert sword after a long and epic fight. It would have been a hard-won, but satisfying victory, and with his dying breath he would have wheezed out those three wonderful words: *I was wrong.*

Somehow this did not feel as satisfying. It felt awkward and humiliating instead. As if she were his victim and not his equal.

She stopped walking and turned to face him, grabbing him by his wide shoulders and thrusting him against the wall. His hands in response locked around her biceps to steady himself. His grip was firm, but not painful, and the heat that radiated from his fingers only angered her further. She thrust him back a second time, the plaster on the little house cracking and crumbling with the force.

'I don't like you!' she snarled. 'I've never liked you! So, let's make this very clear. I don't care if you're sorry or not! Just do as you've promised and get my mother a damn farm!'

They stared at one another. Their breath mingled and the tension between them reached an unbearable weight, neither of them backing down. The only sound was their hot breath shimmering between them in the small alleyway, their big bodies filling the space between and making the squat buildings of the city seem even more fragile.

The dark pools of his eyes locked with hers and then

dropped ever so slowly to her mouth. 'There was a time when you liked me...a lot.'

Her face burned and she almost shoved him for a third time into the wall—not that it seemed to affect the big ox, which only irritated her further.

Then he frowned and looked away from her as if a sudden thought had distracted him. 'Where's your sister?'

She stepped away, dropping his arms as the question drew her back to the present. 'She was just behind us,' she muttered, moving quickly back down the path. Helga wasn't a natural fighter, although she'd been trained to a reasonable level, and a prick of awareness shivered down Brynhild's spine as she hurried out of one alley and straight into the next. Fear was chasing quickly at her heels.

How had she got so distracted? Been so stupid?

Helga wore a heavy purse of silver now and therefore was more vulnerable to thieves, and if she were outnumbered...

Brynhild began to run, the heavy footfalls of Erik following close behind. As the path twisted, she jerked to a halt with a gasp. The air was ripped from her lungs as her vision narrowed at the sight in front of her and all else was forgotten in that terrible moment.

Dimly she heard Erik skidding behind her. He grabbed the walls either side of her head to stop himself from knocking straight into her. She had never been paralysed by fear in battle, but she was now. Terror locked her muscles as she stood on the precipice of disaster, unable to do anything but watch.

'What is it?' he gasped, looking over her shoulder to see what had caused her to stop dead in her tracks.

On the ground was Helga's basket, fresh bread and honey cakes scattered all around. But most disturbingly of all, was her sister's dagger thrust through a piece of linen and into the loaf of bread. Drawn in charcoal was the image of a dragon. Brynhild remembered it from her youth, and it sucked the air from her lungs to see it once again in such terrible circumstances.

Someone had taken Helga.